# CATCH

# What Reviewers Say About Kris Bryant's Work

### Home

"*Home* is a very sweet second-chance romance that will make you smile. It is an angst-less joy, perfect for a bad day."—*Hsinju's Lit Log*

### Scent

"Oh. Kris Bryant. Once again you've given us a beautiful comfort read to help us escape all that 2020 has thrown at us. This series featuring the senses has been a pleasure to read. …I think what makes Bryant's books so readable is the way she builds the reader's interest in her mains before allowing them to interact. This is a sweet and happy sigh kind of read. Perfect for these chilly winter nights when you want to escape the world and step into a caramel infused world where HEAs really do come true."—*Late Night Lesbian Reads*

### Lucky

"The characters—both main and secondary, including the furry ones—are wonderful (I loved coming across Piper and Shaylie from Falling), there's just the right amount of angst and the sexy scenes are really hot. It's Kris Bryant, you guys, no surprise there."—*Jude in the Stars*

"This book has everything you need for a sweet romance. The main characters are beautiful and easy to fall in love with, even with their little quirks and flaws. The settings (Vail and Denver, Colorado) are perfect for the story, and the romance itself is satisfying, with just enough angst to make the book interesting. ...This is the perfect novel to read on a warm, lazy summer day, and I recommend it to all romance lovers."—*Rainbow Reflections*

**Tinsel**

"This story was the perfect length for this cute romance. What made this especially endearing were the relationships Jess has with her best friend, Mo, and her mother. You cannot go wrong by purchasing this cute little nugget. A really sweet romance with a cat playing cupid."—*Bookvark*

**Against All Odds**—*(co-authored with Maggie Cummings and M. Ullrich)*

"*Against All Odds* by Kris Bryant, Maggie Cummings and M. Ullrich is an emotional and captivating story about being able to face a tragedy head on and move on with your life, learning to appreciate the simple things we take for granted and finding love where you least expect it."—*Lesbian Review*

"I started reading the book trying to dissect the writing and ended up forgetting all about the fact that three people were involved in writing it because the story just grabbed me by the ears and dragged me along for the ride. ...[A] really great romantic suspense that manages both parts of the equation perfectly. This is a book you won't be able to put down."—*C-Spot Reviews*

**Temptation**

"This book has a great first line. I was hooked from the start. There was so much to like about this story, though. The interactions.

The tension. The jealousy. I liked how Cassie falls for Brooke's son before she ever falls for Brooke. I love a good forbidden love story."—*Bookvark*

"This book is an emotional roller coaster that you're going to get swept away in. Let it happen…just bring the tissues and the vino and enjoy the ride."—*Les Rêveur*

"You can always count on Bryant to write endearing and layered characters, even in stories like this one, when most of the angst comes from the not-so-simple act of falling in love."—*Jude in the Stars*

"People who have read Ms. Bryant's erotica novella *Shameless* under the pseudonym of Brit Ryder know that this author can write intimacy well. This is more a romance than erotica but the sex scenes are as varied and hot…"—*LezReviewBooks*

"This book is a bag of kettle corn—sweet, savory and you won't stop until you finish it in one binge-worthy sitting. *Temptation* is a fun, fluffy and ultimately satisfying lesbian romance that hits all the right notes."—*To Be Read Book Reviews*

**Falling**

"This is a story you don't want to pass on. A fabulous read that you will have a hard time putting down. Maybe don't read it as you board your plane though. This is an easy 5 stars!"—*Romantic Reader Blog*

"Bryant delivers a story that is equal parts touching, compassionate, and uplifting."—*Lesbian Review*

"This was a nice, romantic read. There is enough romantic tension to keep the plot moving, and I enjoyed the supporting characters' and their romance as much as the main plot."—*Kissing Backwards*

**Listen**

"[A] sweet romance with a touch of angst and lots of music."
—*C-Spot Reviews*

"If you suffer from anxiety, know someone who suffers from anxiety, or want an insight to how it may impact on someone's daily life, I urge you to pick this book up. In fact, I urge all readers who enjoy a good lesbian romance to grab a copy."—*Love Bytes Reviews*

"If you're looking for a little bit of fluffy(ish), light romance in your life, give this one a listen. The characters' passion for music (and each other) is heartwarming, and I was rooting for them the entire book."—*Kissing Backwards*

"This book floored me. I've read it three times since the book appeared on my kindle. …I just love it so much. I'm actually sitting here wondering how I'm going to convey my sheer awe factor but I will try my best. Kris Bryant won Les Rêveur book of the year 2018 and seriously this is a contender for 2019."—*Les Rêveur*

"This is the first story I've read in a long time with a virginal character, and it made a refreshing change both in and out of the bedroom. If you suffer from anxiety, know someone who suffers from anxiety, or want an insight to how it may impact on someone's daily life, I urge you to pick this book up. In fact, I urge all readers who enjoy a good lesbian romance to grab a copy."—*Omnivore Bibliosaur*

**Forget Me Not**

"Told in the first person, from Grace's point of view, we are privy to Grace's inner musings and her vulnerabilities. …Bryant crafts clever wording to infuse Grace with a sharp-witted personality, which clearly covers her insecurities. …This story is filled with loving familial interactions, caring friends, romantic interludes and tantalizing sex scenes. The dialogue, both among the characters and within Grace's head, is refreshing, original, and sometimes comical. *Forget Me Not* is a fresh perspective on a romantic theme, and an entertaining read."—*Lambda Literary Review*

"[I]t just hits the right note all the way. …[A] very good read if you are looking for a sweet romance."—*Lez Review Books*

**Shameless—*Writing as Brit Ryder***

"[Kris Bryant] has a way of giving insight into the other main protagonist by using a few clever techniques and involving the secondary characters to add back-stories and extra pieces of important information. The pace of the book was excellent, it was never rushed but I was never bored or waiting for a chapter to finish…this epilogue made my heart swell to the point I almost lunged off the sofa to do a happy dance."—*Les Rêveur*

**Whirlwind Romance**

"Ms. Bryant's descriptions were written with such passion and colorful detail that you could feel the tension and the excitement along with the characters…"—*Inked Rainbow Reviews*

**Taste**

"*Taste* is a student/teacher romance set in a culinary school. If the premise makes you wonder whether this book will make you want to eat something tasty, the answer is: yes."—*Lesbian Review*

**Jolt**—*Lambda Literary Award Finalist*

"[*Jolt*] is a magnificent love story. Two women hurt by their previous lovers and each in their own way trying to make sense out of life and times. When they meet at a gay and lesbian friendly summer camp, they both feel as if lightening has struck. This is so beautifully involving, I have already reread it twice. Amazing!"
—*Rainbow Book Reviews*

**Touch**

"The sexual chemistry in this book is off the hook. Kris Bryant writes my favorite sex scenes in lesbian romantic fiction."
—*Les Rêveur*

**Breakthrough**

"Looking for a fun and funny light read with hella cute animal antics, and a smoking hot butch ranger? Look no further. …In this well written, first-person narrative, Kris Bryant's characters are well developed, and their push/pull romance hits all the right beats, making it a delightful read just in time for beach reading."—*Writing While Distracted*

"[A]n exceptional book that has a few twists and turns that catch you out and make you wish the book would never end. I was captivated from the beginning and can't wait to see how Bryant will top this."—*Les Rêveur*

"*Breakthrough* delivers satisfying romance, amusing adventures, and a surprising, thrilling change of pace in the latter half of the story. Recommended for fans of 'fish out of water' stories, femme/butch pairings, Great Outdoors immersion, and the television series *Northern Exposure*."—*Omnivore Bibliosaur*

Visit us at www.boldstrokesbooks.com

# By the Author

Jolt

Whirlwind Romance

Just Say Yes

Taste

Forget-Me-Not

Shameless (writing as Brit Ryder)

Touch

Breakthrough

Against All Odds (written with M. Ullrich and Maggie Cummings)

Listen

Falling

Tinsel

Temptation

Lucky

Home

Scent

Not Guilty (writing as Brit Ryder)

Always

Forever

EF5 (Stranded Hearts Novella Collection)

Serendipity

Catch

# CATCH

*by*
Kris Bryant

2023

**CATCH**
© 2023 By Kris Bryant. All Rights Reserved.

ISBN 13: 978-1-63679-276-7

This Trade Paperback Original Is Published By
Bold Strokes Books, Inc.
P.O. Box 249
Valley Falls, NY 12185

First Edition: January 2023

This is a work of fiction. Names, characters, places, and incidents are the product of the author's imagination or are used fictitiously. Any resemblance to actual persons, living or dead, business establishments, events, or locales is entirely coincidental.

This book, or parts thereof, may not be reproduced in any form without permission.

---

**Credits**
Editors: Ashley Tillman and Cindy Cresap
Production Design: Susan Ramundo
Cover Design By Jeanine Henning

## Acknowledgments

No other sport gets my blood pumping more than football. I've loved it since I was a kid. Kansas City is a massive football town. Sure, we have BBQ and we're the city of fountains, but football is the glue that keeps this city united.

I was so excited to write this book! Women in the NFL. Women playing football. I jumped into the research for *Catch* and was stunned. I had no idea there were several professional women's football teams around the country. These leagues aren't supported or sponsored like NFL teams. They don't get million-dollar deals and there is almost no advertising because everything costs money. The players aren't paid. They play because they love the game and want to play. And they're good. I watched the Kansas City Glory play two home games and had a great interview with their head coach and offensive line coach, Keke Blackmon. She has such a positive attitude about coaching, football life, and the love of the game. So, thank you, Keke, for being so helpful and truthful about women in football and the obstacles they face.

I also interviewed Jennifer King, the Washington Commanders' assistant running backs coach and first Black woman to coach in the NFL. She said players don't care that she's a woman. They trust her and know she's there to better them as players. Thank you for your time, Coach King. In such a male-dominated sport, it's nice to hear that women are proving to be invaluable and are taken seriously.

Thank you to my family for being a loving, unified force. I love you, Mom, Dad, and Patty.

I also have the best friends anyone could have. The Nugtastic Four! You will always have my heart. We have the best times together irl and on the thread. Life has been tough, and you all have made it easier by being by my side. I love you, Krystina, Ana, and Morgan. Let's get married. Another massive thank you to my inner circle for propping me up—KB, HS, Friz, Kathy, GFB, Mellie B, Paula, Carsen, Dena, Karen, Cathie, Tagan, all the patrons on Patreon. My BFF Fiona has my heart! I miss our writing sprints, but I know you're pulled in so many different directions. I love you, Jenn & the ginger snaps.

I have a great life and I know not to take things for granted. Molly is still by my side and I kiss her way too much knowing every day is precious. Thank you, Deb, for taking care of me and Molly. We're not easy, but we're worth it.

I hope you enjoy this story and the way I've told it. It's different and I can't tell you how hard I fought to get this book in your hands. Thank you, BSB, for agreeing to publish something unique. Ashley and Cindy worked extra hard to hit the deadlines because I wanted this to land during football season. Great job on learning about sports balls, Ash!

And to my readers. Without you, I wouldn't have the desire to create stories. Your reviews and kind words fill my heart.

# Dedication

To my mom
Who pretends not to care but watches football with us every Sunday and knows more about the game than we do.

## Chapter One—Win the Game, Lose the Girl

*Past*

*Clear your mind, Sutton.*

I had thirteen seconds to get us close enough for Joey Ritchie to kick the tying field goal or find somebody open to run it in for a touchdown to win the game. It sounded so easy. We were down fourteen to seventeen and the winner went to state. Sure, a win and a trip to state would be nice, but my bruised ego and shredded heart wanted Grayson Moats and the Hilltop Hawkeyes to lose. Not because they were a great team and always went to state, but because Grayson Moats took something from me and I wanted him to pay. This was the only thing I could take from him that might hurt.

"As soon as you catch the ball and you see defenders, you drop to your knees and call time out. We're twenty-five yards from the end zone and we need to get to the eighteen-yard line so Joey has a good shot." I grabbed Max's helmet to ensure he was listening. "No showboating. We need these points. If it's not a clear shot to the end zone, drop. Do you understand me?" He nodded and shook loose. We were all on edge. Scouts were everywhere and some of my teammates were looking to get last-minute football scholarships. I wouldn't be given the same football opportunities after high school, so this was my last shot at anything great.

"Just throw me the ball. I'll get it in," Max said.

I couldn't tell if he was being confident or cocky. His eyes narrowed with determination as he wiped the sweat from his brow.

It was forty-two degrees out, but we were all sweaty, dirty, and had hit new levels of stress.

The importance of this moment took my breath away. My lungs refused to fill. I was sucking in tiny gasps of air and fighting the anxiety that bubbled up in my throat. This was our moment. In the huddle, I was the boss. I'd spent three years winning this team over after the starting quarterback broke his leg at the start of our sophomore year. I made the team because of my talent, but most people thought it was because my father was the assistant principal. That is, until they saw me throw the ball.

I looked at the determined faces staring back at me and felt proud. Proud of them for sticking with me even though my linemen were beat up. Beckett had a trail of blood that had dripped from his nose down the front of his silver and blue uniform and our center, Justin, had been pushed to the ground so many times protecting me, his uniform was almost green. I was proud of myself for getting us here. Proud of keeping my focus after such a shitty start to my senior year.

"This is it. This is our time to shine." They were exhausted, bloodied, but determined to win this game. "Stay focused and give Max the room he needs."

He locked eyes with me and nodded solemnly. "Let's get this done, Pumas," he said.

I barely heard the roaring crowd that filled both stands. Two towns had showed up to this game and the seats filled up quickly. Their screams and fist pumps meant nothing to me. I heard the excitement in the announcers' voices, but I couldn't make out their words. My heartbeat was so loud that my ears were throbbing. We lined up in formation.

"We're coming for you, girl!" a tackle yelled, emphasis on the word girl.

A few more unsavory things were said before I got into position. "Blue thirty-two. Blue thirty-two." I looked to my right as the wide receiver lined up and then to my left as Max ran by. "Arizona." The defense pointed at Max and two defenders slid over to cover him. Fuck. It was going to be impossible for him to make anything happen. One Mississippi. "Arizona." Two Mississippi. Justin snapped the ball and pushed at the line fighting to get to me. I fell back into the pocket and waited for Max to set up. He twisted and turned to get away from the two defenders. Nobody was open. When he slipped and fell, instinct took over. I tucked the ball under my arm and ran. Everything seemed to be in slow motion except the clock. The seconds slid off faster than I could run. It was too late to drop and call time out. It was all or nothing.

"Unhitch that trailer, Sutton!" my dad shouted from the sideline.

If it wasn't for the snarling, huffing defensive backs hot on my trail, I would've laughed at his solid advice to run faster, but I was too focused on not getting clobbered. Fifteen-yard line. I opened myself up to get severely hurt every time I ran with the ball. The football world hated female players. I was the first in my state. There were rumors that opposing players were paid by their coaches to knock me down, personal foul or not, but I was fast and my players protected me. In track, I won state two years in a row. Running was in my blood. It was time to add football to my résumé of state wins. Ten-yard line.

"Go, go, go!" Wyatt, my wide receiver, picked off one of the defensive linemen who had been his shadow since the ball was snapped. The other one crashed into them. I leaped over the pile and pushed forward.

I was at the five-yard line when I felt hands brush the back of my jersey. I twisted loose and tucked the ball tight against my body, knowing I was going down any second. Three-yard line. I dug deep and pushed myself even harder. When I hit the turf and the air left my lungs, I wasn't sure if I made it or not. I was on the bottom of a pile, and everyone was screaming. My lungs burned as I fought for a breath. The pads protected me from getting squashed, but it still hurt.

In the distance, I heard Justin yell as though he read my mind. "Get off her."

The crushing weight on me lifted. I tried to take several deep breaths, but the warm metallic taste of blood filled my mouth instead. I gagged and spit it out. My mouth guard had slashed my upper gums when I hit the ground. Somebody flipped me over and I struggled to keep the ball in my grasp.

Max's face came into view. "We're going to state, baby!"

I smiled at him, removed my mouthpiece, and turned my head to puke. He and Justin pushed people away.

"Back the fuck up, man. Back up!" Max yelled. He waved the coach over.

I wanted to tell him I was okay, but I couldn't find my words. I closed my eyes and smiled when I realized all my body parts were accounted for and worked. My lungs were still inside my body even though I thought somebody had squeezed them out.

"McCoy! McCoy! Can you hear me?" Coach's face fell into my line of vision. I never noticed the gray in his stubble or how, from this angle, his face slid slightly forward and his cheeks sagged enough to force open his mouth. He was a nice-looking man, but at this angle, he looked like a fish. A very concerned one.

I took another deep breath and nodded. "We're going to state."

He threw his head back and roared with laughter. "Damn right we are!"

It was nice to see his features back in place when he stood. He whistled for the doctor, but I waved him off. "Somebody just help me up."

"Are you sure?"

I nodded. "I just had the wind knocked out of me. Nothing like five hundred pounds of angry teenage boys tackling you." It was more like seven hundred but I was tough and wanted to play it down. I was lucky and I knew it. I took off my helmet when they pulled me up, anxious to rinse out my mouth.

Coach handed me a water bottle. "Let's shake hands when you're ready," he said.

My team stayed with me until I was ready to lead them to midfield where the Hilltop Hawkeyes waited in defeat. Some of the parents were yelling for their kids to get off the field, but we had media coverage, so their coach made them wait. I rinsed my mouth again until the metallic taste was gone. I tightened my ponytail, grabbed my helmet, and jogged to midfield with my team a half a step behind me.

"Good game." The Hawkeyes head coach hated everything about me.

I ignored his painful grip and smiled, ensuring my dimples popped. What a total asshole! "Thanks, Coach." I moved on, anxious to get in front of Grayson Moats.

Some of the guys muttered "good game" when we shook hands, while others had less than nice things to say like "bitch" or "lesbo." I smiled anyway, making zero friends in the process.

When I reached Grayson, I stopped. "Looks like the better quarterback won." I shrugged like it was no big deal when I knew it was everything. Not only did their offense score a mere seventeen points, but he sucked during one of the most important games of his high school life with home field advantage. He would still go on to play at Michigan State and probably the NFL, but I had him in the moment, and he would always have the blemish of not going to state his senior year because he was beaten by a girl.

He sneered. "You might have won the game, but I won the girl."

I gritted my teeth and shrugged like that didn't hurt more than anything ever in my life. He fist-pumped. "This game meant nothing. I'm still going to college and the NFL while you're stuck here doing what? Working at Marshall's? Oh, maybe you'll get promoted to manager in ten years."

I was six feet tall, but Grayson had at least four inches on me. That didn't stop me from getting in his face. "I have no idea what Parker sees in you. You're just a nasty boy."

"That's exactly what she likes about me." He winked and adjusted his cup. I wanted to puke at his disrespect toward somebody I loved with every part of my heart.

One of his players pushed him along. "Forget about her. This is her moment. The only one she'll have." He turned to look at me. "We'll laugh about how one time a girl thought she could play football while we're living the life playing in the pros." He slapped Grayson on the back and they laughed and moved on.

"A girl who beat the both of you," Max yelled.

They launched themselves at Max. It took three coaches and four players to pull them apart.

"Max, don't. It's not worth it." I loved that he was my biggest supporter, but I didn't want him to jeopardize his scholarship. He was the only one, besides me, who got a full ride anywhere. My scholarship was for Texas A&M's track and field team. I wasn't excited about moving to Texas, but it was a good school for sports medicine and that's what I was going to study. "Let's go celebrate."

Max jogged with me to the stands where our parents and fans waited to celebrate with us. My dad hugged me. "That was brilliant, but also stupid. Don't get hurt over a game. You have your whole life ahead of you."

I accepted hugs from parents I knew and some I didn't. So many people of Oak Grove were in the stands supporting us. I recognized people from the bank, the diner, and even the doctor's office. It was weird to see them in head-to-toe Oak Grove Pumas attire.

"Let's get cleaned up and celebrate." Coach motioned for us to head to the locker room. He pointed to the parents. "Back to the school and then to Tom's Pizza."

I jogged with the team to the locker rooms but not before looking at the sidelines until I found Parker. She was staring at me and gave me a small, sad smile. I looked away. I hated that this glorious moment would forever be marred by Grayson saying he won the girl.

I never knew what she saw in him. I pretended it didn't matter that she crushed my heart at the beginning of my senior year and my anger didn't fuel my need to beat him at his best game, but it was all true. As I jogged into the tunnel to the women's locker room, I made a pact to myself that Parker O'Neal was no longer going to occupy my mind or my heart. I was better than heartbreak and I had an amazing life ahead of me.

## Chapter Two—Rivals

*Present*

"At least you get a nice view."

Human resources director Selma Andrews opened the door to a decent-sized office with neutral tones and sparse furnishings. The smell of fresh paint assaulted me and I had to blink back tears. I was worried the strong scent would cause vertigo. I breathed through my mouth, hoping standing here wasn't killing valuable brain cells.

"Since the windows don't open, it's hard to get the smell out. I'll have maintenance bring over fans," she said. She stepped aside.

"Thank you." I ran my hand over the top of my desk before gently dropping a box of personal items I lugged from the parking lot about a quarter mile away to my new office. The surface of the desk was scratched and slightly dented, but sturdy. I felt it was a good representation of my journey to get to this point. Here I was, day one of being the offensive coordinator for the Connecticut Cheetahs, carrying a box full of notebooks and plays that I knew were going to be beneficial to the NFL expansion team. I was instructed to be here before seven, but judging from the hustle around me, six forty-five was late.

Bill Tatum, head coach for the Cheetahs, stuck his head in the open door. "McCoy, you're with me." He motioned me over, completely ignoring Selma who stood awkwardly in the space between us.

She stiffened at his rudeness. She wished me a good first day and turned on her heel. I gave her a soft smile, hoping it helped. I knew that some men didn't like women invading their territory, but I'd been in the minority my entire life. The things that men have said to me would have made their mothers cry, knowing their sons used such foul language. I wore a suit of armor made of bitter barbs and scars of verbal abuse over the years.

Going into this new endeavor, I was ready for cutting words. Instead, I was greeted with professionalism. I was working as the Vikings' quarterback coach when the Cheetahs offered me their offensive coordinator position. Their former offensive coordinator was caught on video sexually assaulting a woman at a bar one night. I'd like to think I was hired for my abilities, but I knew I was the token hire. The new team needed a fresh start and I was a woman who filled their résumé demands. It made the team look progressive and it directed the negative attention into something positive.

"Yes, Coach?" I asked.

He smiled at me. "Call me Bill. There's a team meeting at seven thirty with everyone. We'll break into position meetings after that. We have a lot to cover. Offense is looking at quarterbacks. Myers tore his ACL so we're looking at other options."

I wondered why I was just hearing about it now. "Wow. When did this happen?" I asked. When the Cheetahs joined the NFL, they were given first draft pick and negotiated a hotshot quarterback from Notre Dame to build the new team around. I thought he was good, but not great. They wanted him because he was young, fast, and hungry. Now that I was officially part of the coaching staff, I had a say in who stayed, who got traded, and who was cut. I wasn't expecting this kind of decision on day one.

"Last Friday. We wanted to wait until we heard back from the doctor to see if it's repairable, but he's toast. So, first thing today we're going to see what scraps are left and who can take us to the playoffs."

My mind was running through a list of possible names I could throw out if they were open to suggestions. The best players were taken, but I was sure there were a few free agents who could fill the spot. Our backup quarterback was average. There was no way he could bring our team to the championship game. He was third-string talent.

I walked into the large meeting room where players and coaches sat waiting for the meeting to start. Bill introduced me. It was a warm reception.

"I'm Sutton McCoy. I'm excited to be here at the ground level of this new team and anxious to get started on our journey." They didn't need to know my résumé. If they cared, they already knew. And I sure as hell didn't want to bring up why I was there. This was a fresh start for everyone. The room rumbled with "Hey, Coach" and "Welcome" and even some applause.

"Okay, let's get down to business," Bill said. He brought up the need for a new quarterback and how it was so important to not make decisions that could result in ending a career before it began. "Meet with your coaches, get taped up, and be careful out on the field today and every day." When he was done with his somber pep talk, we walked across the hall to a small conference room.

"Here's your staff. They'll take good care of you." He opened the door where three guys dressed in Cheetah polos and khaki shorts sat around a table staring at a list of names on a computer screen. The search for the quarterback's replacement had already started. "I think you know everyone," he said before issuing me a final nod and closing the door.

I smiled and shook hands with my staff members. We would expand our staff as we got further into pre-season and regular season, but today, I was meeting with the coaches I would work closest with. I had met with all of them over the last two weeks. Joe Crooks was the wide receivers coach. He was probably my dad's age and sported a stunning comb-over and a mustache he neglected to trim. How the poking, wiry hairs didn't bother his lips or nose astounded me. Brandon Trust was the running backs coach. He was a muscular white guy with the start of a gut. Jamal Pierson was the youngest coach on the team, and the only Black guy on the offensive staff. He was the quarterbacks coach and looked miserable at the hand fate dealt him.

"Great to see you again, Sutton," Brandon said.

"I'm glad to be a part of this. I understand there's a scramble for a new quarterback," I said. I sat and stared at the eight names on the screen that our scouts emailed Jamal.

"Of all the luck. Myers goes four-wheeling, pops a wheelie, and the ATV rolls back and crushes his leg. Even if the ACL heals properly, his knee will never be the same." Jamal sighed and leaned back. "This whole list is nothing but college kids. What about hiring a veteran? Is anybody decent still a free agent? Maybe a veteran can help solidify our team over the next year or two. At least until we can find another young hotshot."

"That's not a bad idea," Brandon said. He flipped through a three-ring binder in front of him. "What about Tommy Colvin or Grayson Moats? They both have been in the NFL for about ten years and have played with different teams. It shows they're versatile."

Today started out amazing. I kissed my sleepy girlfriend good-bye, scratched my dog behind the ears, had a great cup of coffee, found my parking spot, and walked into a spiderweb named Grayson Moats. As a previous quarterbacks coach, and one with a grudge, I was very aware of him over the last decade. His numbers were good, but not great. He played for Miami, Pittsburgh, and had been riding Baltimore's bench the last year before recently announcing his retirement.

"Moats just announced his retirement. Where's Colvin now?" I asked. I already knew but I wanted the focus to be on him, not Grayson. The idea of seeing Grayson with Parker O'Neal at his side made my insides twist painfully.

"He's third string for Kansas City. He'd probably love the opportunity to start at ground level," Jamal said. His sagging shoulders lifted somewhat at the news that there was light at the end of the tunnel. "Should we make some calls? Invite them both?"

"Do we want to let them know they are competing for the same job?" I asked. "Let's bring in Tommy and then if he's not the right fit, we'll invite Grayson." My voice sounded calm even though my anxiety was threatening to explode.

"I'll give him a call right now," Jamal said. He gathered his things and stopped to look at me. "I'm glad you're a part of our team, McCoy. I feel like with you here, we're already improving."

"Thank you. My goal is the same as everyone else's. I want to win games and make the Cheetahs a formidable team," I said. It sounded rehearsed but I meant it. I also wanted to prove that women could do this job, too. I knew everything about football. When I had the opportunity seven years ago to intern at the NFL, I jumped at the chance. It was the opportunity of a lifetime. Women in the NFL weren't popular, but I was more than willing to fight my way to the top and prove to the world that I was just as capable.

"I'm glad you are here, too," Joe said.

My initial conversation with Joe wasn't warm. He believed in old-school football where men were players and coaches, and women were cheerleaders or wives. He refused to shake my hand when we first met and quizzed me on stats of certain players, coaches, and the league. After fifteen minutes of grilling me and me getting every single answer right, he warmed up. By the end of the interview, we were laughing about incredible football games from before I was born.

"Thanks, Joe. I'm happy to be here," I said.

"How about we head outside and see what the team is doing?" Brandon asked.

"I'm in." I jumped up and followed Joe and Brandon out to the field. The Cheetahs had a new stadium, but the training facility and office building needed work. The tax increase on the ballot this fall would give us money for a new office complex. Right now, everything was a Band-Aid, from the fresh paint in our old offices to the hodgepodge equipment room full of secondhand weights and core strengthening machines. For now, training camp was on location, but that would change. Next year we were contracted with a college about two hours away.

"What do you think of the stadium?" Joe asked.

We stood on the fifty-yard-line and looked around. "This is top notch." It was impressive.

"We'll get an upgrade for next season on the rest," he said.

Jamal waved a rolled-up wad of paper he had in his hand to get our attention and jogged over to us. "Colvin is out, but Moats will be here tonight. I've made reservations at the steakhouse for all of us." He turned to me. "You're good with that, right?"

Fuck me. Day one and I was going to be face-to-face with my high school nemesis. It was bound to happen. When the Vikings played against whatever team he was on, I always made it a point to be up in the booth working out plays. I was never down on the field. Now I was going to have to bump elbows with him at dinner.

I forced a smile and nodded. "That sounds great." My stomach churned. "Just coaches or families, too?" I couldn't bring myself to say wife or spouse. Even fifteen years later when I should have been over everything, I couldn't let go of the tug Parker had on my heart.

"Just us and him. It'll be a quick meeting. We'll send a car to pick him up tonight," Jamal said.

"What happened to Tommy?" I asked, hoping my voice sounded normal with just a touch of concern.

"He isn't interested in starting all over with a new team. He doesn't feel like uprooting the family and wants to end his career with KC." Jamal shrugged. I never understood why some players walked away from opportunities after getting this far. I would love to play again, especially for the NFL. Even though I was older, I could still throw a spiral fifty yards.

"Did you call Terry?" Brandon asked.

Terry Scotsman was the general manager of the Cheetahs. I met him once during the interview process and a few times at NFL functions in the past. He was a quiet man with deep pockets and a southern accent.

"He'll be there. Our reservation is at seven so we have a lot of ground to cover before dinner," Jamal said.

I spent about twenty minutes with each coach and his players. My adrenaline had worn off, so by lunch, I was ready for carbs. We went back to the conference room and reviewed practice film. It was going to take a lot to get this new team to gel. According to Brandon, the plays were designed around Myers. With him out and no quarterback signed, it was hard to get the offense excited.

I stood next to Brandon and listened to him bark out today's plans. That was my job, but they were easing me into it. They practiced running plays, trap plays, and our backup quarterback threw several decent passes. The rest of the afternoon was a complete blur. We finally broke at six, but instead of going home and reviewing plays at my leisure, I had to take a quick shower, iron clothes, and head to the steakhouse. Best and worst first day ever.

A look of complete surprise washed over Grayson's face when we were introduced. He broke into a grin that highlighted the perfect five o'clock shadow on his square jaw. "Sutton. Wow. Look at you."

Jamal looked back and forth between us. "You two know each other?"

"You could say we were friendly rivals in high school. It's good to see you again, Coach McCoy," Grayson said. There was no animosity in his voice. I wanted to hate him for our history, for his success, but he seemed genuinely nice. He was still handsome with dirty blond hair that was a touch too long and brushed the collar of his white button-down shirt. He'd aged well and filled out.

"Good to see you, Grayson." The words tasted bitter.

"So, you're in the NFL. That's great. You were with the Vikings before, right?" At my curt nod, he smiled and turned to the other coaches. "This woman gave me a run for my money in high school. She beat me, fair and square, and took her team to state. She knows her stuff."

"Sutton, why didn't you mention you knew Grayson?" Jamal asked.

I shrugged. "First day. I didn't want to sway you all one way or the other." I was amazed my voice sounded so steady.

"Tell us about yourself, Moats," Jamal said after we placed our orders.

"I'm sure you have all my stats and probably know them better than I do or I wouldn't be here."

Joe roared with laughter and slapped his meaty hand on the table. "He's not wrong. Would moving here be a problem with your family? You have children, right?"

"Yes, my wife and I have two girls. Violet and Rose. They are young enough that we don't mind moving."

Grayson looked at me but didn't bring up the past. I smiled, recalling the sweet blond girls I'd seen cheering on their father. Whenever I saw them on TV, it was hard not to look at Parker, but eventually I got to the point where I could ignore her and focus on the children. They looked so much like her.

We didn't talk shop until after we all finished dinner. I was surprised I could even swallow food around Grayson, but I ate my steak and salad and even contributed to the conversation. I wanted to hate him, but he acted like we didn't have a wicked history. He was easygoing and quite charming.

"So, what are you thinking? A year? Two?" Grayson asked.

"A year contract with the possibility of an extension depending on how the season goes, but we'll get into that with your agent. We just want to see if you're interested," Jamal said. He leaned back in his chair and crossed his arms in front of his chest waiting for Grayson's response. I needed to find out what kind of deal we were offering. Everything was happening so fast.

"Well, I'm up for the challenge. I'd like to make an impression somewhere and I can't think of a better place than a fresh team," Grayson said.

Jamal was beaming. I already knew what he thought. Brandon and Joe both gave me curt nods, and Terry folded his arms across his chest. He was measuring Grayson up, but I could tell he was pleased with Grayson's answer. Grayson seemed so genuine and not like the smug asshole I remembered from a lifetime ago.

We finished our drinks and on our way out, Grayson pulled me aside. "Hey, Sutton. I wanted to make sure us working together was going to be okay. I mean, because of Parker."

Hearing him say her name almost made me wince. "Parker was a long time ago, Grayson. I'm fine working with you. We were kids and we've all moved on." I gave him a soft smile to emphasize my point even though I couldn't swallow.

"That's great to hear. Sorry for being such a shit back then. You know, about everything. You were a great quarterback, and I was jealous. I'm glad we're on the same team now. Or maybe soon to be, you know." He held out his hand.

A handshake. Years of despising this guy for taking the one thing I treasured most, and he was offering me a handshake to forgive and forget. It was childish of me to harbor the negativity. They had moved on. Truthfully, even I did. I shook his hand. "I look forward to bossing you around," I said.

He threw his head back and laughed before patting me on the back. "You're okay, Sutton. I have a feeling we're in for a wild ride."

## Chapter Three—Fumble

*Past*

"Why aren't you dressed?" Hayley, my best friend since first grade, asked. She was standing in my doorway, staring at me in disbelief. She looked beautiful in her shimmering silver dress with her hair in an updo. Her cosmetics case was tucked under her arm because I was horrible at makeup. How much time had passed since we spoke on the phone today?

"Shit. Sorry. I got caught up in..." I didn't finish but pointed at my open laptop screen, knowing she would understand. I was supposed to at least be dressed with my hair done, but instead I was still in sweatpants and a ratty T-shirt, sprawled out on the bed watching video clips of me and Parker. Movie ticket stubs, photos of us, and cleverly folded notes surrounded me like a chalk outline on my bed.

Not only had I opened the shoebox vault that stored all our memories, I'd drowned in every piece of memorabilia. Maybe my heart wouldn't feel broken if Parker had been mean to me, but she was kind and sensitive and sweet. I still didn't understand why she dumped me. I lost hours of sleep wracking my brain trying to figure out if I came on too strong, or not enough. Was I that horrible to her new friends? Maybe I should have been more patient? God, I missed her. I missed her arms around me and the tiny kisses she placed on my neck whenever we watched movies together, or how she would always play with my hair when we lay on my bed talking.

"What the fuck is happening here?" Hayley kicked off her heels and sat on the bed. She wasn't pitying me, but I could tell she felt my pain.

"I was getting ready, and legit excited about homecoming, but then I remembered Parker wouldn't be there and then I got caught up in all this stuff I should've burned." I turned my attention back to the one video I had of us kissing. After the third time I hit play, Hayley gently closed the laptop.

"Okay, enough. We have a really amazing night planned and I need you to put Parker out of your mind for just tonight." She tugged on my T-shirt. "Look, I know you're upset about her, but put yourself in her shoes. Her parents aren't cool like your dad is. They think you're a monster corrupting her which you totally aren't." She held up her hands, knowing I hated that description of our relationship. "But she has to live with them."

"I love her and I know she loves me, too."

"Nobody doubts that. It's not you and it's not her. Her parents are the world's biggest Bible-thumping assholes. If it wasn't for them, you'd still be together, right?"

I sat up and sniffled. "That's true."

"Remember that T-shirt we saw in Spencer's last week? 'If you love somebody, set them free. If they don't come back, shoot them.'" Hayley studied my face. "I saw that. It was almost a smile." She was teasing me and it was working. "She's setting you free to have fun your senior year and she's trying to make peace with her parents. I don't envy her. She's in a horrible spot."

My heart felt like a brick. "It's so unfair." Everyone was wrong. Time wasn't healing the heartbreak. Hayley put both hands on my shoulders and made me look at her.

"I know. All this sucks. The girl of your dreams dumped you, and it's hard, but that's why we need nights like tonight. Besides, you're up for homecoming queen. I voted for you so for sure you'll win."

I groaned and flopped back on the bed. "Ugh. I don't have the energy for homecoming right now." Honestly, prepping for homecoming court was the only thing taking my mind off Parker. "I want to hide in my room and look at our photos and reread the notes she slipped into my locker. Remember when she snuck that cute puma stuffed animal in my equipment bag?" It was still on my bed, the one thing that I didn't pack away. I grabbed it and absently played with its tail. Hayley picked up my favorite picture of me and Parker.

"I really like this photo. You look so fucking happy." The photo was of us on the dock last summer. We were completely relaxed. Hayley took the picture. I plucked the photo from her fingertips and held it close to my chest. "That girl is in love with you. There's no doubt about it. She let you go so you can be who you're supposed to be. Maybe someday she'll come back, but right now, her parents call the shots."

Hayley pulled out the dress we found two weeks ago. At five foot three, the junior department at every department store was designed for her size. I was six feet tall. I had to shop in women's evening wear at Nordstrom's and even then, the dress had to be altered.

"Okay, I'll get ready."

Hayley held up her hand for a high five but I ignored it. I wasn't in the mood to celebrate but I owed it to everyone to be there. It was going to take a solid hour to get ready and I was going to need every minute.

"Just so you know, you're going to win homecoming queen. Your competition sucks," she said.

"Oh, okay. Let's see." I counted on my fingers. "Head cheerleader Missy, her sidekick Amberlynn, student body president Tamryn Sykes, and Avon Vue, which I still say is a fake name, and me. I'm a nobody." A nobody who got dumped and whose heart would forever malfunction.

"Hello? You're the only female quarterback in the state! Probably in this time zone. And you have a perfect record this year."

"We're only halfway through the season." Although I pretended I didn't care, I desperately wanted the undefeated season and a trip to state just to show the world I could do it.

Hayley made me sit while she fixed my hair and applied just the right amount of makeup. I knew we were going to be late, but she didn't rush us. When she was done, she pulled me to stand in front of my full-length mirror that hung on the back of my door. "You'll win because you're nice, beautiful, and involved in every after-school sport and activity. And also, look at my amazing skills. Your hair and makeup are sweet!"

Hayley was my rock. She'd been there when we were thirteen and my mom died of ovarian cancer. She was there a few short months ago when I was dumped by Parker. She'd also had my back for every little thing in between. She was always so confident. I'd never seen her knocked down in the twelve years I'd known her.

I slipped on my heels to complete the look. "Look at me. I'm a giant. I'll be the tallest one there." Because of my height I was the best at every sport. The only time I hated it was whenever I had to dress up. Dances, award ceremonies, and away games. Everyone always stared at me.

"Are you kidding me? I don't know why you don't model, too."

"Because I have bumps, bruises, and scars." From September to December, I wore bruises like badges. My teammates winced when, the day after a game, I had a bruised chin or a butterfly Band-Aid on my hairline from one too many hits on the turf. Thankfully, track and softball weren't as physical. But her comment flattered me.

"Still the face of an angel. I'd kill for your wavy hair and dark blue eyes," she said.

"And I would love to be a normal height for the dances."

"You're going to be the big spoon in any relationship. Even if you start dating guys."

I scowled. "Not going to happen." I knew from the time I was little that I liked girls. Hayley even knew and in middle school when our hormones kicked in, we had a list of the girls I wanted as girlfriends and a list of boys she wanted as boyfriends. Our lists never crossed. "I'm sorry I wasn't ready when you got here. Thank you for getting me out of my funk," I said.

Hayley locked her arm with mine. "That's what best friends are for. Funk busters."

I laughed because it was such a corny thing to say. "I love you. Let's go have some fun."

"Oh, you mean like win homecoming queen? Yeah, I'm down for that."

❖

It took every ounce of my being not to tug at my dress. I could see the slight curve of my breasts. Even though it didn't show much, I still taped it down because the last thing I needed was for my boobs to spring free under the spotlight. Max stood next to me on stage and lifted my hand as we accepted our fate as homecoming king and queen.

"Thank you, Oak Grove!" Max pointed to his crown, then to mine. He bowed deeply to me. "And thank you, homecoming queen Sutton McCoy! Not only did we win tonight, but look at you, sis. Damn." He turned back to the crowd and pointed at me. "This is our quarterback!" The crowd whistled and hooted.

I blushed under the heavy, bright lights that illuminated us on the pop-up stage. Max led me down the stairs for the obligatory dance. He was still taller so even though he wasn't as smooth slow dancing, it was nice that I had to look up at him.

"I'm glad you won." Max was my favorite player on the team. I felt like we would stay friends long after high school was over.

"I'm glad I won, too." He laughed and twirled me. "Can you imagine me here with Avon?"

"Absolutely not." Max was dating Becca, a freshman in college, who refused to attend any high school functions. I couldn't blame her. I didn't want to be here either.

"Thank God you got the votes. Here's to the football team crushing everything," he said.

When the dance ended, he hugged me and whispered, "It's nice to see you smile and have fun again."

I hugged him. "Thanks, Max, for being a good friend, especially during the breakup."

He sighed. "That was brutal. And don't even get me started on that douchebag she's dating. Too bad I'm not on defense. I'd break his leg." His words were harsh, but they made me smile. Max had my back on the field and off.

"First loves. Ugh. Am I right?" If I didn't joke about it, I'd cry and Hayley would hate it if I ruined her stellar makeup job.

"Well, she's missing out because you're on fire and one day she's going to regret hurting you," he said.

## Chapter Four—When Past and Present Collide

*Present*

I'd spent the morning looking at films of players out on the field still trying to make our roster. Pre-season started in a few weeks and we were going to have to seriously slash names off the list. Players weren't exactly fighting to play for us, but the ones here had fire and something to prove. I liked being the underdog team because there was only one way to go.

"Well, what do we think?" Bill asked as he surveyed the players running routes, tackling blocking bags, and zigzagging through cone shuffle sprints. It looked completely chaotic to the untrained eye, but there was organization at each station.

Grayson meshed well with the team. He had stayed in shape because the Canadian Football League showed interest in him, but we nabbed him instead.

Jamal walked up before I could answer. "You know, Grayson shows a lot of promise. He's patient, sets up in the pocket, and looks for what he can out on the field. I have a good feeling about this season," Jamal said.

"I think he's going to surprise everyone," I said and meant it.

"We're a young team but we have a lot of talent. And the players have a healthy respect for Moats so we just might win a game or two," Jamal said.

My phone buzzed. I was scheduled to meet with the media in ten minutes. It was the first time I was talking to the press since becoming offensive coordinator. Terry wanted every journalist to be frothing at the mouth to get to me so he kept me quiet to build the suspense. He gave plenty of interviews about me but never put me in front of the microphones.

The Cheetahs' media liaison spent an hour earlier this morning reviewing every question with me that could come up in the press conference. I was nervous because today's interview wasn't about me, it was going to be about the scandal. Sure, they would start off asking me generic, expectant questions like how do you like the job? And then the more personal questions like why you? Did other coaches within the organization want the job? But then they would inevitably ask me about my thoughts on the previous coach. The plan was to redirect attention to me, the first female offensive coordinator in the NFL picked to carry a new team to the playoffs, and not the sex offender whose downfall was still tarnishing the team.

I excused myself when my phone rang. "McCoy." I didn't recognize the number.

"Hey, babe. Good luck today." It was my girlfriend, Lexi, who had moved with me to Connecticut not because we were serious, but because nothing was keeping her in Minnesota.

"Hey. Did you get a new phone?"

"I'm calling you through the app."

"Oh, that's right. Witness protection." I laughed. She liked to use an app for her online business. She was a licensed psychologist and offered both phone and video sessions to customers all over the country.

We hadn't spent a lot of time together since I took this job. My life hadn't slowed down since the minute the Cheetahs approached me. I had only days to find our townhouse, and while it wasn't ideal, it would work until I could find something permanent if my position here was a good fit.

"I won't keep you. I just wanted to say you're going to be great."

"Thanks. I'm still a little nervous. They've prepped me for everything so I can't imagine I'll screw it up."

"That's the right attitude. Don't let the journalists control the interview. They all suck anyway," she said.

Lexi couldn't stand how hateful the media could be toward women. They wanted us to succeed, yet they were the first to attack if we failed. I knew two women who walked away from the NFL because of the pressure that the media put on them, not because the job was too challenging.

"I've been rehearsing all morning," I said.

"I'm sure you'll do great. I mean, what's the worst that could happen? You tell the truth? You give your opinion about a sexual predator? Who's going to be upset about that?"

I sighed and rubbed my hand over my face. "I know I'm freaking out about nothing. I know Terry won't throw me to the sharks. They are extremely sensitive to this sticky situation."

"You're right. They've got your back. It'll be over in no time. What time do you think you'll be home?"

"It'll be another late night." I heard her sigh. She hated my late hours. We almost broke up last year, but once the season was over, I was home by six and we were able to salvage our relationship. Even though she knew the new job would be the same kind of hours, she promised she would try to adjust. "But I'll try to be home sooner." I was greeted with silence. "Do you have a busy afternoon?"

"Just the normal calls. Speaking of which, I should go. Good luck."

"Thanks." I felt off after I disconnected the call. She wasn't happy but I didn't have time to give her right now. Maybe that would never happen. I missed my dog more than I missed her. That probably wasn't the best sign of longevity for our relationship. "Hey, what's the policy on pets?" I asked the group.

"What do you mean?" Jamal asked.

"I guess I'm asking if I can bring my dog to work."

He pointed at me with the rolled-up mysterious paper still in his hand. "Technically, you're the boss. You make the rules."

He was right. And Crowbar would love to curl up in my office or sit by my side during practice. He was the most well-behaved dog on the planet. "Gotcha."

"Too bad your dog isn't a cat. Then we'd have a real mascot." Jamal pointed to the new mascot, Champ the Cheetah, across the field who was taking selfies with the fans who showed up for training camp. People paid good money to be here and watch the new team in action. Some were curious about the Cheetahs, and some were here because of the veterans like Grayson and tackle Jeremy Pickles. It felt like a circus.

"I'm headed in for the press conference." I checked my watch for the thousandth time. "Wrap up practice. It's getting hot and we need to review the film."

He nodded and blew his whistle. I jogged back to the offices and took a moment to look presentable. I shut the door to my office and slipped into a fresh polo and pressed khakis. My tan hid the dark circles from lack of sleep. I added a bit of makeup and brushed my hair. Bill knocked a second before I opened the door.

"You ready?"

"Yes, sir." I matched his stride and we walked into the press room with confidence. It was right there with me until I saw a hundred people with lanyards and cameras around their necks, then it disappeared. The room went from loud chatter to instant quiet when I stood behind Bill.

"Please meet Sutton McCoy, the Cheetahs' offensive coordinator. Let's take it easy this first go-round." Bill stepped back and allowed me to adjust the microphone. I was a few inches taller.

I cleared my throat. "Hello." Hands shot up like a roomful of sixth graders waving to get my attention. Some even called out my name. I didn't know a single person in the room. Did I call them out by what they were wearing? Plaid shirt guy with thick glasses? Woman wearing the hideously bright green dress? Dude who still looked like he was in high school with his baby face and swooping bangs?

"Les," Bill's voice boomed out, alleviating the stress of who to call on first.

A man with a receding hairline wearing a navy polo stood. "Coach McCoy, Lester Moore from ESPN. How has the reception been as the newest coach for the Cheetahs?"

Easy question. I put on a sweet smile and answered him honestly. "The reception has been warm and inviting. I get along well with the other coaches and the players take my advice. It's been a very positive experience. It was a fight to get here, but well worth it."

"A fight to get here? What do you mean?"

First question and I already fucked up. "When you have several people vying for the same job, it gets a little stressful when you are waiting for the call." He sat down satisfied with the answer when more people raised their hands to be next. I knew eventually I would learn all their names, but in the meantime, Bill barked out names.

"Maria."

She stood and looked at her phone. "Maria Cortez, *Sports Illustrated*. Coach McCoy, what's is like being the first female offensive coordinator in the NFL?"

I exhaled and gave the answer I'd practiced. "It's an amazing opportunity. I hope that I'm not the last. In the last five years, the NFL has opened its doors to female coaches, trainers, referees, owners, and even the first female commissioner. It was just a matter of time before one of us had the title of offensive coordinator."

"Any pushback?" Her follow-up question was expected.

"None. The players only want to get better and they trust me and the team of coaches within the organization to make that happen for them. I know football and they know that I do." I clamped my mouth shut and waited for the next question. As planned, they were easy and predictable, and I answered each one confidently. I was on a roll until Duane Spitzer from *USA Today Sports* brought up my past before college.

"You went to Oak Grove High School."

He waited for some sort of confirmation. I nodded. "Yes?" I wanted to say "so what" but that would have been rude.

"You were the first female quarterback in your state. You even took the Oak Grove Pumas to the state championship game where your team put up a good fight but lost seven to twenty."

"Thank you, Duane, for bringing up a painful memory." I chuckled and was met with nervous laughter from the group. It appeared we were all somewhat confused by his line of questioning. "Next question."

He stood and waved his hand at me and them. "Wait. I'm not done."

"Duane, we don't have all day. Final question and then we're moving on," Bill said.

I didn't like Duane. I could tell by his mannerisms and the way he shushed others around him that he was going to be a problem in future press conferences.

"The team has just signed Grayson Moats as the Cheetahs' starting quarterback." He didn't wait for confirmation. He kept talking. "You played against Grayson when you were a Puma, right?"

There was a slight murmur. "It's a small world. We're from the same state. And yes, we joked about it the night before he signed." I glanced over at Bill.

"Sit down, Duane," he said. He didn't seem overly fond of Duane either.

Duane waved again. "No, wait. Last question."

I motioned for him to continue and kept the eye roll in check.

"So, you laughed about it before he signed. Was it awkward seeing his wife, your ex-girlfriend, again after fifteen years?" he asked.

That was a question nobody prepared me for. I tried to breathe. I could feel my lungs clawing for air. I tried not to react. Instead, I looked at Bill for help. He didn't miss a beat.

"Whatever history Moats and Coach McCoy have was a long time ago. They don't have any issues. Coach McCoy was a driving force in getting Moats to play for us. Next question," he said.

Apparently, one scandal per interview was enough because nobody asked the question the liaison prepared me for all morning. The rest of the conference went smoothly. There were even some laughs as we were winding down. Most of the journalists wished me well. I couldn't look at Duane's smug face. I exited the conference room and was immediately ushered into a private office. I wasn't sure if it was for debriefing or just to get me away from the press.

Terry, Bill, and the press liaison walked into the room. I waited for them to sit and braced myself for the onslaught of questions.

"Is there any truth to Duane's question?" Terry asked.

I looked at them. "We were kids. I wouldn't say we were girlfriends. It was a summer romance. And she wasn't out so I don't know how Duane dug that nugget up." I knew that denying would only hurt my career here. "Her very religious parents didn't like me and refused to allow us to be together. Did she move on and date Grayson? Yes. Did it hurt? Yes. But we're all adults now. None of us are giving any thought to who we dated as teenagers."

Bill dabbed at the sweat on his forehead with a handkerchief. "Did you and Grayson really discuss it?"

"Yes. The night we went to dinner to recruit him. He asked if it was going to be a problem. I told him no. That relationship was a lifetime ago," I said.

Terry and Bill exchanged a look. "Find Grayson," Terry said to Bill. Bill nodded and left the room. Terry folded his arms. "Do you think that's something you should have disclosed when we brought up Grayson the day you started?"

I shook my head, refusing to allow his tone to get to me. "I didn't. It was a long time ago. Grayson and I talked about it. It was a private moment between us. We're good."

He pressed his lips together tightly and nodded. "While we wait for them, let's talk about your first press conference. How do you feel about it?"

Other than being completely derailed, it was okay. I leaned back in my chair. "I thought it went well. I'm glad nobody brought up the previous coach."

"What's going on, Coach?" Grayson entered the room followed closely by Bill.

"Have a seat, Moats," Terry said.

Grayson's eyes darted between the three of us. I kept my gaze steady and firm and gave him a very slight head nod. His shoulders lowered in relief.

"We were just informed by a journalist that you and Sutton have history. I understand from McCoy that it's water under the bridge."

He nodded vehemently. "Definitely. We talked about it the night you flew me out here."

"We think that's great, but we want to present a united front," Terry said. He pointed directly at both of us. "If this comes up again, we want everyone to think you are best friends. This team can't handle any more scandals. We're too new and we have a lot to prove this year."

"No problem, Coach. Sutton and I are cool," Grayson said.

I leaned forward. "Yeah, we're fine. Really, Terry."

"Fine isn't good enough. I want the press to believe you're buddies. Best buddies. Can you make that happen?" Terry asked.

I looked at Grayson and shrugged. "Of course."

"No problem here," he said.

Terry looked at Bill and back to us. "Okay. Let's get back to work."

Bill nodded and stood when Terry did. "Let's see how the team did without us." He rapped his knuckles on the table, dismissing us. I couldn't get out of there fast enough. I took a few minutes to catch my breath in my office and then made a beeline for the practice field. Most of the players were over at the stands, signing autographs and taking selfies.

"How was it?" Jamal asked.

"Fine." I didn't want to get into it with him now. He'd find out soon enough. My nerves were shot, and I was jittery. "What's going on?" I nodded in the direction of the fans, irritated that the team was fraternizing with them instead of pounding out plays on the field.

"It's lunchtime and they're feeling famous. Look at them." He shook his head and waved them off.

"They have twenty minutes left of lunch to actually eat and get back to the film room." I took a deep breath and let it out slowly. "But it looks like they are having fun." I was taking out my anger and anxiety on Jamal and it wasn't fair.

"Want to go over there and be seen and heard?"

I waved him off and scoffed. "Hell, no. I've had enough of questions and time in front of cameras today."

"Okay. Well, I'm going to head over there. I'll see you in the meeting."

I shaded my eyes and watched Jamal head over to Brandon and the team as they met the fans and signed memorabilia. I didn't want to stand out on the field by myself and I didn't want to go inside. I was still trying to cool off from the shit show that was my first press conference. My phone buzzed in my pocket. It was Lexi.

*How'd it go?*

Lexi didn't know about my history with Parker. Nobody I ever dated did. I put her in the past and tried to fool my heart that we never existed. I hated that the wound was fresh again. *It was fine. Just a lot of saying the same thing over and over.*

*That's great! I knew you could do it.*

I didn't feel like talking right now. I needed to clear my head. *Thanks. Gotta go. See you tonight.* As I turned to walk into the building, I was surprised to see Grayson on the field holding a child. When it finally registered that he was holding his own daughter, it was too late for me to stop looking.

My eyes darted in search of her even though I tried to tell myself to look away. I saw her and she saw me. Fifteen years later and I was back on that field after winning the game but losing my heart. She had the same sad smile on her face. I tried to look calm. The fluttering of my heart only got worse when our eyes met. I could feel it. We always had that connection in school. I could find her in the cafeteria, or library, or even the football field and we would share a promising look across the large space. It was harder to hide it during our games because I wanted her approval. Everything I did out on the field was for her. Now, she had Grayson.

I broke eye contact first and tried to walk casually back to the offices. I felt more comfortable dealing with the sharks inside who were desperate to derail me with their slick questions than the free-falling I was experiencing inside. At least during the questioning, I had words. I nodded to a few of the defensive coaches still on the field and kept walking until I was safely inside the building. I had to get away from her ridiculously blue eyes drilling into mine, searching for answers to questions never asked from a long time ago.

## Chapter Five—Sacked

*Past*

"Do you think you can sneak away?" I was desperate to see Parker. I missed her and I knew she was having a hard time settling into her new school.

"My dad is constantly checking my mileage. I don't think it's a good idea right now," she said.

Instead of running plays with the team, I was sneak-calling Parker from the empty girls' locker room. We had tried blocking our numbers with *67, but her parents checked the phone records and threatened to take away her phone. Now I called the pay phone on her school campus fifteen minutes after the last period let out. We only got a few minutes each day so we treasured them.

Parker's parents told my dad that I wasn't allowed to call or have any contact with her. They didn't approve of my gay lifestyle and blamed me for making Parker doubt Jesus and the word of God. Their words, not mine. On top of that, they thought a girl playing football was an abomination. My dad told them I would keep my distance.

Now, I was curled up in a ball on the locker room floor hiding from my responsibilities, begging the person who mattered most to me in the world to defy the rules just to be with me. "Not even halfway? I mean, I can meet you at the park later today."

"I can't. I want to, but I have cheer practice later and then a bunch of us are going to like grab pizza or whatever." She paused as though she said too much.

I sat up when I heard one of the outer doors to the gym open. "Well, I mean you have to have friends, right?" Even though her squad was a bunch of mean, bitchy girls, at least she had her cousin Emilia to lean on.

I rubbed my hand over my face. Everything about this sucked. When she left, my stomach was in knots for weeks. I forgot to eat for three days, which made me pass out at practice. Coach was pissed.

Hayley stuck by my side and assured me this wasn't the end of my life. She said if we were meant to be, then Parker would be back. It was like she and my dad had a conversation about me because both were saying the same thing.

"I'm trying to fit in. Mom says it's not healthy to mope and I need to be social. I don't want to upset them. Dad's pretty mad and I still need their help with college."

"So, you're going to let them hold you hostage for the next five or so years? I know they're your parents, but they're homophobic jerks. They're going to do everything in their power to keep us apart. Forever, not just high school." I was pouting and I knew it.

"This is hard on me too. I miss you. At least you can talk to everyone about it. I'm alone here, Sutton."

"I know. I'm sorry. I just hate that you let them continue to make your decisions for you. Are you going to let them dictate your whole life? If you don't stand up to them now, they're going to forever be a pain in your ass."

It was hard enough that she moved away, but trying to find alone time with her when our schedules were so packed was almost impossible. She had cheer and a new life to start while I hung back, fearing my heart would simply give out because we were apart.

She sighed. It wasn't the sweet kind of sigh, but the kind that signaled she was irritated with me. "I'll sneak away this weekend. Maybe we can meet halfway in Spencer? In our normal place?" she asked.

I should've been excited that she was willing to go against her parents, but I wasn't. I felt like it was a pity meeting and my anger flared. "Don't worry about it. Listen, I have to get out on the field. I'll talk to you later." I hung up, grabbed my helmet, and jogged to the field.

When we finally met at the park in Spencer the following weekend, I forgot about all the heartache of the last few weeks. Parker looked amazing. She slipped into my front seat and pulled me into her arms. I cried as I held her.

"How are you? Are you okay?" I asked.

She nodded before her lips captured mine in the kind of kiss that reminded me why I would do anything for her.

"I'm doing all right. I'm fitting in, but it's so hard to start senior year at a different school," she said.

She stroked my face and ran her fingers through my hair. I felt the love in her touch. I'd forgotten how blue her eyes were. I used to tease her that they were the same color as the cornflower crayon because I'd never seen eyes that color before.

"Your parents suck." I was being nice. They were awful. Her dad got transferred to a different branch of whatever insurance company he worked for, but Emilia told Parker that he requested it. She overheard her mother and Parker's mom discussing the reason behind the move. It was because of me, the sinner who defiled their sweet, innocent daughter. Again, their words, not mine.

"I know this is hard, Sutton." She started crying.

A wave of protectiveness bubbled up from deep inside me. I hated that they hurt her, hurt us by keeping us apart. "One day when we're done with high school, we'll be together. Nothing's going to keep us apart. Not them, and not the world," I said.

She sobbed against me and I thought we were crying about the same thing, but I was wrong.

"I can't do this anymore, Sutton. It's just so hard."

I pulled out of her embrace, stunned. "What do you mean? What can't you do?"

"My parents treat me like I'm worthless. It's hard making new friends. I'm an outsider trying to fit in. I have cheer practice every day and finding time to sneak away is almost impossible. I feel like I'm lying to everyone in my life."

She tried touching me, but I pulled back. "Are you breaking up with me?" Fresh tears popped up in the corners of my eyes but I didn't care.

"I have to, Sutton. I can't live like this. It's not fair that I have to keep you a secret because of my parents. You deserve to be out and proud. This is your senior year. You're supposed to have the best time of your life, and I know that keeping you in the closet is holding you back."

"But it's only for eight months. Until we go to college," I said. Her parents would only let her apply to Christian colleges. She was applying to Abilene which was only about three hours from A&M, and to Calvin in Michigan which was a whole world away. She made a sobbing noise.

"I'm going to Calvin. My parents said they won't help me at all if I go to ACU."

"Wait, what?"

"It's not fair to you to ask you to wait for me. Michigan and Texas are thousands of miles apart."

"So, you just want to give up? You're eighteen. You can pack your stuff and move in with me and Dad. Then we can go to A&M together. You don't need their money."

She shook her head and grabbed my hands. "They're my parents, Sutton. I'm all they have. I can't just leave them." I watched the tears trickle down her face and knew I was losing her. There wasn't anything I could do about it. "I love you and that's why I'm doing this. Trying to date long-distance is impossible. This is hard enough and we're only a hundred miles apart."

Everything she said made sense, but my heart wouldn't concede. I was too invested. I put my head on my steering wheel and cried. I felt her arms wrap around my body as she cried with me.

"I will always love you, Sutton."

I looked at her through the tears that wouldn't stop falling. "How can you do this to me?"

"I'm doing this for both of us. You'll always have my heart." She opened the door and slowly slipped out.

"You're making the biggest mistake," I said. When I realized that this wasn't a joke, I got angry. "Go ahead and forget about me. Forget my face, forget everything that happened, and lose my number!" I watched as she walked to her car and drove away without so much as a backward glance. I sat in the parking lot wondering how my heart slipped out of my grasp so effortlessly when just a few short minutes ago it was something I held onto for dear life.

## Chapter Six—First Meeting, Again

*Present*

I was dreading tonight. Like on a scale of one to ten, I was at an eleven. Lexi felt my tension even though I tried to hide it.

"Come on. It'll be fun. I promise to be on my best behavior," Lexi said.

I smiled because she was charming and I knew she would look good on my arm. "I know you will." I kissed her softly. "You make me look good."

She posed and slowly spun so that I could see her amazing dress and heels and how perfect her hair and makeup were. Her auburn hair, when curled and styled, touched her shoulders. Her hazel eyes shifted from blue when she was happy to green when she cried. She was hot, no doubt about it, but I was also getting bored again. I didn't have time for a girlfriend, but I didn't know how to tell her that either. Our fights were becoming more frequent.

Tonight, she was being nice. We were going to a black-tie event in downtown Bridgemont where coaches and starters were introducing their charities to the public. It was a big event and tickets were by special invitation only. If you weren't on the list, you didn't get in.

"Now, hurry up and get ready. I don't want to be late," Lexi said.

I dropped my towel and slipped into the cream-colored double strap one-shoulder fit evening gown that Lexi wanted me to wear. I didn't have a lot of time to mess with my hair so I blew it straight, applied makeup, and slipped on strappy heels. I stood in front of Lexi when I was ready.

"Well, how do I look?"

She ran her hands down my sides and rested them on my hips. "You look incredible. I'm going to have to fight everyone off tonight."

"I'll be the wallflower standing by the bar," I said.

"You'll be the one surrounded by all the football players who want to talk shop with you." She rolled her eyes and smirked. It seemed odd that she wanted to start a fight tonight.

"Well, it is about football. All of this," I said.

"I'll just hang back with the girlfriends and wives and we'll talk about how we never get to see our partners during the season."

She was in for a rude awakening when she found out the players were home by six or seven. The coaches hung back to talk about the day's practices and how to improve plays. If we could, we'd stay there all night. A new team was exhausting, but we were all so excited to make this happen. Lexi would never understand.

It also didn't help that tonight I was most certainly going to run into Parker. It was inevitable. I had managed to avoid all gatherings with her until tonight. As I drove into town, I thought about how I was going to handle seeing and talking to Parker after all these years.

"Is there anybody I should avoid? Or be mean to? Are you on anybody's shit list? Because I won't stand for that," Lexi said. She put her hand on my thigh and gave me a small squeeze.

"Nope. It's all good." I hoped that was true. The closer we got to the event, the more I sweated. I turned up the air.

"Oh, babe. You'll ruin your makeup." She touched my brow and adjusted the vents to blow on me. "Are you that nervous about tonight? I mean, you're going to be around your people. If anyone should be sweating, it's me. I'm going to meet your boss and the owner of the Cheetahs."

She wasn't this self-centered when we first met. "It's a lot for both of us." I turned my attention back to the road and got us to the event right on time. I gave the valet my fob and a hefty tip to keep the car close. If things went south, I wanted to get out as quickly as possible.

"Looking good, Coach." Anthony Quinn, our running back, stopped to introduce us to his girlfriend, Crystal. She was friendly and they looked stunning together.

"You both look amazing." I introduced them to Lexi who turned up the charm.

"It's so nice to finally meet you. Sutton talks about you all the time," she said.

Anthony beamed with pride. "It's been great having her on our team," he said.

There was a comfort walking into the hotel with another couple. I was sure they would break off from us as soon as we got to the ballroom, but having Anthony next to me helped me relax.

"Are you excited to talk about your charity? Running Back Packs, right?" I asked him. If I remembered correctly, the organization gave food-insecure children packs of easy-to-prepare food for the weekends.

"It's near and dear to me." He emphasized by placing both hands over his heart.

"I think it's great," I said. I reached for Lexi's hand when we found the ballroom.

"Your hands are sweaty, babe." Her hand grew limp in mine and I knew it was only a matter of seconds before she dropped it.

"Sorry. I'm a little nervous."

"Sutton, over here." Brandon waved me over to a table with the offensive coaches. The large table was already littered with glasses of wine, water, and longnecks. I wondered what time everyone arrived. "This is my wife, Tina."

I shook her hand and introduced Lexi to the table. The men smiled at her appreciatively and the other wives, once introduced to us, seemed snobbish except for Tina. Lexi wasted no time in finding a waiter and ordering a glass of chardonnay. I asked for water. The last thing I needed was alcohol.

The room quieted as Terry made his way to the podium at the front of the room. There were easily three hundred people in the ballroom. I relaxed a fraction when I didn't see Grayson or Parker.

"Thank you all for coming this evening. As a new team, we are anxious for you all to get to know us and learn about our charities. It's important for us to spend time with our community and give back. I'm sure you saw the tables in the hallway with the different charities. Please chat with the players and coaches if you have any questions. You'll find them floating around. Cheers, everyone!"

Just what I didn't want. Free time. I thought it was an organized event where we spoke briefly about our charities, ate dinner, and left after an hour. Instead, it was an upscale buffet with a full staff behind each station to serve us. Lexi wanted to wait to eat and I was fine with that. I was good sitting in my chair the whole evening with the rest of the room behind me.

Lexi stood and leaned over my shoulder to take my drink order. "Do you want anything to drink? I'm going to socialize and grab another wine."

"I'm fine with water." I smiled and nodded. I turned my attention back to Tina. "So, you plant the bulbs in the fall?" I was getting a lesson on tulips and, right now, it was everything to me.

"Well, if it isn't homecoming queen turned NFL pro."

I turned when I heard Max's voice. "Max! What are you doing here?" I jumped up and hugged him tightly. I pushed him away only to pull him back for another hug. "Why didn't you tell me you were coming?" I'd talked to him on the phone during my first week with the Cheetahs. He was so happy for me. He had just opened his fifth gym in the northeast this spring.

"I wanted it to be a surprise. I have business over in Boston and thought I'd swing by and see how my favorite quarterback is doing."

"I can't believe this. I'm so freaking happy!" I took his hand and squeezed. "Let me introduce you to everyone." He shook my staff's hands and had a little something to say about each coach, noting a great call they made during their careers.

"You were great in Dallas. I'm sorry your career got cut short," Jamal said.

Max had blown out his knee during his third year. He waved Jamal off. "I'm still blessed. I miss football, but I don't miss the pain every week."

"How do you know McCoy?" Brandon asked.

"We went to the same high school," Max said.

"Small world, huh? Grayson Moats is from around your area, too. Do you know him?" Jamal asked.

Max smiled. "We've shared space before." He turned to the table. "It was nice to meet you all, but this one needs to show me her charity." He locked arms with me and escorted me out into the large hall where tables with information on our charities were available to scan or take home. The administrative staff worked with all of us and were in charge of staging tonight. They did an incredible job. It was hard to get through the crowd to get to my charity, Book Ends, which encouraged kids to read more and also gave them a sense of social responsibility. For every book they read, a book was donated to a school in need.

Max smiled. "Why did you pick this? I don't remember you reading a lot in school."

"I love to read. I was too busy in high school but read a ton in college. Now I listen to audiobooks to and from work."

"Do you sleep?" He moved closer and lowered his voice. "Is Lexi still around?"

I shushed him as I looked around in case she sneaked up on us. "She is. She's even here tonight." Max had met her once when we first started dating and told me to run the other way. He got bad vibes. Hayley felt the same. She'd helped us move here but was completely perplexed about why I was okay with Lexi moving to Connecticut with me. Lexi overheard and they got into a huge fight. Hayley ended up leaving early and now we only talked on my lunch breaks or on my way home, never when Lexi was around.

He pulled me close. "I don't want you to freak out, but Parker and Grayson are here."

My back was to the crowd which gave me time to prepare myself. "How does she look?"

He raised his eyebrow and paused. "You look better."

"Shit," I muttered.

"Uh-oh."

My heart stopped and the blood in my veins turned to ice. "What does that mean?"

He smiled and nodded. "She's coming over," he said through clenched teeth as he kept a smile on his face.

"I'm not ready."

"Not an option." He turned me slowly to face Parker.

I held my breath, knowing she would take it away if I didn't. I knew she would grow into a beautiful woman and I'd seen a few photos, but I just wasn't prepared to see her this close and in person.

"Hi, Sutton. Hi, Max," Parker said. She looked stunning. She still had the brilliant eyes that could sear right through me. She was wearing a short black dress that clung to her and landed right at the knee. She accessorized with gold jewelry including a small brooch of our team's logo pinned to her dress. Motherhood had given her nice curves. She was cute in high school, but as an adult, she was a knockout. Her long blond hair was highlighted and pulled over one shoulder.

"Hi, Parker. It's good to see you again," I said. I wished I would've had that glass of wine.

"Hey, Parker. It's so good to see you again after all these years," Max said. He leaned forward and gave her a stiff hug. I didn't move. It took my stomach ten seconds to stop quivering. Once my body relaxed, my anxiety at seeing her again after so many years vanished. I knew it was my brain protecting my heart. We had all moved on, but my guard was still up.

"Congratulations, Sutton. I always knew you would make it big. If anyone could break the glass ceiling at the NFL, it would be you," she said.

After fifteen years, that's what she said to me? I forced a smile. "Thank you. It's always been my dream." I was going to say something likewise, but I knew nothing about Parker's life on purpose. Bits and pieces of hers popped up only because of Grayson.

After a long awkward pause, Max spoke up. "What's Grayson's charity?" he asked Parker.

She pointed behind her to the obnoxiously large Keeping in Motion banner. The organization donated bikes to kids to promote exercise and health. There was a crowd around Grayson in his booth. He looked happy and handsome as he flirted with the press.

"It's getting a lot of attention. The idea is to get kids away from electronics and back to nature. You know, exercise and adventure." Parker stared at me the entire time. It was unnerving. I tried to look bored, but not rude. I had no idea what to say.

"I think it's great," Max said.

"Max! What are you doing here?" Lexi swooped into our conversation and looped her arm around Max's shoulder. He was nicer about my relationship with her than Hayley was.

"Hey, Lexi. Good to see you again."

Lexi reached her hand out to Parker. "Hi, I'm Lexi. I'm with her." She gave me a small hip bump and waited for somebody to introduce her to the sexy woman standing close to me.

"Hi, I'm Parker Moats, Grayson's wife." Parker shook her hand.

Lexi held Parker's hand with both of hers. "Wow. Nice rock." She studied the giant diamond ring embarrassingly hard. "I'm so glad to meet you. I need a friend to sit with during the home games."

The absolute last thing I needed was for my girlfriend and my high school ex-girlfriend to be friends.

"Hey, Coach. Congrats on your charity," Grayson said. I hadn't even seen him slip up behind Parker until he put his arm around her shoulders. There wasn't any animosity in his body language or his demeanor. Apparently, I was the only one who still harbored any anxiety over the situation. "Max, right?" Grayson shook Max's hand. "Good to see you again, man."

I felt Max tense. Maybe not the only one.

"Congrats on signing with the Cheetahs. You have the best coaches in the league." Max bumped his shoulder gently against mine.

"No doubt," Grayson said.

He seemed so charismatic and friendly and the longer we stood chatting, the more it seemed like I was being the childish one. Lexi held my hand which didn't go unnoticed by Parker, but nothing on her face gave me any indication that it bothered her. Parker asked Lexi questions about her therapy practice and seemed genuinely interested in everything she said. She turned those deep blue eyes on me and opened her mouth to speak when we were interrupted.

"Coach McCoy, Grayson Moats. Would you mind if we did a quick interview?" Grayson and I turned to find a local TV reporter poised and ready to film with a cameraman three steps behind her. I'd seen her on the ten o'clock prime time news. She was blond and attractive. Grayson looked at me and I nodded. The reporter wasted no time in directing us to a more private place away from the traffic by the tables.

"You two used to play football against one another, right?"

"She destroyed me in high school." Grayson was being overdramatic, but it was done in jest and we all smiled. "I'm so fortunate to be on her team this time." I was impressed with his acting skills. The reporter turned to me.

"I'd say it's mutual. Grayson is an excellent quarterback," I said.

"Are there any hard feelings between you two?" she asked.

Grayson put his arm across my shoulders. He made it seem friendly rather than invasive. "Not a single one. I've admired her for a long time. First in high school then in the NFL. I can't think of a better offensive coach to take us far our first year."

I smiled through my nerves and almost convinced myself I was having a good time. "Even when we were teenagers, Grayson was a powerful leader. I can't wait to see what he does with this team."

"It sounds like you two have a great history." The reporter moved to my other side so the cameraman could get a shot of the crowd behind us. "So, tell us about your charities. Let's start with you, Coach McCoy."

Grayson and I said wonderful things about each other's charity and it was easier to relax once I had something else to talk about. Grayson was engaging and the reporter was obviously smitten. She thanked us for the interview and moved on to find Jamal to do a segment on his athletic program for children.

Grayson leaned closer. "I wasn't lying. I think you're one of the best."

It amazed me how different he was now as an adult. He was almost too nice. "Thanks, Grayson. I appreciate it." I didn't know what else to say. He either really took what Terry said to heart, or he meant it.

We walked back to our partners and Max. The moment he was visible, people started calling Grayson's name. "Well, I hate to break up this reunion of sorts, but I need to get back to the table. Parker, I want to introduce you to a few people. Excuse us."

"It's so good to see you again, Sutton," Parker said. Her voice was a little more mature, and I still got a chill when she said my name.

"You, too."

"Come on, babe. I need food so the wine doesn't go to my head," Lexi said.

"You two go on ahead. I'm going to talk to a few of the players I know," Max said.

Lexi and I slipped back into the ballroom and got in line for the buffet. The thought of food wasn't appealing, but I had to keep up the pretenses. I ordered a white wine and welcomed another in-depth conversation about tulip bulbs and mums with Tina. I ended up eating half of what was on my plate.

Just like I was always able to do back in high school, I immediately felt Parker when she stepped into the room. I watched as she and Grayson weaved through the tables until they sat with the other quarterbacks and their dates. She didn't engage in conversation with the wives. Every time I glanced her way, she was staring at me. Her attention released feelings I had buried. Was she happy? Was she living the life she wanted? Did she finish college? Why was I so invested?

"I think I'm going to go. That's okay, right? If I don't leave now, I'm going to eat all the dessert," Lexi said. She sounded bored. She didn't know anyone and she lasted longer than I expected.

I was freaked by the rebirth of my fascination with Parker, but I remained outwardly calm and even managed to give Lexi a smile. "That's fine. I need to find Max and see what his plans are."

"Maybe I should take a Lyft home. I don't think you should leave yet," she said.

I wasn't going to fight her. "Do you want me to order you one?" I pulled out my phone, knowing the answer already. "It'll be here in six minutes. By the time we get to the lobby, it will be out front." I stood and held out my hand. We took the long way around the room, careful to avoid running into Parker again.

"I won't be out too long." I kissed her as she slipped into the Lyft. "Let me know when you make it home." I stayed outside for a few moments before going back inside. I needed fresh air.

"Oh, good. I thought you left without saying bye." Max walked out on my way in.

"I was putting Lexi in a Lyft."

He put his hands on my upper arms. "How are you doing?"

I walked right into his arms for another hug. "It's been an emotional night. What are your plans?"

"I'm going to hang out with you. Let's promote your charity." He escorted me inside and walked me to my charity table. He took a couple of photos and posted them along with a link to my website that asked for donations.

"Sutton, can I talk to you a minute?" Parker asked.

I turned and found her about five feet from me. I looked at Max.

"I'm going to grab a beer. Do either of you want anything?" he asked.

My mouth was dry and swallowing was impossible. "I'll take a water," I said. Parker shook her head and Max slipped away quickly. "What's going on?"

"I'd like to sit down and chat with you sometime if that's all right. I know it's been a long time. If you don't want to, I understand." She touched my arm briefly but pulled her hand away when I looked down at her fingertips on my skin. As though she recognized my waffling, she added, "I want to know what your life has been like since high school. It sounds like it's been an amazing ride."

My anxiety was at a ten when I first arrived and now I couldn't feel anything at all. Maybe the initial shock of sharing space with her was over. Our relationship was half a lifetime ago and maybe we really could be friends. It would be good for Grayson, the team, and honestly, good for me. I loved her deeply a long time ago and I did want to know about her life since we split.

"Yeah, that sounds nice. I'd like to hear what you've been up to as well."

She found a pen on the table and wrote her number on one of my charity flyers. "I know you're busy with the season starting up, but let me know when you're free to have coffee or lunch." She turned as Max approached with a beer and a tall water. "Bye, Max. It was good to see you again."

He handed me the water as we watched her leave. "How do you really feel about that?" He faced me and waited for my reaction.

I felt defeated when I looked at him. "I honestly don't know right now. I'm too overwhelmed. But we both know I'm going to call her anyway."

## Chapter Seven—Turnover

*Past*

We met Parker's new friends at a mall by Hilltop High. It was so hard not to grab Parker's hand or pull her close.

"This is my best friend, Sutton McCoy. She's the quarterback for Oak Grove."

"Hi," I said.

One of them stood. She was pretty and had an adorable smile with pronounced dimples. "I'm Emilia. It's nice to finally meet you." She gave me a quick hug.

"Hi. I've heard so much about you."

Amanda looked me up and down and smirked. She nudged Kirsten with her elbow. What was it about cheerleaders and their bitchiness? "You're tall," she said.

I shrugged. "I model in my spare time." Even though it was a total lie, Hayley would be so proud of me. "But not during football season." Their eyes widened and I could tell they were trying to figure out if I was lying or not. I fluffed out my hair and struck a pose.

Parker snorted. "She's just playing around although she totally could," Parker said. She winked at me. "Modeling is way better than pageantry."

"You were Miss Mountain View, weren't you?" I asked.

Parker held up two fingers. "Twice."

Amanda and Kirsten looked at one another. "That's really cool." They were clearly impressed by the pageant wins and not my sports career, which told me exactly what I needed to know about them.

Amanda and Kirsten were obviously the type who gave all cheerleaders a bad name. Despite the bitchiness, I could understand why Parker joined cheer. Her parents gave her an option. She could either cheer or join their youth ministry. Cheering was easy, and even though she didn't like it, it kept her occupied. And with Emilia on the team, it made fitting in a lot easier. It made my heart happy that she knew somebody else going to her new school. Parker told me she'd told Emilia about us. Emilia thought it was great and said our secret was safe with her. After two minutes with Amanda and Kirsten, I doubted the rest of the squad would react the same.

"Are you dating anyone, Sutton?" Kirsten asked.

Sbarro smelled delicious and I regretted succumbing to peer pressure and ordering an Orange Julius like the rest of Parker's friends. Kirsten's question rattled me. I held my finger up as I swallowed. "Not at the moment."

"Even with all those yummy football boys around?" Amanda asked.

I laughed a little too loud. Clearly, Parker hadn't told them I was a lesbian. "After you play football with them, they don't smell so yummy."

"We should find you somebody. Parker already has a few guys interested. It's just a matter of time before she figures out which one she likes," Amanda said.

Red splotches appeared on Parker's cheeks. "It's only because I'm the new girl." She refused to look at me.

Kirsten leaned forward. "Speak of the devil." She waved at a group of guys. "Hey, Grayson."

A tall, good-looking guy with sandy-blond hair walked over to the table. Based on his build and Hawkeyes shirt, I immediately knew he was the quarterback of their school. He was flanked by oversized guys who were clearly his linebackers.

"What's going on?" He nodded at everyone, but his eyes landed on Parker. She avoided eye contact. He smiled confidently. "Parker, it's good to see you out. I didn't think your parents ever let you do anything." He pulled up a chair and sat on the end of the table closest to her.

"My best friend came up to visit so we're all hanging out." She seemed so nervous around him. Something felt off.

"Get this, Grayson. Sutton is a quarterback, too," Amanda said.

He busted out laughing and covered his mouth with his fist. The two goons howled. "You? You're a quarterback?"

"Yeah, so?" I asked. I wanted to verbally drop my résumé in front of him, but something told me he didn't care.

He crossed his arms. "I've never heard about you. Are you new? What school?" One of his buddies punched him.

"This is my third year leading the Oak Grove Pumas."

More snickers. "Divisions must kill you. I've never heard of Oak Grove. I've been the quarterback for Hilltop since sophomore year and we've gone to state the last two years. We'll go again this year. There's no competition." He waved his hand at me. "No offense."

I bit my cheek to keep my anger in check. I silently counted to five. "None taken. Maybe I'll see you this year." I shrugged and looked around, bored. That made the guys laugh even harder.

"Be nice, jackasses," Amanda said even though she was laughing, too.

"I heard she's actually really good," Emilia said.

I was irritated that Parker was silent while Emilia defended me. I was having a miserable time, but I promised Parker I would try. I knew she was trying to fit in, but at what expense?

"So, there's a party tonight if you want to come," Grayson said. He looked at me pointedly. "You can come, too."

"Gee, thanks. That sounds swell," I said. I couldn't hide my sarcasm, nor did I want to. After spending ten minutes with the superstars of the Hawkeye football team, I was done. I needed a change. "I'm going to grab some coffee. Do you want to come with?" I asked Parker.

"What? You can't do it by yourself?" Grayson pointed to a Starbucks across the food court. "It's right there."

"I thought my friend would like some fresh air since you seem hell-bent on breathing in her space." I stood and waited for Parker to decide.

"Sure. I could use a pick-me-up," Parker said. We crossed the food court. "I'm sorry. I don't know why everyone is acting like that," she said.

I could tell she wanted to touch me, but all eyes were on us. I could feel my anger ramping up. I hoped Parker would come to terms with her sexuality soon. Her parents were homophobic. Her church was homophobic. I felt like I was fighting a losing battle some days. Today was one of those days.

"I know it's hard for you and I'm really trying, but your friends are different than what I'm used to," I said.

"I know." Her shoulders slumped.

I wanted to hug her, but I knew the rules. "I'm sure you will find your people, but I just don't think they are them. And what's up with Grayson hitting on you?"

We stepped up to the counter and Parker didn't answer my question.

"Can I take your order? Oh, hey. Parker, right?" The barista was friendly. There was a rainbow bracelet on her left wrist.

Parker smiled. "Hi, Brianna. Yeah, Parker. This is my friend Sutton from Oak Grove."

"Hi, Sutton. Welcome to suburban hell. Can I get you something?"

"One coffee with two cane sugars and two creams, and one coffee with hazelnut syrup," I said.

"Coming right up," Brianna said.

Parker and I moved to the side. "She's nice. Why can't you pick somebody like that to be friends with?"

Parker folded her arms. When she did that, I knew an argument was coming. "I'm trying to fit in. This is my third high school. Third. I have no long-term friends because my dad keeps getting relocated. If I don't stay friends with those cheerleaders, they can get me kicked off the team. Staying on their good side is the easiest way to get through senior year."

I couldn't help myself. I put my hands on her shoulders. I was careful to keep my hands loose so it looked like I was consoling her. "I get it. I'm just saying that it's hard for me, too."

She smiled. "I know this isn't easy for you either. I just need time to adjust. Let's skip the party and do something else. Somewhere quiet and dark." She wiggled her eyebrows at me. Her smile was adorable and my heart raced.

"That sounds way better than any party."

"Here you go." Brianna set the cups on the counter. "Nice to meet you, Sutton."

"Thanks, Brianna. Nice to meet you, too."

"You're so fucking charming." Parker playfully elbowed me in the ribs. I almost spilled my coffee but it felt good to joke around.

"Oh, my God. You were talking to that gay girl." Amanda looked repulsed.

Counting to five did nothing to curb my anger this time. "Her name is Brianna and she's really nice."

Amanda leaned back. "Relax, Sutton. I've known her for years and she's weird."

"Why? Because she's gay?" I asked. Grayson and his entourage made gagging noises.

"She's always been weird. Look at her hair. I bet she never showers. She always smells." Kirsten waved her hand under her nose.

"Leave her alone. She's fine," Emilia said.

"She's nice." Parker's voice was soft, but at least she said something. She held up her cup of coffee. "And she got my order right."

Grayson laughed. "That doesn't make her friend material. That means she's great for the service industry. I still don't want a lesbian making my coffee. She needs to bury that shit deep."

I squeezed the back of the chair. "So, if she wasn't gay, you'd be best friends with her, right?"

"Oh, God, no. She still stinks," Grayson said.

"Well, I can smell your linebackers from here so I don't think anyone here has room to talk." My voice was clipped. I wasn't backing down. Not from this. Not even for Parker. Sometimes things were bigger than worrying about fitting in for nine months.

"Burn!" Grayson pointed to his friends. "She's not wrong. You should try soap during the showers instead of gaying it up with each other."

"Shut up, man." The one with the buzz cut pushed Grayson's shoulder, pissed that the conversation turned to him.

"It doesn't feel good, does it? People making fun of you," I said. My stomach was in knots, but I wasn't backing down.

Grayson held his hands up. "Okay, truce, QB, truce."

"We should probably go," Parker said. She picked up her empty smoothie cup.

I smiled at the group and batted my eyelashes. "Emilia, it was so nice to meet you. I'm glad Parker has you around." I gave the rest of the table a bored look. "Nice to meet you all. Buh-bye." I followed Parker. We walked in silence out to the parking lot. "I know I'm supposed to support you, but they're horrible."

She yanked open her car door and slammed it shut behind her. I slipped inside, thinking we were in for another argument, but I was surprised when she reached for my hand.

"I know and I'm super mad at them. Come on. I know the perfect place where we can be ourselves," she said.

We left my car at the mall and Parker drove us to a small movie theater that was playing *Breakfast at Tiffany's*. There was an older couple sitting in the front so Parker and I found a dark corner where we could hold hands and kiss. It was two hours of pure bliss. She kissed me in the dark and my moan was swallowed up by the movie's loud volume.

When Parker drove me back to my car at the mall, we held hands the whole way. I almost forgot how irritating her friends were.

"I'm glad we got to hang out today," I said.

"I know. This sucks. My parents are the worst. They have this idea of who I should be. I want to stand up to them, but I can't. They're my parents, you know?"

I had to look at it from her perspective. I had a wonderful dad. Parker was under the thumb of her parents. "I love you. I know you're strong and one day you'll figure things out and stand up to them."

We had slipped back into Sutton and Parker, two girls in love. We were always going to be together regardless of the Graysons, Amandas, and Kirstens of the world.

## Chapter Eight—The Defense

*Present*

Parker peeked her head into my office and waited for me to wave her in. "Since you aren't going to call me for coffee, I thought I'd bring the coffee to you."

I stood when she placed a cup of coffee in front of me. "Parker. What are you doing here?" I tried not to gape or think about what I looked like at the moment.

"I had to drop something off for Grayson and decided to force you to have coffee with me. I mean, if you have time." Parker was wearing a blue dress, short heels, and had her hair loose around her shoulders. It was hard to miss the giant diamond on her hand or the tennis bracelet on her thin wrist.

I looked at my watch. The team meeting after lunch started in half an hour. "I have about twenty minutes." I tossed the rest of my energy bar into the trash and pointed at the chair in front of my desk.

"I'm sorry to barge in but I figured you probably didn't have the time with the season starting. And it's just coffee."

I smoothed back my hair and tightened my ponytail. I looked like I was still in high school, and she looked like a quarterback's wife. I took a sip and had to stop myself from smiling. The coffee was perfect. She remembered how I liked it; two creams and two sugars. Not refined sugar, but cane sugar. I took another sip and tipped the cup in her direction. "Thanks." It was extremely hard to keep eye contact.

"Where do we start?" she asked.

"What do you want to know?"

"For starters, how was college?"

I leaned back and folded my arms. "This sounds like an interview." Her smile always gave me butterflies. I was guarded this time, but a few flutters made their way inside. I smiled in return. "College was exactly how I'd thought it would be." Minus the relationship with her. "I've been working every day since college."

"And look at you now. First female offensive coordinator for the NFL and you're only thirty-three years old. I know this might sound silly, but I followed your career. I was worried that you were working too hard and not having any fun."

That was offensive even though I knew she didn't mean it to be. "I did. What about you? You're married and you have two daughters. Tell me about that."

"The time has flown by. My daughters are amazing and incredibly smart. I can't believe how perfect they are." Her voice grew softer and she turned her face and averted her gaze just a little bit as she thought about them.

"You always wanted children," I said.

"You would love them. Their personalities are so different and yet they complement each other so well. They are best friends, and I couldn't be prouder of them. I'm sure that will change as they grow older, but now they still play with each other."

"Will you show me photos?"

She opened her purse and pulled out her phone. I studied her face while she scrolled through her photos. She always tanned better than I did and her sun-kissed skin made her blue eyes even lighter. Her lips were still full and the tiny laugh lines around her eyes grew more pronounced when she found a photo she wanted to share. She handed me the phone. "The one on the left is Violet, or Vee, and Rose is the one petting the goat."

They looked just like her with blond hair and blue eyes. Rose had Grayson's square jaw, but the rest of her features were Parker's. "They're beautiful. And this is such a fun age."

She tilted her head and pursed her lips. "Speaking from experience?"

"Not me. Hayley has three boys all under the age of ten. I try to hang out with them as much as possible."

"How is she doing?" Parker asked.

I smiled. "She loves being a mother like you. They live in Rhode Island, so I get to see them whenever I have a break."

"Which is rare because of your new job. I've got to give it to you, Sutton. I always knew you'd end up in the NFL. I'm proud that you made it to this level."

She was proud of me? I figured she never gave me a single thought after she hooked up with Grayson. "Thanks." I didn't know what else to say.

"How's your dad?"

For the first time since she sat down, I gave her a genuinely happy smile. "He's great. He also moved to Rhode Island, and he started dating again."

She returned my genuine smile with one of her own. "That's so wonderful to hear. I always admired him. He was cool and supportive. Did he ever write his novel?"

"Funny you should bring that up. He's finishing it right now." He was also working on a book about me, but nobody needed to know that. Half the proceeds would go to my charity. For the first time since she walked into my office, I was able to keep eye contact with her in a way that didn't feel like a challenge.

"And your charity is getting books in front of children. I guess I didn't realize you liked to read."

I threw my hands up in mock disbelief. "Max said the exact same thing. I love to read. I just have zero time for anything but football." I crossed my arms. "I'm listening to a true crime novel in my car right now. I get to hear forty minutes of it a day. Twenty minutes on my way in and twenty minutes on my way home."

"Huh. I guess I never knew that about you," she said.

"Honestly, I'm not surprised. It's all about football. I can have fun after I've proven myself." I didn't know when that would be.

"But you still make some time for yourself, right? More than forty minutes of audiobooks a day, I mean. What about vacations? Have you been anywhere exciting?" she asked.

I realized she was invested in the conversation. This didn't feel like a reach out because Grayson was told to be friendly toward me. This was a door opening. Slowly and carefully. "I went to Portugal about four years ago."

"With Lexi? That's your girlfriend's name. right?"

"No. Well, yes, Lexi." I nodded. "She's my girlfriend now, but I didn't go with her. We've only been dating for about two years. I went with my dad. He needed to get away from everything for a bit, so he picked Portugal and we hung out there for two weeks. It's now one of my favorite places on Earth."

"We've been to Spain, Mexico, Canada, and we usually head to Disney World with my parents after the season ends."

My lips twisted when she mentioned her parents. I'd tamped down my feelings for them for so long that hearing her say "parents" took me by surprise. I couldn't hide my reaction quick enough.

Parker frowned. "My parents are still the same. I'd like to say they've gotten better with age, but I'd be lying. Only two things give them happiness. Their church and their granddaughters."

This fledgling relationship was too tender for bad memories. "I'm sure it's great for your daughters. I remember how much fun I had with my grandparents when I was little," I said.

It was surreal to see Parker, a grown-up with a family, sitting in front of me. She was calm, like always, and looked amazing, like always. We settled into a nice conversation about her daughters, football, and Crowbar, who was sprawled in his bed oblivious to the anxiety in the room. We were keeping it light. I think she was just as scared of dipping below the surface as I was.

We were startled when Brandon knocked on my open door. "Meeting starts in five, Sutton. Hi, Parker. Nice to see you again."

"Hi, Brandon," Parker said. She stood and grabbed her purse. "Thanks for letting me crash your lunch, Sutton. It was good to see you again. Give me a call if you free up any time for something other than football." She smiled playfully.

I nodded at her and held up the cup of coffee. "Thanks for stopping by." I was surprised it was already time for the meeting.

It had been fifteen years, but we had easily fallen back into conversation. It felt like no time had passed.

I waited until she left my office before I followed Brandon to the team meeting room. We were reviewing this morning's full scrimmage. Our first game was this Sunday, and we were playing the Cleveland Browns. Their defense was average, and they relied on zone offense. We'd have to start off conservatively, much to everyone's chagrin. The players wanted to go out and wow the NFL, but us coaches were hoping we would safely get through the game without getting hurt.

We had lost all three of our pre-season games. Pre-season didn't matter. We needed to finalize the team and several players were fighting for spots. Now that we had firmed up our roster, we had to strategize about our first game. There was an energy in the room. The players were itching to show the world their worth and I was nervous, knowing so much was riding on me.

"Sunday will be here sooner than you all think. I expect you all to act like professionals on and off the field. Don't do anything reckless. All eyes are going to be on us on Sunday, and I want to bring home the win. Now let's go over the film and try to figure out how we can give Grayson more time to fire the ball," Bill said.

"Should I cancel my skydiving trip this weekend?" somebody yelled playfully. It was enough to make everyone laugh and relax a bit.

"Okay, okay, settle down," Bill said. He was smiling though and that meant everything in the moment.

We focused on the pocket and pointed out things the offensive linemen could do to give Grayson that extra second or two he needed to get rid of the ball. The defensive coordinator, Marcus Atkins, laid into the defense about hitting hard and getting through the line.

By the time we broke apart for the afternoon, we were all mentally exhausted. The offensives coaches had stayed until eleven the night before. I didn't think there was anything else we could cover before the game on Sunday. We decided to head home early knowing tomorrow we probably wouldn't leave the stadium until after the game on Sunday. I dreaded telling that to Lexi. The night before, she'd ignored me when I got home so Crowbar and I spent the night in the guest room. The transition from work life to home life was shitty. I was happier at work.

I started bringing Crowbar to work because I missed him and I doubted he was getting the love and nurturing he deserved at home. He managed to make an entire NFL franchise coo like babies when they saw him. Terry loved him the most. He was forever sneaking him treats even though I explained that we were watching his weight. He waved me off and gave Crowbar another treat right in front of me every time I said something.

"Ready to go, boy?"

Crowbar lifted his head from the couch and plopped back down. I didn't blame him. I didn't want to go either. Another night of Lexi shutting me out didn't sound fun. And the new couch I had delivered to my office was extremely comfortable. I grabbed my bag and patted my leg for him to follow. He begrudgingly slid off the couch and slowly worked his way over to me. I turned off the lights and shut the door.

"Good night, Coach." I waved to Bill on my way out. The players had left hours ago.

I opened the back door of the BMW and Crowbar took his sweet time crawling in. He was the most chill dog on Earth. Hayley and I found him on the beach three years ago. He didn't have a collar or a chip. After a month of passing out flyers with no results, I decided he belonged with me, knowing full well I didn't have the lifestyle for a dog. The vet thought he was about two years old when we found him so he was about five even though he lumbered through life as though he was already a senior dog. Unless a squirrel was in the picture.

I made sure he was secured in his harness before driving home. I called Hayley even though she was probably elbow deep in baths and getting the boys ready for Friday movie night.

"Is everything okay?" She sounded panicked.

"Yeah, why?"

"Because it's early and your first game is Sunday and you never call me at this time."

"We decided to knock off early because tomorrow is going to be a bitch of a day. I swear I know more about the Browns than they do."

"I'll be watching."

"Guess who showed up today to visit me?"

There was a pause before she answered. "Shut up. No, she did not." Hayley emphasized every word.

"Yep. I was on my lunch hour going over the playbook and she plopped down a cup of coffee, saying she knew that I would never call her, so she decided to stop by."

Hayley huffed into the phone. "That's so rude."

It had been a week since I told her about the charity event and how Parker had given me her number. "It wasn't too awkward. It was a nice conversation given our past."

"Just be careful. You never got closure with her and I don't want you to get hurt."

I instantly frowned. I couldn't decide if I was upset because she didn't think I was emotionally ready to have a friendship with Parker, or because there was some truth to her words. I took a deep breath. "I'll be careful." Crowbar interrupted our serious conversation by sneezing twice.

"How's the doggo doing?" Hayley asked.

"If we weren't the Cheetahs, we'd be called the Crowbars because this dog has won over every single heart in the place, including the owner."

"I can't believe you picked that name." She chuckled.

"Hey, the dog chose the name. You know that."

"Well, you tried to call him Melvin. Nobody likes that name. Not even a dog," she said.

I looked at him in the rearview mirror. "He looks like a Melvin." When we found him and put him in Hayley's car, he refused to get out. We tried pushing him, pulling him, and giving him treats, but he wouldn't leave the car. I said that I would have to get the crowbar to lift him off the seat. His ears perked up and he stared at me. "Crowbar?" He wagged his tail and jumped out. "You should hear me try to explain his name to the team. The owner looked at me like I abused him."

"Back to Parker," Hayley said. She muffled the phone and gave somebody instructions on what bag of chips to grab and how many they each could have. "What did you talk about?"

"She talked about her kids and showed me photos."

"Heartless!" Hayley hissed.

I tried to pretend it didn't sting. "She asked about you. We talked about my dad. It was kind of a catch-up conversation. She seems happy."

"Yeah, well, I'll forever hate her for what she did."

I smiled. "I know. It was a shitty time in my life. But you know what? We went down the paths we were supposed to. She was supposed to get married and have kids and do churchy things with her parents and I was supposed to coach football and live an authentic life. Even if I need to break up with my girlfriend soon because we're totally unhappy. I know I'm only delaying the inevitable."

"You'll figure it out. You always do. And I'm super proud of you for all your accomplishments. Speaking of football, the boys are excited to play catch with Auntie Sutton."

Hayley's husband, Mike, was a very successful engineer but he was athletically-challenged. He couldn't throw, catch, or kick a ball. The responsibility fell to me. "Bring them by the practice field anytime. I'll have them run plays with the guys."

"Let's wait until Cameron is a little older. He has zero life skills. What four-year-old runs directly into traffic? Mine, that's who," Hayley said. I heard a commotion in the background and something heavy shattered on the ground. "Sis, I have to go. Major cleanup ahead. Just kill it on Sunday and know that I'll be watching like always."

"I love you. Kiss the boys from Auntie Sutton."

"I love you, too."

I disconnected the call as I pulled into the garage. I paused before opening the car door. I didn't want to have the conversation with Lexi because my stress level was already at a nine. "Hi. We're home," I called out when we walked in. I was greeted by silence and was relieved. I checked the Lyft account. Lexi had taken one downtown an hour before.

"Are you hungry, boy?" Crowbar was always hungry. I made a turkey sandwich and poured kibble for him, but we both knew he would get half of my dinner. I kicked off my shoes and fell onto the couch. I turned on the television, not even sure what was on. Crowbar curled up next to me and within minutes of finishing my half of the sandwich, I was asleep.

"Hey, wake up, babe."

I blinked to find Lexi standing over me. "What time is it?"

"It's almost one. What time did you get home tonight?" she asked.

"Early. About eight."

"Why didn't you send me a message? I could've come home earlier."

I sat up and rubbed my face. Crowbar didn't budge. "I figured you needed to get out. Where'd you go?"

"I took a Lyft and met some friends. Didn't you notice my car in the garage? Weren't you even worried? I mean, if I got home and saw your car but you were nowhere to be found, I would legit worry. This is exactly what I mean. You don't care. You don't care about anything but yourself and your world."

I hated that she wanted to start something at one o'clock in the morning. I knew she'd been drinking and I didn't want to take the bait. "That's not true. I care about you."

"You care, you just don't love me. You're emotionally unavailable. You always have been. I thought Bridgemont would be a fresh start for us, but that was naive. I hate that I'm a therapist doling out advice to people who are exactly in this position, and yet I can't even get my own life straight." She threw up her arms and refused to look at me.

I shrugged and brought my dishes to the kitchen. She wasn't wrong. Relationships were hard and she wanted too much of my time. "You knew I would be super busy with my new job here. We've talked about this a dozen times."

"Why do we always have to do what you want? How come your career is more important than mine?" she asked.

Her voice boomed across the empty space between us. She was close to breaking down. I knew the signs, but I held my ground. "It's not, but this has been my dream since I was a little girl. My whole life has been football. This is who I am, Lexi." I softened my voice. "Don't make me choose."

Her shoulders drooped. "You're right. You deserve to live the life you want." She looked at me for the first time in over a minute. "I know it's late, but we really need to talk."

I knew she wasn't happy, but it never occurred to me that she was actively looking until I saw the guilt in her eyes. I rubbed my face with both hands and tried to feel something besides relief. I found nothing. She was right. "I don't think we need to say anything. I just hope you're happy. You deserve it."

"Look, I'm sorry but I need somebody who's present in the relationship. I'm so lonely."

It stung that she didn't break up with me first, but I was a coward, and I wasn't going to do it. My defenses went up and even though I knew I was to blame, I lashed out. "Well, it doesn't look like you're lonely anymore." I patted for Crowbar and marched into the bedroom, locking the door behind me. She could sleep in the guest room for a change.

## Chapter Nine—Touchdown

*Past*

Waking up with Parker tucked in my arms was the definition of heaven. She was snuggled against me and the small hairs on the back of her neck tickled my nose. Her breathing was even and low. I placed a small kiss on her temple and held her closer. School was starting in a couple of weeks and both cheer and football had grueling schedules over the summer. We spent every minute together knowing that once school started, our precious time would become scarce.

Parker's breathing changed and I smiled when she stretched against me and pulled my arm closer to her breasts. "I could wake up like this every morning."

I wasn't used to sleeping next to another person and the excitement of her nearly naked body was too hard to resist. Sleeping wasn't a thing. We'd make love, take a quick nap, eat food, make love again, fall asleep for a few hours, repeat, and repeat. This was our fourth Sunday morning together, our fourth overnight as a couple, and a month since we both lost our virginity.

I looked at the clock. "It's almost time for you to leave." I held her closer, praying just once she'd want to forget about family obligations and several hours of church to stay with me.

"I know. Plus, I hear your dad downstairs. He's up early this morning." Her voice was soft and quiet in the early morning stillness. She tapped my leg and slipped out from beneath the covers. I watched her reflection in the bathroom mirror as she brushed her teeth with the red toothbrush she had stashed in my bathroom. She winked when she noticed me watching her.

"Are you sure you don't want to stay?" I playfully pulled her back on the bed and was rewarded with a refreshing kiss.

"I would love to, but God needs me." She laughed.

"I need you more." My pout had no power which made me pout for real. "Okay, I'll call you later." I fell back on the bed when she left, hoping to catch another hour of sleep, but my dad had other ideas. He knocked but walked in before I had a chance to say anything. "Dad." I scowled and pulled up the covers.

"I made pancakes. Come on downstairs. We need to talk." He sounded sad.

"Okay. I'll be down in a minute." I threw on sweats and a sweatshirt and met him at the kitchen.

He placed a plate of peanut butter pancakes and bacon in front of me. "Did you sleep well?"

Barely, but I wasn't going to tell him that. "Yes. It's nice to have one day where I can sleep in."

He poured us orange juice and sat at the table. "Sweetheart, I know you need your privacy and your freedom, but given your relationship with Parker, she can't stay the night anymore unless her parents sign off on it." He held up his hands. "I'm not comfortable with her parents not knowing." He knew her parents were religious and were vocally against homosexuality. While he knew I was responsible and respectful, I could tell he was worried about how they would take the news.

"They just think we're friends, Dad. It's not a big deal."

"If it's not a big deal, where do they think she was last night?"

I blew out a deep breath. "Missy's."

"I'm sorry. I'm just not okay with you lying. Even by omission. I don't want them to ruin your chances at getting a scholarship and I definitely don't want to lose my job if they start talking. People are looking at you closely because of who you are. You need to be careful, kiddo."

"Okay, no more overnights." My heart dropped to my stomach at the news, but I didn't want anything to happen to him. Parker's parents were the kind who would cause trouble and the last thing he needed was the community getting up in arms about him promoting gayness or whatever.

"You can have sleepovers. As long as her parents sign off on it."

"That's not going to happen. I don't think her parents like anything about me."

He gave me a sad smile. "I'm sorry they don't try to get to know you. You're a wonderful person and you have so much to offer the world. It's their loss."

I smiled because he genuinely believed it. He was proud of me. "Thanks, Dad. Why are people like that?"

He shook his head. "I don't understand it either. Some people's belief system is so rooted into religion that they can't believe anything else. If they are challenged, they fight even if they hurt the people they love."

"Sounds stupid. Parker tells me all the time how her parents shame her. They sound like horrible parents," I said.

"It's not an ideal situation for her, but she'll be an adult soon enough and hopefully can make her own decisions. Life changes once you go away to college," he said.

It dawned on me that I would be going away and leaving him all alone. "What about you, Dad? Maybe you can transfer to a school down in Texas." The realization that we would be apart made my heart sink into the pit of my pancake-filled stomach.

"Don't worry about me. I'll be fine. I can retire early and write that book I've always wanted to write." He wasn't joking. Ever since I could remember, my dad wanted to write the next great American novel. Since becoming assistant principal of Oak Grove, he never had the time.

"Please retire to a beach somewhere so I can visit. But don't be one of those reclusive writers who forgets to bathe and walks around town muttering to himself, okay? Like that's just going to be too much for me. I can't field daily calls about your well-being."

My dad pretended to be crushed. "I'll try my best to not be an embarrassment to you."

"Do you have a five-year plan?" It was a question he always asked me.

"I plan to get you off to college, sell the house, maybe move down to Florida to be closer to Uncle Ronnie."

I barely hid my gasp when my father mentioned selling the house. We had moved into this house when he became assistant principal six years ago, a year before my mother died. We needed more space and my mother wanted a larger kitchen. She wanted to start a catering business but when she got sick, that dream was forgotten. I didn't hide my surprise well enough.

He patted my hand. "We're not doing anything for a while. Let's get you through college first."

I finished my breakfast and drove to the gym to work on core strengthening exercises. My phone started ringing loud enough to cut into the alternative rock on my headphones. I took off my headphones and flipped open the phone.

"Hey, you're finally up." I sat up on the weight bench, excited that Hayley called.

"You only called me like six times. Not all of us get up at the crack of dawn to work out and pump iron," she said.

"Sorry. A lot went down this morning. Parker can't spend the night anymore unless her parents know about us and that's not going to happen. And my dad is thinking of selling the house and moving to Florida when he retires."

"No way. Is he retiring soon?"

"No. We were just talking about going away to college and it came up," I said.

"Got it. What about Parker? Does she know where she's going?"

"Fingers crossed for Abilene but wherever she goes, we'll make it work." We were in love and nothing was going to keep us apart. She had more options and more money than I did.

"But what if she goes somewhere else? What if her dipshit parents ship her to some remote Christian college in Canada or something?"

My heart slipped a bit at the thought of her being so far away but revved back up when I realized nothing could keep us apart. We were destined to be together. "I'll just have to make sure I get a passport."

## Chapter Ten—The Coach and the Cheerleader

*Present*

My alarm went off at six, but my eyes were wide open. I was lying on my couch in my office. We had been up until midnight discussing plays and strategies for today's opener. I hadn't been this nervous in years. The sports world would have a lot to say about my debut as offensive coordinator, and a win would go a long way toward proving my worth. Fuck, I was tired. I was physically and emotionally drained and the day hadn't even started.

"Come on, boy. Let's get you outside." Crowbar was on his bed by the couch.

I stretched and grabbed my toiletry kit and game day clothes and headed toward the women's locker room. Crowbar lumbered behind me. I dropped my things off and unlocked the door to the practice field. There was a tiny area beside the building that Crowbar deemed his. Since the place was going to be crawling with people soon, I made him come back inside. I took a quick shower and slipped into a fresh Cheetahs polo and pressed khakis. I knew I would change at least one more time before the game. We had an interview with media at ten while the team warmed up.

Brandon was in the hallway when I left the locker room. "Good morning, Coach. You ready for your big day?" he asked. He surprised me by hugging me. It felt nice and relieved a lot of pressure. He was a pound hugger with the guys, but with me, he excluded the handshake.

"As ready as I'll ever be. I can't imagine shoving anything else in my brain," I said,

"We'll adjust as the game gets underway. I feel good about today."

Brandon was the kind of guy who would stick by you no matter what. I knew we were going to be friends. Tina was very nice and it was refreshing to see somebody support their partner one hundred percent. I hadn't talked to or texted Lexi since she informed me she met somebody and was moving out. How was that possible? We'd only moved here two months ago. My ego was bruised, but honestly, I was relieved. It was one less conversation I had to have with her. Besides, she never liked Crowbar. Since coming to the office with me, he had a bit more spunk. I had more important things happening than Lexi at this moment. I followed Brandon to our meeting room and looked at the excited and worried faces in front of me.

"Players and coaches, are we ready?" I wasn't prepared for the whoops and hollers that answered me. The special teams coach joined us for the pep talk before we met with the media. When we broke to meet with the press, I seriously wondered where the time went.

"Coaches, follow me," Bill yelled.

The five defensive coaches joined me, Brandon, Jim, and Jamal. We followed Bill to the press room. I did a quick scan of the reporters but didn't see Duane Spitzer. The shit storm he'd tried to stir up had died down since the interview Grayson and I gave at the team charity night. Hopefully, no one else would try to revisit Duane's line of questioning.

At the large table Bill sat in the middle. I was on his left, Marcus on his right, with the rest of the coaches standing behind us. I wasn't going to say a thing unless I was addressed, and even then, I was going to keep my answers to a minimum.

"Welcome to the Cheetahs press room. This is a big day for us and for the NFL. We're excited to show our team to the world." Bill pointed to a reporter. "Maria, why don't you start us off?"

"Coach Tatum, was it difficult switching up your offense after Myers's accident? You built up your offense based on his abilities."

"Grayson Moats is a veteran player. He stepped into the position with poise and confidence. There wasn't a single hiccup when he took over," Bill said.

Bill wasn't wrong. Grayson fit in well and picked up the plays with ease. He even made a few suggestions on plays Jamal designed. He was going to surprise everyone watching today.

After minutes of answering questions, I looked at the clock and started bouncing my knee. We needed to get out on the field and ensure our players were stretching and practicing and getting mentally prepared for the game. I needed it as much as they did.

"Good luck, coaches." Several reporters echoed Maria's sentiment.

Bill nodded and we followed him out to the field. The gates were open and fans were filing into the stadium. People wanted to see the new NFL team in action. We tested our microphones with Grayson and with the other coaches. Marcus was calling the plays from upstairs and I would walk the sidelines with Bill.

"Let's pump the guys up," Bill said.

We'd practiced them running onto the field twice on Friday. We were making our much-anticipated debut, and nobody wanted to screw it up. Bill and I walked into the locker room. The guys looked at us for words of encouragement. They were brimming with excitement. I was, too.

"We're here to play ball. We're not here to showboat or do backflips in the end zone. Does everybody understand me? You have one job for the next four hours. This is what we've trained for. We're all at the start of something great here. Let's do our jobs and come back with a win." Bill's encouragement got the entire team pumped up. We were taking the field in five. I'd never felt energy like this before. "Put your helmets on and let's get ready to show the Browns and all the fans who we are and what we want. Who are we?" He cupped his hand behind his ear and waited for the team to yell.

"Cheetahs!"

"What do we want?"

"A win!"

He repeated himself until the entire team worked themselves into a frenzy yelling and fist-bumping one another. It was like the end of a rave and I made sure to stay clear. I stood back and waited for them to charge out of the locker room. They lined up in the tunnel, waiting to be introduced to the football world.

I was bursting with pride. I had a good feeling about today. One of the hottest singers, Bristol Baines, was singing the national anthem. A local high school was singing "God Bless America," and three stealth bombers were going to fly over before the start of the game. My dad texted that he was in the stands even though I told him he could be escorted to me. I would catch up with him after the game.

"Cheetahs! Cheetahs!"

Hearing the fans scream gave me such a rush. I wasn't expecting my introduction to make such an impact, but when I was announced, I was given a standing ovation. I waved and smiled, swallowing the lump that lodged itself in my throat. If I cried now, nobody would take me seriously. I found my dad on the fifty-yard line wearing a Cheetahs polo and whistling. I blew him a kiss and waved back. This was a big moment and as much as I hated attention, I loved every second. I was the first female offensive coordinator and people were celebrating my milestone. I wanted to fall to my knees and cry for every success and every failure I ever had on the football field. Instead, I took my spot on the sideline with the Cheetahs and waited patiently until kickoff. There were still another ten minutes of pre-game rituals before the game even started. The Browns won the toss and deferred. We were getting the ball first.

"Get out there and get good field position," Bill yelled. He looked patient waiting for the kickoff. I was ready to jump out of my skin.

Ian Camper, our kick returner, caught the football and was off. It was so hard not to race beside him on the sideline. He broke through the first wave of tacklers. When he got to the forty, all of us started yelling. Not only was he slipping through holes the special teams created, but he was on track to run it all the way to the end zone. I clutched Bill's arm unprofessionally as we watched the twenty-two-year-old walk-on from my alma mater stiff-arm the kicker and run it in for the first touchdown in the Cheetahs' history book. Everyone went wild.

"If that doesn't motivate all of us, I don't know what will," Bill yelled.

Ian raced over to Bill and handed him the ball. "That one was for you, Coach." Fuck. I started tearing up. I turned my back and grabbed my tablet from the bench just to remove myself from the moment. We still had a whole game to play. I couldn't afford to be outwardly emotional.

When Grayson threw the winning touchdown pass with forty-two seconds left in the game and our defense took the field to sack their quarterback, I celebrated. I wiped away tears and laughed as the linemen surprised Bill with the ceremonious Gatorade shower. I ran when I saw them coming.

I asked security to bring my dad down on the field. I smiled as I absorbed the atmosphere of our stadium and the fans who stuck around to watch our first win. I did my first solo interview with NBC's Monica Meadows who was one of the few journalists I trusted. She was a reporter on the sidelines on big games and I knew she wasn't going to blindside me with sexist questions.

"Coach, congratulations on the win. How important was it?" Monica asked.

"Nice to see you again, Monica. Today's win was everything. It showed the world that the Cheetahs should be taken seriously and that we aren't stopping and we're not giving up."

"You led the entire game. Was it hard to adjust to the game as it progressed?"

"Not at all. I feel like we had the advantage."

"How so?" she asked.

"We watched games of the Browns from last season to get ready and they didn't have any games of us to watch. They adjusted well, just not enough to win the game."

"I know you have some celebrating to do. One final question. How's the journey been to get here at this point?"

"It's been both wonderful and strenuous, but worth it."

"I know you've worked hard, Coach McCoy. Congrats again on a very memorable and emotional win." I heard Grayson behind me so when I turned to congratulate him on a great first game, I wasn't expecting Parker and their daughters to be on the field with him. I hated that she looked so perfect. She was wearing shorts and a Cheetahs jersey with Moats across the back. Seeing them kiss cut my great mood in half.

"Great game, Grayson." I nodded at him.

"Same to you, Coach!" He had to yell over the crowd of reporters who surrounded him.

"Sutton!" my dad shouted.

Brandon was escorting him to me. I met them halfway and hugged my dad tightly. We were both crying. I didn't care that we were in a field of cameras and interviews. My dad, the person who inspired me the most and stopped living his life so we could focus on mine, was here.

"I'm so proud of you. You did it, Sutton. You did it." His aftershave took me back to when I was in high school. I could tell he'd lost weight. He said it was to be healthier, but I thought it was because he was slimming down for his new girlfriend.

"Wait a minute. Judy's here and you left her in the stands?"

He wiped away his tears and laughed. "Well, security only grabbed me."

"Dad, I'm going to have to give you dating tips because leaving your girlfriend in the stands isn't going to get you any brownie points."

"Mr. McCoy?" Parker said from behind me. "Hi. I don't know if you remember me, but I used to go to Oak Grove with Sutton."

My worlds were colliding again. I never told Dad that Grayson and Parker got married. The look of surprise on my father's face couldn't be faked.

"Of course, I remember you. Parker O'Neal. It's good to see you again," Dad said.

She put her hand on his hand briefly. "You look happy and well."

"So do you. Sutton didn't tell me you all were back in touch," he said. He was perplexed and I was scrambling, afraid he would say something inappropriate.

"She's married to Grayson Moats now, Dad."

"Oh. Okay." He was slow to cover up his surprise. He noticed the kids wearing matching Moats jerseys. "And you have a family. That's great."

"Yes." Parker put her hands on their shoulders. "These two little cheerleaders are so proud of their daddy and team."

I squatted so I wasn't so formidable to a six- and an eight-year-old. "And you must be Violet and Rose Moats." I pretended to size them up. "I mean, unless I'm wrong and you're actually here to try out for the team." Their sweet, shy giggles made me smile.

"Cheerleading runs in the family," Dad said.

"I'm sure football will, too," Parker said. She turned her attention back to me. "Congratulations on your big win, Sutton. Are you celebrating tonight?"

"We'll probably grill at my house. What about you?" It was easier to talk to her now since our spontaneous coffee break.

"We'll probably go back to the house and do the same. I hope you get a chance to relax. I know Grayson's been working hard, but he says the coaches are the last to leave and the first ones in," she said.

She was literally pulled from the conversation when Grayson grabbed her hand. He said something low to her and kissed the girls. "Coach McCoy, they're calling us," he said to me. He nodded his head toward a reporter standing ten feet away. "Are you up for it?"

"Yeah, sure." I followed him and waited for the reporter to cue us in. It was a live feed so I took several deep breaths and made myself focus. My emotions were all over the place.

"We won because we have great coaches and some of the league's best players. Coach McCoy was instrumental in getting me here so I think she's got pretty good instincts." Grayson winked. "The Cheetahs might be a new team, but we played like champions today."

When the reporter turned to me, I answered truthfully about how proud I was of the team and how Grayson was a true leader. My life was so strange. Here I was, again, after one of the biggest games of my life, with Grayson Moats. Only this time, we were on the same team. It was hard to wrap my head around it.

## Chapter Eleven—First Touch

*Past*

"Aw, they're beautiful." I took the bouquet of roses before Parker kissed me senseless. I loved it when she locked her fingers behind my neck and pulled me closer.

"Where are you taking me on this secret date?" she asked.

I wrapped my arms around her waist and kissed her firmly on the mouth. At my house, we could be ourselves. My dad wasn't due home for another twenty minutes so, for the moment, we were alone. "I was thinking of taking you to the swimming hole." Her pout was too cute not to kiss. Max was having a barbecue at his house so I knew most people would abandon the swimming hole for his giant pool and free food. "Everyone we know will be at the party, so we don't have to worry about a bunch of people there. Plus, I get to see you in that amazing bikini and have you all to myself."

She crinkled her nose and kissed my neck. "I must really love you if I'm going to splash around in muddy water."

I smiled. "The water's spring-fed so I promise it's not muddy." She raked her nails across the back of my head. It felt so good my knees threatened to buckle. "We'll head to Max's after we've had a few hours to ourselves." She gently pulled me down the hall to my bedroom.

"What are we doing?" I was equally panicked and excited about what she had in mind. We'd been on several dates and we'd reached the hooking up stage of our relationship. I was careful not to do anything she was uncomfortable with, but so far, I'd done everything right.

"I have to change into my bikini." Parker's parents didn't allow her to wear a bikini, so she stashed one here. She raised an eyebrow and my heart leaped in my chest at the possibilities. I didn't think we had enough time to fool around, but I was willing to see how far we could get before my dad got home.

"And I'm going to help you every step of the way," I said.

Parker was shy and uncomfortable about her body. I understood because I was very self-conscious about my height and my muscles. But I thought she was perfect.

She found her bikini in my dresser and took it into the bathroom. I was sad that she shut the door, but I sat on my bed and waited for her to come out. She did not disappoint. I held my breath when she opened the door.

"How do I look?" she asked.

I pulled her so that she stood right in front of me. "You look incredible." I ran my fingertips over her flat stomach and placed a soft kiss above the waistband. We both were shaking. "This is my favorite thing you've ever worn."

She smiled shyly and put her hands on my shoulders. "I want to look good for you."

My blood rushed to my face and spread out to all my sensitive spots, making them pulse with heat and desire. I ran my hand up the small valley between her breasts and brushed my fingertips over her soft cleavage. Most of our previous make-out sessions were over our clothes, in the back seat of my car, and in the dark. This was new. I put my hands on her hips and pulled her closer to my mouth. "Is this okay?"

"Definitely okay," she said.

I ran my tongue alongside the hem of the top before she got frustrated and pulled the material to the side. I didn't hesitate. Her skin was hot against my mouth. Chill bumps spread over her skin and her nipple hardened as I kissed my way over to one breast. I held back a moan when I felt the softness and hardness on my tongue for a hot moment before she pulled away.

"I'm sorry. I went too far," I said.

"No, Sutton. Your dad's home. I just heard the garage door open."

She scrambled back into the bathroom and I raced to the kitchen on wobbly legs. I opened the refrigerator as though looking for a snack.

"Hey, kiddo. I thought for sure you'd be at Max's party by now," Dad said.

"Parker's changing into her swimsuit now. I'm just hungry." Food was the last thing on my mind. I pulled out a bowl of grapes. "How was your golf excursion?"

He was in a school district fundraiser to collect scholarship money for students who otherwise wouldn't be able to attend college. I was proud of myself for sounding and acting normal when my body tingled with desire.

"It was good. We came in second, but we raised about five thousand dollars."

"Dad, that's amazing." I dialed it down when I realized I sounded a bit too enthusiastic. "What are your plans for the rest of the day?"

"I'll fix the sink in the utility room, and probably take a nap. It's been a long day." We both turned when we heard footsteps. "Hi, Parker," he said.

I could only grin and blush.

"Hi, Mr. McCoy. How was golf?" She had slipped back into her shorts and T-shirt and looked as innocent as she did when she first got here, even though she wasn't. We weren't. My cheeks flamed at the memory of what just happened in my room.

"It was fun but I'm tired. Have fun at Max's. I'm going to take a shower." He kissed me on my forehead and left the kitchen.

I stared at Parker.

She smiled shyly at me. "That was close," she said.

That was everything. It was perfect. She was perfect. Every part of me fluttered when our eyes met.

"That was amazing," I said.

The tension left her shoulders as she walked over to me. "Your dad has terrible timing."

I kissed her softly. I couldn't tell which one of us was trembling. It was a big moment. "The worst." I looked into her blue eyes and saw love. We said "I love you" last week, but it felt like the words didn't do justice to the feelings inside me. Three little words weren't strong enough to describe how she affected me.

"I'm looking forward to this special place that we've never been to before even though we've been dating for over a month." She was teasing me.

I loved her so much. I was trying to keep my cool, but it was hard. I found love. I found what my mom and dad had and here I was standing in my kitchen eating a grape and trying not to cry. I coughed to dislodge the lump in my throat. "Me, too. Is there anything you need?"

She touched my cheek. "Just you."

This emotional roller coaster was equal parts terrifying and exhilarating. I kissed her again, tasting her warmth and eagerness. "What are you doing to me?"

"The same thing you're doing to me. Now let's go before your dad catches us. The water will cool us off."

Happy that she felt it, too, I practically skipped out to the car. The swimming hole was fifteen minutes away. As soon as I put the car in drive, Parker reached for my hand and held it in her lap. Warmth radiated from her bare thighs.

"I'm going to warn you now that the water is cold. Like scream at the shock cold."

She looked at me in alarm. "You know I hate being cold."

I pulled her hand up to my lips and kissed her knuckles. "I promise to keep you warm."

She squeezed my hand. "I know. Even if we don't go in, time with you is always amazing."

"What time do you have to be home?" I asked.

"Nine."

"Oh, my God. I'm surprised they didn't offer to drive you to Max's and pick you up." I rolled my eyes.

Her parents didn't like me and told Parker to find other friends. She was on the cheer team, after all. I wanted to talk smack about them, but I also didn't want them to screw up this amazing high I was on.

She squeezed my hand three times. I sighed and instantly forgot about her awful parents. Three squeezes meant "I love you."

## Chapter Twelve—Turnover

*Present*

"Will somebody find out where in the hell our quarterback is?" Bill's voice boomed in the giant team room.

Jamal jumped up and left the room to do exactly that. I looked at my phone. I hesitated but pulled up Parker's number and shot her a text.

*Hi. It's Sutton. Grayson isn't here for the team meeting. Do you know where he is?*

I didn't want to scare her, but I wanted her to know that we were concerned. He didn't strike me as a player who would disrespect his job or his teammates, but today was a big day and our biggest player wasn't here. I saw bubbles pop up and then disappear. At least she saw my message. I didn't want to let my imagination run wild, so I waited and listened to Bill talk about yesterday's game. Eventually, we'd get to review plays on screen, but right now we were just reviewing what the team did well and areas we needed to improve. Grayson was in both categories and was missing it.

*I'm so sorry. He's on his way. Give him twenty minutes.*

That was it. No explanation. Nothing. I texted Jamal and told him. Thirty seconds later, he returned to the room.

"He'll be here in twenty." Jamal looked at me and nodded thanks.

Winning the first game was great, but missing practice the day after was inexcusable. Hopefully, Grayson had a good reason. I didn't want him to miss my film discussion, so Marcus and the defensive coaches went first. I almost missed Grayson slipping into a seat in the back row. I gave a general impression of the offense and let my individual coaches talk about improvements they wanted to see. We threw in clips of great plays and every score to boost morale. It was important to improve, but we wanted the team to know they did a good job overall.

"Let's break for lunch. This afternoon we'll review Miami's game. Moats, stick around," Bill said.

Jamal and I hung out because we needed to find out what was going on with Grayson. He moved from the back of the room to the front.

"Why weren't you here on time, Moats?"

Grayson ran his hands over his face. "Coach, I'm sorry. I ate bad food last night and wasn't feeling well." He held up a bottle of Gatorade as though that explained everything.

"Let's get the rules down. If you have a tummy ache, let us know. You call in just like you would if you had any other job," Bill said, emphasizing tummy ache with a whiny voice.

"I'm really sorry. It won't happen again, I promise."

Jamal pointed at him. "I expect this from a rookie, not a veteran. You have everyone's number so there's no excuse for not letting us know. In the future, text or call me first, and if I don't respond, text or call Coach McCoy, and if she doesn't respond, then you text or call Coach Trust. Are we clear?"

"Yes. I'm sorry." Grayson nodded humbly.

"Go try to eat something," Jamal said.

We watched him walk out of the room. Bill stomped away. I turned to Jamal. "That wasn't on my bingo card today."

"Let's hope it's a one-time deal. The last thing we need is a flighty quarterback."

"I'm sure this was a slip up. He looks fine though," I said.

"This was his freebie."

"Come on. Let's grab something to eat. I feel like I've been here longer than five hours."

I was exhausted, but not from this morning's meeting. Last night was a complete disaster. I got home to Lexi pulling out of the driveway in a U-Haul. She was bitter and accusatory, which confirmed that splitting was the right thing to do. I felt nothing. That's not true. I felt relieved. She wasn't wrong about me not being available, and it was a relief to stop pretending I was ever going to make that space for her. I removed her access to the house security system, changed the passwords to all my online accounts, and finally crashed about one. I got five hours of restless sleep. Even Crowbar wasn't in the mood to go to work. Yesterday was a lot for both of us.

"How did you celebrate last night?" Jamal asked on our way to the cafeteria.

"I had dinner with my father and his new girlfriend."

"That sounds nice. What about your girlfriend? I didn't see her at the game."

I never wanted my personal life and professional life to collide, but that went out the door when we signed Grayson. "We broke up. She moved out last night when I was at dinner."

He stopped and put his hand on my shoulder. "Are you okay?"

"Yeah." I waved him off. "I don't know why she moved here with me. We were on the rocks anyway. I'm fine with it. Really." I was angry last night, but I woke up and felt such peace. This was a fresh start for me. I could focus my energy on football and making sure I was doing everything in my power to take this new team to the playoffs. We just needed to make sure Grayson was feeling better. I grabbed a salad, fruit, and a chicken breast and went back to my office. Crowbar probably needed to go out and I needed the world to go quiet.

*Did Grayson make it?*

I leaned against the open side door to enjoy the sun and answer Parker's text. *He did. Said you tried to poison him last night, but he survived anyway.* I quickly followed up with a wink emoji because I didn't know her humor anymore.

*Ha ha. I'm glad he made it.*

It was weird that she would ask and not know herself. I wondered if Grayson had a habit of saying he was going to work and going elsewhere instead. Or maybe this was her way of reaching out to me since she now had my number. I was too emotionally exhausted to try to figure it out.

Crowbar trotted past me and went straight to my office. I found him sitting and staring down the chicken breast I had on my plate. "Of course, you're getting a bite." He gave a low woof and gently took the piece from my hand.

I bit into an apple and pulled up my email. I had over two hundred emails congratulating me on the win. Terry's assistant's emails were flagged to be at the top. I had three from her. One was the congratulatory email on the win, the second was a coaches' meeting I was expected to attend at the end of the month, and the third was a reminder about the Empowered Women in the NFL group I had signed up for when I signed my contract with the Cheetahs. Members gave talks to area schools to encourage students to pursue their dreams. I groaned because that meant extra work, but I knew I had a responsibility that went above coaching. Four schools would get me for an hour every Tuesday for the next month. The event would be recorded by the NFL for a documentary on diversity in the league.

I sent the organization my approval and added the visits to my calendar. The first one was tomorrow at a private elementary school, Wellington Academy. It was in a posh neighborhood about twenty minutes away from the office. I shot an email to Terry's assistant to see if we had any giveaways for the kids and asked that anything be brought to my office by the end of the day.

The team spent the afternoon studying the Dolphins. Even though it was our first away game, I had a feeling we'd win. Miami looked sloppy. Our defense would easily be able to break through and pressure the quarterback. I took notes, pointed out weaknesses, and worked with coaches on tweaking plays.

It was a long afternoon and all I wanted to do was go home and sleep. Since we didn't run plays on Mondays and the players were off on Tuesdays, the coaching staff decided to break early. Crowbar and I headed home at six. After eating leftovers, I crashed on the couch and woke up hours later with a kink in my neck and a dog partially on top of me.

"Come on, buddy. Let's go to bed." Since Lexi was gone, Crowbar was back in the bed with me. We were both fine with that decision.

❖

"The important thing to remember is that if you work hard enough, you can achieve your dreams."

Of all the schools in the entire city, of course Parker's kids would attend this one, and of course, Parker was a room volunteer. I didn't know if the universe was punishing me, but it sure felt like it. Hopefully I masked my reaction at seeing her in the gymnasium when I met with the principal and the cameramen who were filming the event.

"Does anybody have any questions?" I had a stack of coloring books for the kids about Champ, the Cheetahs mascot, but I couldn't pass them out until after I was done because I would lose their attention. A little girl in the front raised her hand. I pointed to her. "What's your question?" I asked.

"You don't look very big for a football player. Do you play football?"

Nothing like a five-year-old to knock my confidence down a few notches. "That's a great question." I avoided Parker's eyes because I didn't want a simple glance to make me fall back in a hole that took years to crawl out of. "In high school, I was a quarterback. I was tall enough to be a football player and I could throw a football a long way."

"Can you still throw a football a long way?" She was very inquisitive.

"I can."

"Then why aren't you still a quarterback?" She shrugged.

"I'm too short and probably too old to play now."

"Rose's dad is a quarterback. Maybe you can play with him." A small girl with short brown hair and big blue eyes spoke. She immediately covered her mouth, realizing she should've raised her hand first. We'd already established Grayson was a quarterback because almost every child pointed it out when I first got there.

"Yes, Mr. Moats. I work with him. He's taller and bigger than I am."

"Is he a good quarterback?"

This line of questioning was starting to make my eye twitch. "Yes, he is. We won our first game because of him."

"How come the quarterback isn't the coach?"

"Because the coach has more to do than just be a quarterback. They have to make sure the entire team does well." I made sure no little digits were raised before I changed the subject. "I brought a friend with me today. Would you all like to meet him?"

"Yeah!"

About one hundred and fifty students in little navy polos shared their enthusiasm loudly without even knowing who was here with me.

"Champ the Cheetah, come on out and say 'hello' to these students." Champ threw aside the stage curtain and did a goofy wave. "Champ, meet the great kids that attend Wellington Academy."

He high-fived the kids in the front row. Mascots didn't speak. They waved, did backflips, danced, and tried to get the crowd excited. The kids were thrilled. I kept the smile on my face even though Parker was fifteen feet away. We made eye contact several times and even though her smile was hesitant, it still stirred something inside me. It was the same light, fluttering joy I got when I knew somebody was interested in me.

"Students, let's give Coach McCoy and Champ a round of applause for taking time out of their day to spend it with us." The principal got the children to clap for our short, but fun visit.

I stood back while Champ took photos with the different classes. A young teacher with long dark hair and hazel eyes slid over to me.

"Congratulations on your accomplishments. I love football and respect what you've done so much." She tilted her head and looked at me coyly. I found everything about her charming from her crooked smile to the small smattering of freckles across her nose.

"Thank you. Are you a Cheetahs fan?" It was a stupid question because we had played only one regular season game.

"Believe it or not, my family has season tickets. We were at the game so we saw your first win."

I could tell she was not only excited about the team, but I got the feeling she was interested in me. "Where are your seats?"

"Section one forty, ten rows up," she said.

I nodded. "Those are good seats. How do you like the team?"

"I'm so excited. Good quarterback, great coaches, especially the offensive coordinator. I mean, I can't imagine you won't get us to the playoffs. You're going to slaughter Miami. They are a hot mess on the field."

She really did get it, and as much as I wanted to relax and talk football with her, I knew better than to open up quickly. Besides, I was working and a cameraman was lurking about ready to pick up anything interesting, not to mention the teachers with their iPhones out recording everything.

"We certainly hope to bring home another win."

She touched my arm lightly. "We're rooting for you, Coach. My friends and family are going to be watching on the big screen." She bit her bottom lip and smiled at me.

"Our first official fan. It's nice to meet you. I'm Sutton." I held out my hand and she shook it.

"I'm Ruby. I teach kindergarten."

"Do you have children that go to school here?" When she laughed at my question, I automatically looked around hoping we weren't being loud. I locked eyes with Parker. She didn't look amused. I quickly looked away, guilt pricking my conscience.

"I'm twenty-five and very single. No kids, no girlfriend. One day, maybe, but right now I just want to have fun and watch football and teach these little goofballs fun things," Ruby said.

There was so much in that delivery. If we were at a bar and my girlfriend hadn't just moved out forty-eight hours ago, I would've asked her out. But we were both at work and the weight of my dreams was on my shoulders. I didn't have time for her. Right then, Champ waved me over. I excused myself but turned to Ruby. "I'll see you at the games."

"I'll look for you," she said.

We took photos with the students, and I wrapped up our visit by passing out coloring books about Champ's journey from tiny cheetah cub to NFL mascot. We waved to the children and followed the principal back to the front of the school. Champ excused himself to slip out of the costume. I sat in a conference room by the principal's office and smiled, remembering how many times I sat outside my dad's office waiting for him when practice was over and I needed a ride home.

"Thanks for coming out to the school."

I stood, knowing that voice. "Parker. How are you?" Right in the middle of Wellington Academy, Parker gave me a slow up and down and was obvious about it. I took a step back at her forwardness and stumbled over the chair I just vacated.

"I'm doing well. I was surprised to find out that you were going to be here," she said. She looked sexy as hell in a cream-colored accordion skirt that grazed her knees and a black, thin sweater. Her hair was pulled back in a low, messy bun and she was wearing glasses. If I could have dreamed up the perfect sexy librarian, today's Parker would have been it. She made my mouth water.

"I completely forgot about it until yesterday. Hopefully we kept the kids entertained," I said.

She touched my arm and gave me a sweet smile. "You did a great job. The kids loved you."

I looked at her hand on my forearm. "I get to do this three more times at other schools. Any suggestions for improvement?"

"I think you're perfect just the way you are," she said.

She squeezed my arm twice which was probably innocuous, but I tensed as I waited for that third squeeze. It never came. She dropped her hand but didn't move out of my space. I looked around to see if anyone else witnessed her flirting through the glass wall. We were still alone. My shoulders dropped in relief. "It's been fun, but I need to get back. We have our first away game and we have so much to cover."

"I know. Grayson's pretty excited about it."

His name on her lips splashed over me like cold water and I took a step back and almost fell over the chair again. "I should probably find Champ."

Her hand was back on my arm. "Listen, Sutton. I know things were bad between us years ago and I'm to blame for that, but we're going to be sharing so much space in the future. Can we try to get along? You were always so important to me." There was warmth in her voice that suggested more than a friendship. How she could stand in front of me with our history swirling in the space between us and flirt was confusing. She was married to one of my players. I was dumbfounded. "For whatever reason, we are back in each other's lives. I know Grayson thinks so highly of you and your coaching abilities," she said.

I stared at her. It had been fifteen years. Why was this so hard for me? "I have peace in my life, Parker."

She waved her hands at me. "And I'm not here to disrupt it. I genuinely miss you in my life. Coffee the other day was great and I'd really like for us to be friends. Do you think we can do that?"

Before I could answer, Brad busted into the room. "Hey, you ready?" His eyes darted between us until they lit up with recognition. "Hey, you're Grayson Moats's wife. I'm Brad, you know me as Champ."

Even though he was sweaty and smelled like wet carpet, Parker shook his hand and gave him the warmest smile. "It's nice to meet you, Brad. I'm Parker."

"It's an honor. I think your husband is great and I'm so glad he's on the team."

"I'm glad he's a Cheetah, too. You look like you love your job," she said.

I had to agree. Brad didn't skimp on energy while in the suit.

"Those who can't either coach or become giant, hairy animals who run around football fields." He grabbed his bag and looked at me expectantly.

"I guess we're out of here." I looked at Parker. "We'll talk soon."

"I'll hold you to that, Sutton." Her voice was low and laced with promise.

It took everything to not turn around and look back at her. When Ruby stopped me in the doorway of the school to ask me out, I immediately looked for Parker, but she was already gone. Ruby was nice, pretty, into me, and available. Even though my breakup was new, maybe in a few weeks or months, I might be ready to date again. I handed her my phone to add her contact information. She didn't send herself a text from my phone. She was leaving it in my hands and my respect for her grew.

## Chapter Thirteen—First Kiss

*Past*

My final track meet was postponed so this was my first free weekend. I didn't hesitate. I found Parker in between classes.

"Are you cheering this weekend? Do you have any plans?"

Parker leaned against her locker and held her chemistry book against her chest. "Nope. Nothing." She lowered her gaze and then looked up at me. She bit her bottom lip and right then I knew for sure she was into me. I always suspected, but she had been spending a lot of time with Harrison, one of our offensive linemen. But even in our group, she always gravitated toward me.

"Would you like to go out with me Saturday night?"

Parker looked around to see if anyone overheard. "Sure. What did you have in mind?"

My heartbeat was so loud that I barely heard her question. I hadn't thought that far ahead. Working up the nerve to even ask her was the only thing on my mind. "Uh, I'll come up with something." Thankfully, the first bell rang. "Talk to you later." I shoved off her locker and scrambled to my next class with my heart full of excitement and possibility.

I wanted to do more than just take Parker out for burgers and a movie, but I was severely limited financially and creatively. I'd never been on a date before, nor tasked with the responsibility of planning one. I decided on a picnic at the lake and asked my dad to whip up some of his chicken salad with grapes and walnuts. Just in case she had food allergies, I packed fruit and cut up some vegetables. By the time I was ready to go, the basket weighed a solid ten pounds.

"Are you secretly moving out and not telling me?" Dad asked.

I wanted to scowl at him, but I was too excited to play the disgruntled teenager and smiled at him instead. "Nope. Just trying to make a good first impression."

He slung the dishtowel over his shoulder and leaned against the counter. The ribbing had only just begun. "So, this is the girl who's been occupying your head for the last several months. What's her name again? Patty?"

I gave him the obligatory eye roll. "Parker, Dad. And you've met her a thousand times. She's a cheerleader and new to the school." He gave me a blank stare.

"I've seen all the cheerleaders and they're all blondes. Which one is she?"

I pushed his shoulder playfully because he knew a lot of the students in the high school. "They're not all blond."

"Is she?"

I looked at him. "Yes, with really pretty blue eyes and red lips."

He shook his head. "Still doesn't ring a bell."

"Well, she's beautiful and smart and funny." I smiled just thinking about her. It took months for me to work up enough nerve to ask her out. We'd hung out a bunch of times, but it was always with our group of friends. Tonight, it would be just us. I grabbed a blanket from the front closet and was met with my father's raised eyebrows. "It's for the picnic. This is our first date. You don't have to worry about that."

"Take some bug spray and at least one flashlight. And make sure your car is gassed up."

"If we can't find anything to do after we eat, we'll just come back here and watch a movie. That's okay, right?"

"Of course. I'll even make myself scarce." He used the dishtowel as a cape and pretended to vanish like a magician behind it. He held it up and ducked behind the kitchen island as it floated down to the counter, giving the appearance that he disappeared. I was impressed but also appalled that he might try to be this cheesy tonight.

❖

"This is yummy. Your dad is a good cook," Parker said, taking another bite of chicken salad on a croissant. She wiped the corner of her mouth with a napkin from Taco Bell I found in the glove compartment of my car. I remembered everything for our date except napkins. We were sitting on a bench in Tilly's Park. It had rained when I was driving to pick up Parker so the romantic picnic I planned fell apart. I knew Parker was nervous being out in the open so I found a bench tucked away from the road. Discretion was a must and I didn't care. She wanted to go out with me and that meant everything.

"My dad is amazing." I meant it. If the assistant principal gig didn't work out, he could start the catering business my mother never had the chance to get off the ground.

"Tell me about your mother." Parker's smile was gentle and encouraging. I missed talking about my mom.

"She used to read to me every night. Even if I was mad at her. I pretended I wasn't listening, but I clung to her every word. She had all these great voices and acted out each part. She was wonderful." I smiled at my memories. I was fortunate that I still had them.

"Did she support you playing sports?"

"She loved it because I loved it. She hated when I got knocked down, but honestly, it didn't happen that much. I think she would have a hard time watching me play high school football though. Pop Warner was hard enough for her."

"So how long have you been playing?" she asked.

"Since I was five. I was fascinated with the game and spent every weekend watching college and NFL games. It was how my dad and I bonded."

"You don't look like a quarterback."

"Thank God." I pretended to wipe my brow in relief.

She touched my hand. I froze. Her fingertips were soft. I almost melted when she linked our fingers. "I like that about you. You always look so sweet and innocent on game day in your skirts and dresses."

I blushed at her appraisal. "I feel so awkward."

"Why? You look amazing," Parker said.

"I'm one of the tallest students in the school."

"So?"

"It's embarrassing to have everyone staring at you when you walk by." I groaned and put my head down on the table. I smiled when I felt her fingers touch my hair.

"It's because you're gorgeous and tall."

I looked up at her and got lost in her wildly blue eyes. My cheeks burned and I took a long drink of iced tea, but it did nothing to cool the rush of lava. "You're just saying that."

"Are you kidding me? I have a hard time keeping eye contact with you."

Her voice trailed off, making my heart swell. She was beautiful and shy and here with me. She was nervous but so was I. We'd figure this out together. "I think I'm the lucky one here. Popular girl, cheerleader, smart, funny."

"Let's just agree that we're both lucky," she said.

I laughed nervously. "We are. And since this park turned out to be kind of a bust, let me salvage the rest of this date by taking you somewhere less buggy and humid."

"What did you have in mind?"

"My dad made cookies and said we can hang out over there. I'm sure there's a good movie we can watch. I know it's not the best first date, but it's private." She helped me pack up the food and raised her eyebrows at me when she saw the blanket in the back of my car. I shrugged sheepishly. "I had visions of a nice picnic by the lake before today's downpour."

"It was a great idea," she said.

"I'm sorry the weather ruined our date," I mumbled and closed the trunk. I stopped when she put her hand on mine.

"It's not ruined at all. Plus, the dates that don't go according to plan are always the most memorable."

I didn't think it was possible for me to fall harder for Parker, but in that moment, with the sun setting behind her and the soft chirp of crickets beating around us, her words weaved inside and squeezed my heart. She was fine doing whatever as long as we were together. I crawled into the driver's seat hoping the five-mile drive home would be quick. Being this close to Parker was driving me wild. I didn't know what was acceptable first date behavior. I wanted to hold her hand again, but was that okay?

When we pulled up at my house, my dad was out front weeding the garden beds. "You girls go on in. Fresh cookies are cooling in the kitchen."

"Thanks, Mr. McCoy."

Parker didn't seem nervous around my dad, whereas I was a hot mess. I brought home a girl. My first date. My dad winked at me as we walked by and I blushed. I was equally proud and mortified.

"What kind of movie are you in the mood for?" I asked and pointed to the living room.

"Sutton McCoy. Are you not going to give me a tour of your house? Look at this kitchen. It's beautiful." Parker ran her hand over the granite countertop. "I love this kitchen and the color."

"My mom picked the scheme."

"It's perfect."

I looked closely at the blue flecks in the granite. "Your eyes are this color." I pointed and looked at her.

"Your eyes are blue, too."

"No. Yours are prettier." I didn't know who moved, but suddenly we were in each other's space. I wanted to kiss her. I had been kissed once before, but it was a long time ago, and the kiss was with a girl who didn't care about me. The girl who stood in front of me now made my knees weak. I'd been dreaming of kissing Parker since I saw her in the office on the first day of school. I didn't know the first thing about making a move. Did I ask first? It would be so easy to just lean down and press my lips against hers. She was doing that thing where she bit her bottom lip and looked at my mouth.

"Can I—" I never finished because she threw her arms around my neck and kissed me. My hands automatically snaked around her waist. I had to hold her for fear that I would float away. When I felt her tongue gently stroke my lip, my knees threatened to buckle. I put one hand on the counter to brace myself. When she pulled away, I felt disoriented and completely invigorated. It felt like my blood was bouncing in my veins and a new energy spinning inside me. "Uh, that was nice."

"That was really nice." Parker took a step back. She took my hand but looked down at the tile as though shy or embarrassed. "And the first time I kissed a girl."

I felt a little cocky and a little empowered by her confession. She touched my jawline slowly and brushed my cheek with her thumb.

"I like the way you kiss," she said.

"Come on. Let's go find a movie." We snuggled under a blanket and watched a movie I'd seen a million times, but the only thing I could think about was how wonderful it was to finally kiss her and what it meant to be hungry for another person.

## Chapter Fourteen—The Same Team

*Present*

"Coach, we need to talk."

I looked up to find Anthony standing in my doorway. I looked at the time. He should be out on the field practicing. Something was wrong. I stood. "What's going on?"

He looked down at his cleats and put his hands on his hips. I waited for him to drop whatever horrible news he had. "Moats is drunk."

"What?" It wasn't even ten in the morning. I was still processing our game with the Bills. It was our first loss of the season so I was in a horrible mood. It wasn't just a loss. We were annihilated 37-14. I refused to stop taking notes about what went so wrong. Three wins and one loss was still a good start, everyone assured me. But they didn't have anything to prove. I did.

"I don't think everyone knows, but I wanted to tell you before it got out." He ran his hand back and forth over his buzzed head out of nervousness.

"You did the right thing by telling me. Let's get him in my office. Does Jamal know?"

"He told me to get you."

"Okay, let's go." I followed him out to the field where Grayson was propped up on the bench trying to down Gatorade. "Okay, stop trying to sober him up with that. That's not going to work." I looked around to ensure the press wasn't on the field. "Let's bring him inside." Anthony and a third-string linebacker half-carried him into my office. I called Craig, one of the Cheetahs' medical staff, and told him to bring IV fluids.

"Wow, Sutton. This is such a nice couch." Grayson ran his fingers up and down the pattern in the fabric. He slid down and put his head on the armrest and tried to put his legs up on the cushions.

"Somebody take off his cleats, please," I said. Once Grayson was settled, I told both players to get back on the field. We didn't want to draw any unnecessary attention. They left as Craig was coming in with fluids. "Shut the door please." Craig shut the door and immediately got to work hooking Grayson up. He protested only a bit before his eyes hooded and his breathing got heavy. "Don't drool on my couch, Moats." I grabbed a trash can and put it next to him. Craig took his vitals and sat on the chair opposite him.

"I'll just hang around to make sure he doesn't knock out his IV," he said. I appreciated that he was here. Grayson was a big guy and I couldn't manage him on my own. I debated texting Parker but decided to wait and see how Grayson was after the treatment. I turned my attention back to the video of the worst game I'd ever coached. The Bills were amazing. We were everything but. We looked sloppy. Grayson got sacked four times. He was sluggish, and for a brief moment, I thought maybe he was drunk during the game. We needed to have a serious heart-to-heart when he was sober.

The door opened and Jamal let himself in. "How's he doing?" He quickly closed the door behind him. Nobody wanted this to get out.

"He's sleeping it off right now. What's the policy on this?" I asked.

"Therapy and detox. This hasn't been a problem before. Maybe he got shit-faced last night and is still drunk this morning."

"That might have happened in college, but not in the NFL." I was so mad at him. Grayson had everything I wanted and he was blowing it.

"I guess I'll run Archie through the drills and make sure he's up on the play changes. Get him warmed up in case the penalty is Moats missing a game or two. I'll gently bring it up to Bill."

"Did he drive here? Is his car outside?" I hoped he was dropped off by a Lyft or a friend. I inwardly huffed. What kind of person let a friend drive or dropped them off knowing they were drunk?

"I'll go check," Jamal said.

Grayson went through an entire bag of fluids before his eyelids fluttered open. His throat was thick with phlegm as he tried to talk. "Where am I?"

Craig leaned over him to hook up another bag. "You're in Coach McCoy's office," Craig said.

"How did I get here?" He was more coherent, but still out of it. He struggled to sit up. Craig offered him a hand.

"Why are you drunk at work?" I hissed.

He dropped his head into his hands and started sobbing. Craig excused himself, but I stopped him before he opened the door. "Craig, please keep this under wraps until we know more."

"Yes, Coach." He nodded and quickly disappeared.

I didn't like being alone with Grayson, but I knew Jamal would be back soon. I didn't know how to handle a grown man crying and I didn't want to pry. "Look, whatever's going on with you, we have people who can help you." That only made him cry harder. When he started making a choking sound, I handed him the wastebasket just before he heaved. There wasn't a lot, but enough to make me take a step back and pray he didn't spew on my new couch.

"He didn't drive here." Jamal entered my office and was startled to find Grayson awake.

"Well, at least he didn't endanger anyone." I squatted so I could look into Grayson's red-rimmed, teary eyes. "Grayson, how did you get here?"

He sniffled and wiped his eyes. "I think Matt dropped me off."

"Who's Matt?"

He shrugged and tried standing but wobbled and fell back onto the couch.

"We need to get him out of here," Jamal said. We stood in front of him with our hands on our hips, not knowing the proper protocol.

"It's lunchtime. If we can get him into my car without drawing a lot of attention, I can take him home," I said.

"That's right. You're friends with his wife." He looked everywhere but at me. Apparently, he knew about our past, too. I was sure the entire team knew, but nobody said anything because there wasn't anything to say.

"I'll text her and let her know we're coming." We had to get him off campus before rumors got out about his state.

"How are we going to get him to your car?" Jamal asked.

"I'll get it and drive it as close to the building as I can. Meet me by the side door. Give me ten minutes." It was lunchtime so most of the players and staff were in the cafeteria which was in a different building. I drove up on the grass and parked about twenty feet from the door. Jamal was waiting there with Grayson's arm draped over his shoulder.

"Watch Crowbar for me. I should be back in an hour," I said.

Jamal set a small wastebasket on Grayson's lap. I'd texted Parker to meet us in case she was at the school or out doing whatever she did nowadays. A quick check showed me that she hadn't seen my message yet.

"Be careful." Jamal clicked Grayson's seat belt into place.

I knew to drive slowly. I didn't want him throwing up in my car. The office was bad enough. "Grayson, I need you to keep your eyes open." I plugged his address into my navigation system and groaned. Nineteen minutes.

"Fresh air," he said and fumbled at the buttons on the car door.

"Let me do it." I rolled down his window and he stuck his head out and smiled. "You remind me of Crowbar right now."

"Who...why is your dog Crowbar?" He laughed as though it was the most hilarious name. "It's so weird." At least he was communicating.

"He picked his name."

Grayson frowned. "That doesn't make sense." He rambled on about how people should name dogs because dogs couldn't speak.

"Do you have a dog?"

He smiled again. "I love Buttercup. She's so good with the girls."

"What kind of dog is she?"

"A golden retriever," he said.

Of course, he had a golden. Perfect everything. "Those are great family dogs."

We were quiet for a few minutes. I looked down at the estimated time of arrival. Twelve minutes. "How are your parents?" I didn't know anything about them, but it was a neutral topic that we could probably talk about until I coasted into their driveway.

He snorted. "I don't talk to them much." Or maybe it was a bad subject. Before I could switch topics, he turned to face me. "I don't like Parker's parents. They're awful people."

I almost laughed. I wanted to agree with him but I had to keep our conversation from getting too personal. I wasn't sure what he would share with Parker. "I remember them from high school. They didn't like me."

"They didn't like you because you're gay and they thought you were trying to convert their daughter. I can't tell you how many times they brought that up." He moved the visor down to block the bright sun that had poked its way through the dark clouds. "We're going to get storms tonight. I studied meteorology in college."

Three more minutes. My phone dinged and the text from Parker showed up on the screen. *I'm home.*

I was glad Grayson was slumped in the seat with his eyes closed. By the time we got to the entrance to his development, Parker had texted me the code to open the gates. Their house was gorgeous. I pulled up into the driveway. Parker opened the garage door and waved me inside. That made sense. Privacy. I could control the narrative somewhat at work, but nosy neighbors liked to gossip.

"I'm so sorry about this," Parker said.

I tried not to focus on her leggings and tank top. She was either on her way to the gym or had just got back. "Where do you want him? I'll help you drop him off somewhere."

She might not have wanted my help, but she needed it. Grayson was a big dude and no way could she get him into the house without another person. I opened the passenger door and pulled him out. I put his arm around my shoulders and walked him into the house. Parker walked on the other side of him in case he wobbled. She directed us to the couch. He stretched out and started snoring.

I looked at Parker. "Is this a thing with him? I can't begin to tell you how much trouble he's in."

"No. This isn't normal for him at all. We've just got a lot going on right now." She sat in the chair opposite him. She looked defeated. Her normally bright eyes looked dull and her features sad.

I wanted to comfort her but that wasn't my job anymore. We were friends, that's it. "I don't want to pry. At all. But as his coach, I need answers. I need to go back and figure out what we're going to do about this. He needs help. Even if this is a one-time thing, we have to treat it as though he has a problem. Nobody wants an alcoholic quarterback." Her eyes welled up and I felt like a real ass. "Truly. We only want him to succeed." Me, for selfish reasons, and the team because they needed a leader to guide them to a winning season.

"His problems aren't alcohol or lack of commitment to the team. He loves being a Cheetah." She looked at him slightly snoring on the couch with his forearm covering his eyes and shook her head. "I'll have him call Coach Pierson later tonight."

I took a deep breath. "I'm here if you need to talk. Either as his coach or as your friend. Take care of him and reach out if you need anything." I meant it. Our past was the past and I could put any lingering feelings to the side to help somebody who needed it.

"Thank you."

I stood and had to brace myself for the giant fluffball of a dog that barreled toward me. "You must be Buttercup." The dog stopped short in front of me and wagged her tail. I smiled and let her sniff my hand before I petted her.

"You know our dog?"

"Grayson was mumbling a lot about dogs on the drive over here."

She cringed. "I'm sorry, Sutton. I'll talk to him when he sobers up."

I stood. "I have to get back to work, but keep in mind what I said." I couldn't believe I was opening myself up like this, but a long time ago, I loved this woman. She didn't deserve to go through whatever this was alone, and she probably didn't have a lot of friends since they just moved here.

She put her hand on my arm, something she always did to soothe me. "Thank you. I appreciate your help and discretion."

"Bye, Parker." I was more enthusiastic when I said good-bye to Buttercup. I rubbed her ears playfully. "And you'll have to swing by and play with Crowbar. He's getting all the attention at work, but I have a feeling you would steal their hearts away."

I slid into my car and waited for the garage door to fully open. I looked everywhere but at Parker who was standing in the doorway looking at me. When I put the car in reverse, I finally looked at her. She was leaning on the doorframe waiting for me to back out of the garage. Her shoulders were slumped, but there was an iciness in her blue eyes that I hadn't seen before. I didn't envy Grayson when he sobered up.

"Did you find out anything?" Jamal asked me before we started our afternoon coaches' meeting.

"No, but I told his wife that there would be repercussions. I told her we had therapists available for all the players." Mental health in sports was finally getting recognition. Too many players struggled with the stresses of the game. There was a lot of pressure to stay on top because there was always a willing player to take your spot if you failed. It was time for Grayson to take advantage of that. "And I told her to have him call you when he sobered up. What did Bill say?"

Jamal shrugged. "He said we have to sit down and talk to him about it and that he might have to miss the next game."

"Fuck," I said. I wanted to believe it was an isolated event, but I didn't know anything about Grayson. I didn't think Parker would lie to me, but she might lie to protect her husband.

"I know. This sucks. At least no one got hurt and we kept it under wraps. Maybe he does community service and attends AA meetings. We can only hope this is an isolated incident," Jamal said.

"In the meantime, let's get back to football," I said. I didn't want to talk about the Moatses. "We had a shitty away game. Let's go over plays that will work against Chicago's defense." I could barely concentrate on anything. My mind kept wandering to Parker and what was going on in her marriage. We spent two hours reviewing the Bears' four games this season. They also had a 3-1 record, but they were favored to win thanks to our recent colossal loss.

Halfway through the meeting, Jamal held up his phone. "It's Grayson." He jumped up and stepped out into the hall.

Out of habit, I checked mine for any text messages. There wasn't anything. We didn't even try to continue to talk about football. We wanted to hear Grayson's excuses. When Jamal finally opened the door, it took all my energy not to jump on the table, lunge for his shirt, and yell "spit it out!"

"His best friend died. One of his friends drove to tell him in person and they drank until the early morning. Another friend who wasn't drinking dropped him off this morning," Jamal said.

"What do you say to that? What's our policy?" We had bereavement leave, but it didn't cover showing up to work drunk. I didn't want to lose Grayson as a quarterback. If we had to go with our backup, we would be lucky to win two more games this season. With Grayson healthy and his head in the game, we had a chance to make it to the playoffs.

"Let's get Bill in here and figure it out," Jamal said.

I was extremely nervous. The five minutes it took for Bill to make his way to us felt like five months. We were all tense.

"So, what's his story?" Bill's voice boomed in the small conference room. He slid into the chair at the front of the table and looked at us expectantly. I looked at Jamal.

"Apparently, a childhood friend died last night, and he and his buddies got together to commiserate. Sutton had a conversation with his wife who assured her that this wasn't like him at all," Jamal said.

Jamal knew to only give facts and keep explanations short. Most coaches didn't have time to deal with this kind of bullshit, but we needed Bill to make a decision about playing him. If not, we had to scramble to get Archie ready for the game on Sunday.

"Let's have him meet with a therapist first thing tomorrow morning. He is coming in tomorrow, right? If he doesn't, we'll put in Archie."

Jamal nodded. "Yes, he'll be here. And he apologized profusely for screwing up practice today."

I cringed and willed Jamal to stop talking. Coach made a decision and now we could move forward with the game plan.

Bill pointed at Jamal. "Make sure he gets into a therapist tomorrow. He doesn't leave here until he sees one."

"Will do, Coach."

Bill nodded to us and left the room. We all let out a deep sigh followed by a nervous laugh.

"That wasn't as bad as I thought it was going to be," Brandon said.

"If it gets out to the press, what do we say?" Jamal asked.

It was like they'd never coached in the NFL before, but everyone here had. "We'll tell them he missed practice for personal and private reasons and he's excited to play Chicago this weekend. We don't owe them anything." I snarled just thinking about Duane Spitzer.

Joe, who had been quiet most of the day, wrapped his beefy knuckles on the table. "Then let's get back to coaching."

The pressure in my chest lifted, knowing Grayson was still in as a starter. We could build back up after our loss and get a few more wins under our belt until our bye week when we had the weekend off. I got out of there at seven, desperate for sleep. Today felt like a week. Even Crowbar was yawning as I locked my office. My phone dinged and when I saw the message, my heart almost stopped. It was from Parker.

*Thank you for your help today. We know that's not in your job description. We'd like to have you over to dinner one night as a thank you. The last thing we need is a scandal.*

Shit. I couldn't be rude. Not to her.

*That sounds nice. We have a bye week coming up. Maybe that weekend.*

Bubbles instantly appeared. *That would be amazing. Feel free to bring a date. Lexi, right?*

I didn't want to get into why I was no longer with Lexi. I simply said okay and put my phone away. I couldn't wait to tell Hayley on my drive home.

## Chapter Fifteen—Neutral Zone

*Past*

"Okay, everyone scooch closer. I can't get you all in the frame," Parker's mom said. She was trying to snap a few photos of the ten of us before we headed out to junior prom. We squeezed as close together as we possibly could without wrinkling our dresses. "Nobody move and everyone smile. Wait. Sutton, honey, why don't you switch places with the young man next to you." She meant Joey. "There. Now you all look proportionate." She looked through her camera a million times before taking about fifty photos.

"Okay, Mom. That's enough," Parker said. She stepped out of the line and motioned for us to leave.

"I feel like I'm in a really bad episode of *The O.C.* with rich, snooty parents," Hayley whispered on our way out to the limos.

"Yeah, her mom is fake and mean." I scowled.

"It's like she knew you wanted to be near her daughter and she put a stop to it. Clam jam." Hayley made a screeching sound and threw her hands up as though something blew up.

I shushed her. "It's not like that." But it made me laugh. We were going as a group, but she was hoping to hook up with Zay, the only guy in our group who wasn't into sports. He was in a garage band and was terrible, but Hayley went to all their concerts anyway. Whenever I wasn't at practice, she dragged me too. I was fine with that because I just wanted to make sure she was safe.

"I want to be famous and have limos cart me everywhere." Hayley opened every compartment and bounced from bench to bench. It was obviously her first time in a limo.

"Me, too. I'm going to play in the NFL," Joey said.

"Same." Max high-fived him.

"Me, too," I said. Everyone looked at me. I was expecting them to fall into fits of laughter, but every single person supported me. Even Zay.

"If anybody can do it, it's you, Sutton," Zay said.

Hayley squeezed my knee. "You're totally going to make it. I just know it."

"Even if I have to cheer," I said. That's when everyone laughed. Tonight, wasn't about serious stuff like our futures. It was about having fun and letting loose. One of the seniors was having a party that we were for sure going to. When we pulled up to the hotel, we had the limo drivers take photos of us and as I hoped, Parker worked her way over to me.

"You look amazing tonight, Sutton. And really tall," Parker said.

I didn't know how to react to her compliment. I was so nervous around her. "Thank you. I love your dress. It fits you perfectly."

She wore a red dress that hit at her knees and flared out a bit at her waist. I thought she looked amazing, but I figured her parents probably flipped out.

"Thank you. It's a rather bold dress, but how many times will we go to prom?" she asked. She wasn't wrong. She leaned closer to me. I wasn't prepared to see a hint of cleavage, but there it was. The dress clung to her like silk. Parker looked like an adult, not like a seventeen-year-old.

"Maybe one more time," I said. I was hopeful that next year I would be with somebody special—like her.

"Let's head inside before people start leaving. I want the world to know we were here," Joey said, interrupting our moment. He linked arms with us and escorted the group into the foyer. The line to get photos was long and I didn't feel like standing in it. I ditched the group and slipped into the ballroom. The decorations and twinkling lights made me smile. It seemed like a fairy tale. My dad gave me a head nod and turned the other way to give me privacy.

"Sutton, over here." Two cheerleaders dressed in floor-length, tight sequined dresses waved me over.

"What's going on?" I asked Missy and Amberlynn.

"Did you hear about Sam's party?"

I nodded. "I think we're all going later."

"Missy's parents got us some Smirnoff Ice and I have beer stashed in the back of my car."

I wasn't sure what they wanted or why they waved me over. I wasn't going to drink. The last thing I needed was to get caught with a beer or worse, be drunk around Parker and make a fool of myself. She'd been asked by several people who she was interested in, but nobody got a clear answer. Until I knew, I didn't want to make a pass at her and make her uncomfortable.

"So, what's going on with Parker?" Amberlynn asked.

I cocked my head as if I didn't understand the question. My heart sped up and my palms were instantly sweaty. What did they know? "What do you mean?"

"Who is she into? She's flirted with a few of the guys, but Andrew wants to know if he had the green light to ask her out and you're close to her."

That was news to me. Andrew was the captain of the soccer team. He was kind of a jerk. At the beginning of the year, I overheard him say something negative about girls in sports and got in his face. He laughed it off until my linemen showed up behind me.

"I don't know if she'd be into somebody like him," I said.

"Why?"

They were baiting me, but I didn't care. "He's a jerk about women athletes, including cheerleaders."

Missy made an exaggerated point to look around before asking me the obvious question. "Who are you here with? Did you finally agree to go out with Katie?"

"No, I'm just here with friends. They're in line for photos." After an awkward pause, I excused myself. "I should probably go."

Missy gave me a half-smile. "We'll see you at the party."

I had no choice but to head back out to the photo staging area. I pushed on the door as Parker was pulling it open and bumped into her. "Oh! I'm so sorry." I grabbed her hand to keep her from stumbling back.

"I was just coming to get you. We're almost up for photos."

"And I was headed your way for that very thing."

She nodded in the direction of the ballroom. "What's it like in there?"

I shrugged. "Lots of pretty people dressed up standing around and waiting for Sam's party to start."

"Are we all going?"

"I feel like we have to. I'm not going to drink though."

"I'm staying at Shannon's tonight. I'm sure she'll want to close the party down," she said.

"Well, if you need to leave early, let me know." I smiled and clenched my jaw to keep my teeth from chattering.

"You'll rescue me. That's sweet." She smiled.

I felt heat rush over my skin. Either I was crushing hard and imagining it, or she was into me. "That's what friends do." It was a dumb thing to say but I was nervous.

"Sutton! Parker! Get in here," Max yelled. He waved us over and ten of us crammed into a prom photo that I knew I would keep forever. Parker was pressed against me. Her body heat gave me chills. When the photographer snapped the photo, I felt like she was my date even though we were both whisked away in different directions as soon as the photo was done.

We danced for an hour or so before Shannon wanted to head to Sam's. The limo stopped in front of a house that had at least a dozen cars in the driveway and on the street. Loud music was coming from the house. Our driver stopped and said he would park a block over.

Hayley dragged me into Sam's saying that if I stood around waiting for the second limo to arrive, I would look desperate. I was the high school quarterback and the quarterback didn't wait for anyone. She assured me Parker would find me and she wasn't wrong. Five minutes after we went inside, Parker found us in the kitchen. She smiled at us and accepted a hard lemonade from Sam when she walked into the kitchen.

"Here's where everyone ended up," she said. She took a sip and grimaced but hid it well. I was studying her too hard to miss. She had freshened her makeup and let her hair down. I didn't care that I was staring until I felt the sharp elbow jab from Hayley. She leaned over and scowled. I smiled and shrugged. She gave me an eye roll and a sigh. I shook my head.

"What's going on over there?" Parker asked. She wasn't clueless, but I don't think she was ready for the truth either.

"Nothing." I gave her what I thought was my sexiest grin, but it fell quickly when Andrew slid up behind Parker and put his arm around her shoulder. I swallowed hard and looked away.

"Looks like prom was a hit." He made a production of looking Parker up and down appreciatively. She leaned away from him. I wanted to punch him.

"Gross. Don't be creepy, Andrew," Hayley said. It was obvious Parker was uncomfortable. "You should ask people before you paw them." She pulled Parker away and tucked her safely between us. Parker's arm brushed mine and chill bumps raced along my skin.

"Parker doesn't mind. I always put my arm around her." He took a long pull from his longneck. His eyes never left her.

"Parker's too nice to tell you to fuck off," Hayley said.

Zay walked into the kitchen and brushed his long bangs out of his face with his slender fingers. He wasn't a big guy, but he was tall and scrappy. "What's going on here?"

Andrew laughed. "Nothing. Just girls being girls. I'll see you later, Parker."

Hayley made a gagging noise when he left the kitchen. She turned to Parker. "Tell me you're not into him."

Parker looked alarmed. "No. He's too…" She paused trying to find the right word.

"Predatory?" Hayley suggested.

"Gross?" I added. We all laughed knowing we were on the same page. "Don't worry, Parker, we'll make sure you aren't alone with him."

"Thanks." She took another drink and hissed.

"You know, it's okay not to drink if you don't want to." I held up my red Solo Cup. "It's ice water. I put it in a cup so nobody questions me."

Parker put her hard lemonade on the counter and took a sip from my cup. "This tastes so good."

I grabbed another cup, added ice cubes, and turned on the filter on the sink. "Would you like your own?"

She held up my cup and took another sip. Her tongue darted out to catch a small drop of water on her upper lip. I was mesmerized. "No, I'm good with this one if you don't mind."

Hayley, standing behind her, gaped at me and quickly pushed Zay out of the kitchen. "We'll catch you later."

When it was just the two of us, Parker turned to face me. "What did you think about prom?"

We had danced as a group and every time I got close to Parker, she got pulled in a different direction. It was as if something was purposely pulling us apart. Hayley joked that Parker's parents were probably watching us the whole time on hidden cameras and I was convinced she was right after three failed attempts of trying to dance with her. "I'm glad we're here and not there."

Parker tilted her head at me. "Why?"

It was now or never. It was just the two of us standing in the kitchen. I leaned my hip up against the counter and before I got lost in her blue eyes and tight body, I said, "Because I finally get you all to myself."

## Chapter Sixteen—One Minute of Truth

*Present*

I grabbed Hayley's hand and pulled her to me before we walked up the driveway. "Thank you for doing this for me. I know you had a hard time getting away for the night."

Hayley smiled at me and patted my hand. "I love you, but I did this for me, too. I'm invested in this now. This way, I have firsthand knowledge of how she is, how you are, and if you can have a friendship with somebody who destroyed you." She gave me an angelic smile, but underneath her halo was a fierce woman who was used to fighting for her family. She blinked at me three times and increased the intensity of her smile.

I rolled my eyes. "Come on. Let's get this over with."

"The reunion of a lifetime. How do I look?" Hayley looked amazing. She had gone all out for tonight. She had her hair done, spoiled both of us with mani/pedis, and even though fall was here, she wore a sleeveless dress. She gained fifty pounds when her last was born but worked hard to lose it and, in the process, came away with a lean, muscular body.

"Too bad you're married with five hundred kids. I'd take a crack at you."

She kissed my cheek. "I wouldn't leave Mike to raise my devil children alone. Nobody deserves that punishment."

I knew she was joking. They were a handful, but they were sweet and fun. I reminded myself to get over there and play with them soon. Coaching was important, but I had to remind myself that it wasn't everything. "Are you ready?"

She turned to me. I saw the fire in her eyes and something sinister perched on her smile. "Oh, I've been waiting for this for fifteen years."

I gave her the look. The same you-better-behave-or-else look she bestowed on her boys. "Play nice. I have to work with him for the next several months," I whispered. We walked up the stairs to the front door in silence. Grayson opened the door before I even rang the doorbell, and for a moment, I wondered if they heard our conversation on their cameras.

"I'm so glad you're here." He looked pointedly at Hayley. "I know you. I remember you from the high school games from way back when."

She studied him for a brief second before holding out her hand. "I'm Hayley, Sutton's best friend since grade school. I went to all her games."

Hayley was being kind. I begged her to go to my games. "My biggest cheerleader." Fuck. Did I really just say that?

She looked at me wide-eyed. "This is a lovely home, Grayson. You have children, don't you?" she asked, quickly changing the subject.

"Yes, come on in. Unfortunately, Vee and Rose are already upstairs and in bed."

I looked at the time. It was only eight and a Saturday night. Grayson must've seen my reaction.

"They played in a soccer tournament all day. They were exhausted. Can I get you anything to drink?" He motioned for us to follow him into the living room. It was an open floor plan and both Hayley and I aimed for Parker in the kitchen. She pulled something out of the oven and I was able to study her for a moment without her seeing me. She wore a red V-neck cashmere sweater and high-waisted jeans that hugged her curves. Her hair was pulled back in a casual ponytail and her accessories were minimal. Grayson was wearing a dark blue button-up and jeans. They complemented each other well.

"We brought a nice red if it fits the meal." Hayley handed Grayson the bottle.

When Parker put down the oven mitt and joined us, I felt my heart thud. She still had it. That undeniable hold over me. I knew Hayley felt it, too, because she tapped her foot against mine.

"Oh, my God. Hayley. What a nice surprise," Parker said. She offered a hug, which Hayley accepted. Parker turned to hug me, too. It would have been too awkward to refuse so I bit down and held my breath as she gently pushed her body against mine. I forgot how tiny she was until I felt her in my arms again.

"Surprise! I'm Sutton's date tonight," Hayley said.

"Where's Lexi?" Parker asked. She quickly intercepted Buttercup from jumping on us and sent her upstairs to be with the girls.

"We broke up," I said.

Parker's eyes widened. "I'm so sorry to hear that. You seemed so…" She dug around for the right word. "Connected."

I barked out a laugh. "She didn't like my work schedule or my dog so I had to kick her out."

"You didn't kick her out." Hayley put her hands on her hips. "Lexi met somebody else because Sutton is apparently emotionally unavailable."

"Or that," I said, knowing Hayley was trying to make it sound like it wasn't my fault, but in the process, made everything sound a lot worse. Grayson shot Parker a look. She returned it with an equally puzzling one. Hayley glanced my way and furrowed her brow. Great, Hayley was going to make something out of nothing.

"I'm sorry to hear that," Parker said. She meant it. Her features were pinched in concern for me and suddenly the dinner party felt more like a pity party.

"Really, it's okay. We weren't meant to be together. I don't know why she moved with me to Connecticut." I felt like a failure because I was talking to an ex and her husband about the woman who just left me.

"Well, I commend you for being professional at work. I had no idea you were going through anything personal." Grayson shrugged. "I wish I had better control over my emotions."

"Breaking up and dealing with a death are two very different things," I said.

"Why death?" Hayley asked, even though she knew. It was her way into the conversation without telling them she knew.

"Grayson's childhood best friend died very recently and he showed up to practice intoxicated. Sutton tried to sober him up and sneaked him home," Parker said.

Grayson blushed at her explanation. "So, Parker's excellent cooking is our way of saying thank you. I don't want to lose my job over one stupid mistake," he said. He stood by the bar in the sitting room. "What can I get everyone to drink? Dinner should be ready in about thirty minutes. We should save your wine for dinner. How about a martini?"

"I'll have one dirty," I said.

"Tanqueray?" he asked.

"Perfect."

"Same," Hayley said.

"I can't believe you have three boys. I think it's amazing. What's it like raising them?" Parker asked.

Hayley laughed. "It's exactly as horrible and wonderful as you think. Sometimes they want to cuddle and other times they run away when I get too needy. They're smart, funny, and very caring."

I took the martini from Grayson and tried to get into the conversation. I was nervous around them only because of our history. It was ridiculous, but I couldn't help the way I felt. "They are wonderful kids. My goal is to get them interested in all sports."

With Hayley's slight frame and Mike's small stature, they would never be big enough to play football, but there were other sports they could excel at if they wanted to get involved. I smiled thinking of the camaraderie I had with other team members when I was growing up. It made middle and high school tolerable.

"With Mike's brain, Sutton's athletics, and my confidence, my boys are going to be quite the force in whatever they decide to do,"

Hayley said. Her eyes were shining bright with pride and love for her family. The same light was in Parker's gaze.

"I know exactly what you mean. The girls love football and soccer, but they also love homework and school in general. They'll probably be more social than I was," Parker said.

"You were a cheerleader. I'm pretty sure it doesn't get more popular than that," I said.

"Unless you're the quarterback who takes the team to state," she countered smugly.

"Touché." I toasted her martini glass against mine and quickly toasted Grayson, too, since she probably meant him. I ignored the embarrassment that crept up my throat and warmed my cheeks. "I'm sure that with the parental support in this room, all the kids will turn out great." Parker gave me a heated look over the large rim of her glass. It was obvious to me and when I felt Hayley's knee press slightly into mine, she saw it, too.

When the timer chimed, Grayson pointed to the dining room. "Let's get caught up over dinner." I watched as he pulled the chair out for Parker. I expected a jab to the heart, but it didn't bother me as much as I thought it would. They were married and obviously cared for one another.

Hayley sat across from Parker and I sat across from Grayson. It worked for me. Seeing Grayson didn't sting like it used to. We were friendly and since we worked together, he was starting to become just another player on the team. I hoped to get that comfortable with Parker.

"So, thank you again, Sutton, for saving my ass," Grayson said.

"We all do them. Make bad decisions," I said. I shrugged. "We're not perfect."

"Leaving my husband alone with my boys is a bad decision, but I need alone time. It's nice to get away, but I dread going home. The house will be in complete disarray and the kids one step away from *Lord of the Flies* characters," Hayley said.

"Can I see photos of your kids?" Parker asked. Hayley quickly pulled out her phone and showed them her family. "Oh, my gosh. They are so adorable. And they look just like your husband." Parker handed the phone back to Hayley. "What does he do?"

"He's an engineer. He does well enough so that I can stay home with the boys."

"That's great. You seem happy. You always had a motherly instinct about you. Even when we were kids," Parker said.

"She was always protecting me, that's for sure," I said.

"Even when you didn't need it," Hayley said. A tender moment passed between us and I squeezed her hand.

"I'm so happy you two are still so close. Hayley always had your back," Parker said.

"So, you know about my life, tell us about yours. I'm assuming you dated in college and got married shortly after," Hayley said. I knew that I could get through this with her beside me.

Parker seemed so relaxed. "Grayson was drafted right out of college. We got married after his first year in the NFL and had Vee and Rose. We've moved quite a bit but I'm hoping we make Bridgemont our forever home so the kids can have stability."

"You started in Miami, right?" I asked.

"Yes. I was there for five years, then got traded to Pittsburgh. Took Miami to the playoffs three out of five years, and Pittsburgh twice. I was second string in Baltimore so I didn't see a lot of playing time."

"You've had a solid career and should be proud of it." Was I really pumping up Grayson Moats?

"Blah blah blah. Football, football, throw the ball, catch the ball," Hayley said. We laughed at her theatrics. She knew football almost as well as I did, but nobody knew that except me, my dad, and her husband.

I tuned out the conversation for a moment. Parker's vegetarian lasagna was amazing. I couldn't remember the last time I had a home-cooked meal. I was a DoorDash VIP and that wasn't something I was proud of.

"Sutton?" Parker asked.

I jerked my head up and looked directly at Parker. "What? Yes? What'd I miss?"

"Have you had any time for yourself? I know the Cheetahs have you working seven days a week. Will that slow down for you?"

I wiped my mouth and took a sip of water. "I don't want it to slow down. Once I've proven myself and Grayson and I take the team to the playoffs, then maybe I'll settle down. Until then, I don't want to."

Hayley shoulder-bumped me. "During the summer, she spends about a month with me and her dad in Rhode Island. He has a beautiful house on the beach. He's so good with the boys. I make sure Sutton tunes out the world and just relaxes. The NFL gives their coaches time off right before training camp starts."

"So, if you just broke up with Lexi, was there anybody else that you had a long-term relationship with?" Grayson asked.

Why would Grayson Moats be interested in my love life? This conversation was taking a weird turn and I didn't know how to handle it. "I've had a few girlfriends but nothing serious. Lexi is the only woman I've lived with and that was more out of convenience." I could feel the sweat starting to form in the small of my back.

"I remember you dated that one girl in college who worshipped the ground you walked on. What was her name? Kristin? Katherine?" Hayley asked.

"Kristin." I shook my head. That was a terrible time in my life. "I wouldn't say she worshipped me, but she was a bit much."

Hayley looked at me. "Seriously? The girl planned everything from your wedding to finding a donor for your four children." She looked at Parker and Grayson and thumbed in my direction. "After that fiasco, Sutton took a step back from the dating world. And she got off social media."

"I got off social media because people were saying terrible things about women in the NFL," I said.

"That totally sucks because you're amazing, but you're also missing out on fun platforms. Instagram is great. And I can't even begin to tell you all the amazing things you could do as a coach on TikTok."

I rolled my eyes at her. "And yet I still manage to live a full life without being controlled by my phone." Hayley and Parker both put down their phones. "No, no. I don't mean you two, I just mean I don't need that in my life. You both have beautiful families and sharing them with the world is a gift. Crowbar is adorable, but who wants to see pics of him every day?"

"Every single person in the world does," Hayley said.

I looked at Parker who nodded and back at Hayley. I shook my head. "Stop. Grayson, are you going to weigh in on this?"

He shrugged and grinned. "Sorry, Sutton. It's the way of the world now."

I leaned back and sighed. "Who has time for this?"

"Every single person in the world does," Hayley said again. She reached for my phone. "Let me be in charge of your social media. Send me pics of coaching, Crowbar, and you in a bikini and I'll post them for you."

I snorted and reached for my phone, but she shooed me away. "Hang on. Let me at least download a few things for you." I dropped my head in my hands, completely embarrassed.

"Fine." I felt warm fingers on my hand and knew they weren't Hayley's. Parker had reached between the wine glasses and briefly touched my hand out of support. Her body was always warm. Years ago, I used to snuggle against her for body heat.

"It's okay. I avoided it, too. I was busy raising kids. But we moved a few times and I missed my friends so I jumped on the social media train to stay in touch and haven't looked back," Parker said. She stood to clear the table. "Who wants dessert?"

"Please," Grayson said. Hayley and I nodded.

Parker grabbed her and Grayson's plates, and I grabbed ours and followed her to the kitchen. My eyes darted up and down her body. She'd matured nicely. She had curves and took care of her body. I knew that Hayley struggled a lot after each birth with body image. Being a quarterback's wife came with a stupid set of unwritten rules. Parker obviously took that to heart because she looked the same size as she did in high school, only more curvy.

"What's for dessert?" I asked, not really knowing what to talk about.

"Boston cream pie." She looked at me expectantly as though daring me to question why she chose that particular dessert.

"Oh." Boston Cream Pie was my favorite. It wasn't a coincidence. I didn't take the bait. I couldn't. "That sounds delicious. Homemade or store-bought?" I knew it was homemade. She made me one for my eighteenth birthday. It was lopsided and the chocolate frosting melted because she put it together while it was still warm, but it was perfect because she made it for me.

"Homemade. I've come a long way in the last fifteen years." She sounded angry at me.

I walked around the island and stood beside her. "You really have." My voice was low so that only she could hear me. When she looked at me, I saw how vulnerable she was. Her happy-go-lucky attitude over the last few months was a front. We stared at each other for a long time. I wanted to reach out and pull her to me, but it wasn't my place now. I wasn't her safety anymore. She had a different life and as much as I wanted things to be different, she was untouchable.

"Things are different now, Sutton." She was always good at reading my mind.

"Are they? Because they look the same as they did when we were kids." I took a step back. Whatever was happening in this kitchen was something that we put behind us a long time ago and needed to stay there.

She took a step forward. "Things aren't as black and white as you think. I would love to grab dinner with you one night, just the two of us, and tell you things that should've been said a long time ago."

My heart steeled itself against her words. No wonder Lexi said I was emotionally unavailable. The moment I started feeling things, I shut down. "I think we should just leave things the way they are. I don't need to know whatever is going on in your marriage. We should keep things simple. It's the smart thing to do." I smiled ruefully and headed back to the dining room where Hayley and Grayson were talking about NFTs. "It's like I recognize the words but they mean nothing to me," I said, jumping into the conversation as if the last minute didn't happen.

Grayson laughed. "My agent wants to do something with them, so maybe I'll actually start paying attention."

"Okay, enough of that." Parker walked in with the pie.

"I never understood why it's called pie when clearly it's a cake," Hayley said. The knee bump under the table let me know that she was aware that Parker made my favorite dessert, too.

"It looks delicious," I said and gave her a soft smile. Even if it was horrible, I was going to eat every last bite. It tasted as yummy as it looked and as much as I wanted more, I refrained.

We spent the rest of the night laughing and having a good time. I tried to put the conversation with Parker to the back of my mind, but I kept catching her looking at me. She wasn't looking at me like a friend. Thankfully, Hayley and Grayson were strong reminders of why Parker was off-limits. So I just focused on good company and good conversation. As much as I'd dreaded the evening, it turned out to be fun.

"Thank you again for letting me crash your party. It was good to see you again." Hayley pulled Parker into a hug and accepted one from Grayson.

I hugged both, too. I knew Parker needed friends and if I could get through this night, then having a friendship with her was doable. Hayley and I were silent until I pulled out of the driveway.

"Holy fuckballs! She's so into you still!" Hayley squeezed my leg. "I mean, I was waiting for the room to explode. So much chemistry."

"Fuck. I can't have that, sis. She's married to my quarterback. I'm technically his boss. Please tell me you're just reading into it."

Hayley turned to me, this time squeezing my arm. "Are you kidding me? The tension was there when we walked in the house. At first I thought he was oblivious, but did you see that look they shared when I said you and Lexi broke up?"

I clenched the steering wheel, refusing to let my mind wander. "He knows we have a past. I'm sure that's all it is. We even talked about it before he took the job. I told him there wasn't a problem with us working together." I paused, thinking back to Parker searching my face for answers in the soft moment we shared in the kitchen.

Her guard was down for a minute. Mine was down for fifty-five seconds. I looked at Hayley. "She's off limits."

Hayley sighed and flopped back in the seat. "I know. And all this sucks for you. It can't be easy."

"It's weird really. At first, I was avoiding her at all costs. I locked away the feelings I had for her. I never let go and seeing her again just brought everything to the surface. That's why I'm suffering now."

Hayley's soft voice punctured the momentary fairy tale. "She's suffering, too. Maybe if we stay up all night and talk things through, you'll feel better about your situation. That always worked when we were young."

I took her hand. "Thank you for being the best friend in the whole world."

"Ride or die, sister."

I nodded. "Ride or die."

## Chapter Seventeen—The Snap

*Past*

Even though I was the assistant principal's daughter, I still had to fill out all the forms for the gay club I wanted to start at Oak Grove. I was stuck on the line for faculty advisor.

"What about Mr. Everett? He's pretty cool and he knows you're gay," Haley asked.

"He's old," I said.

"So what? Old people can't support gay and lesbian students? My grandmother loves you."

"I'm pretty sure choir and band take up his schedule. He doesn't have time to add another club to his schedule. Do you think your grandmother can get a job up here? Then we can just sign her up." I was nervous to ask anyone.

"What about your dad?"

I shook my head. "Against school policy. I already asked."

"Let's just ask Mr. Everett. The worst he can say is 'no' and then we'll ask someone else. Oh. We can also ask Ms. Hill, the librarian." She nudged me down the hallway to the choir room.

"I don't think the library is the best place for us. We won't be able to be quiet." I didn't mention that the library was in the middle of campus. If we met there, anyone could see who was in the club and hassle us. I wasn't as worried for myself because I had the football team behind me, but I didn't want to put anyone else in a bad position.

"Then we should try to get the choir room. It's carpeted and virtually soundproof," Hayley said.

"Does getting the choir room have anything to do with Zay being in the choir? You're not going to do some weirdo 'oh, my God, he stood right here in this spot' or 'his fingers were all over this piano.'" I made my voice high to emphasize I was pretending to be her. Truthfully, her voice was deep and raspy for a girl. I smiled when the red splotches appeared on her cheeks. It was fun to tease her because I rarely got the chance.

"Stop it," she muttered.

I gently squeezed her cheek but refrained from saying anything more. She was sensitive and I knew when to back off. "You're adorable and I love you. Let's go find Mr. Everett and see about the room. You should probably let me do the talking."

"What does that mean?"

Hayley was a bit much at times, and even though she was wonderful, I thought it best coming from the assistant principal's daughter. "Because nobody's going to tell the assistant principal's daughter no."

She nodded. "Good point. Okay, you schmooze him instead. I'll go touch the piano keys." We both laughed. "Serious faces. Ready?" At my nod, she knocked on the door.

"Come in," Mr. Everett said. He ate his lunch in the choir room partly for quiet, but also, he wasn't friendly with the staff. When my dad thought I couldn't hear, I heard him talk about how disagreeable Mr. Everett was.

"Mr. Everett, hi. We're starting a new club at the school and we were wondering if you would be our faculty advisor. It would be every other Tuesday at lunch. I already checked with Ms. Clarissa and it's the one day you don't have practice."

He looked suspiciously at me as though I had an alternate agenda and after a seven-second stare down, he said "What's the club?"

We didn't have a name yet so I threw one out that I had seen online for other high school and college clubs. "Gay-Straight Alliance. We need a safe place."

"That's interesting," he said. He showed zero emotion which was better than disdain or disgust. "I guess that's fine but no food in here."

I looked down at his sandwich and smirked at him. "We'll clean up any messes. I'm pretty sure my father would kill us if we destroyed any school property."

He folded his arms in front of him and leaned back in his chair. "If you need my help with anything, let me know." I got his first genuine smile. It was short-lived because Hayley started tinkering on the piano. The scowl returned.

"Please don't touch that," he said.

Hayley looked guilty and held her hands up as though at gunpoint. Mr. Everett didn't know that she could play the shit out of a piano and as much as I wanted her to show him up, I wanted to get back to the front office so we could get rolling on our new club. I gave him the form to sign. He filled out the faculty portion.

"Thanks, Mr. Everett. We promise to take care of things and not touch the instruments." I grabbed Hayley's hand and we ran out of there. We managed to get all paperwork finished and turned in before lunch was over. When we came out of the office, I bumped Hayley's arm. "Look, there's Parker."

"Okay. So?" Hayley wasn't a fan of the new cheerleader.

Parker was on my radar because she was so nice, smart, and gorgeous. Plus she jumped to help me when I desperately needed it. We'd spoken a few times since she was part of the cheer team and in my AP English class. I was so nervous around her. I wanted to get to know her better.

"She seems cool," I said.

Hayley gave her an up-and-down and pointed her nose up in the air. "She's straight as an arrow. Let's find you somebody who won't emotionally destroy you. Is there anybody else on your radar?"

"At this school? Not really." That wasn't entirely true but just because there was another lesbian here, didn't mean I had to date her.

I gave Parker a small wave when we walked by. She smiled at me. It was a genuine smile and I felt it flutter around inside me.

Nobody else gave me that feeling. Hayley was right. I was crushing on the new girl.

"Don't do it. That girl is going to break your heart." Hayley clucked her tongue and shook her head. "She's trouble. Plus, she has the attention of every single dude at our school."

"So?" I was offended that Hayley wasn't open to the idea that maybe there was a chance that Parker was into me.

"Invite her to the first Gay-Straight Alliance meeting. If she shows up, she's at least open to the idea of gayness. If she doesn't, then she's straight."

Great idea. "Hey, Parker." I turned around and jogged after her.

"Hi, Sutton." She brought her books up to her chest and held them close.

"Hayley and I are starting a new club at school and we're looking for people to join or help make posters to spread the word. I wanted to know if you were interested in either?" I loved the way she nervously bit her bottom lip. If she only knew how nervous I was asking her, she would know she had the upper hand here.

"What's the club?"

Oh, boy. If I was wrong about this, Hayley would never let me live it down. Before I had a chance to launch into the description, Hayley jumped in.

"It's called the Gay-Straight Alliance. I'm the vice president because I'm an ally. So even if you aren't on the rainbow somewhere, you can still join in support." Hayley either sensed my nervousness or wanted to give Parker options.

"I'd be more than happy to help make posters. We had so much fun making them for the football games. When's the first meeting?"

"It'll be every other Tuesday in the choir room at lunch. We haven't been approved as a club yet, but when we are I'll be sure to let you know. Does Sutton have your phone number?" Hayley asked.

I couldn't tell whose face was more angelic: Parker, because she was perfect, or Hayley who knew exactly what she was doing and was playing innocent. I leaned up against the locker for support when Parker looked at me with her piercing blue eyes.

"No, but I can give it to her." We watched as Parker tore off a corner of a history study guide and wrote down her number. She handed it to me and I held it as though it was the most precious thing I'd ever held.

"Thank you," I said.

"We'll let you know final details." Hayley shoved me away. "Could you please embarrass yourself more?" she hissed when we were out of earshot.

I shoved the number in my jeans pocket and couldn't stop grinning. "Thanks for doing that."

Hayley shrugged like it wasn't a big deal. "Now you have her number, and you can text her. Maybe strike up a conversation."

I threw my arm over her shoulders. "Come over tonight and we'll design a flyer that we can pass out and hang around school."

She stopped and spun me around to face her. "Just be prepared for some people to be dicks about this. Not everybody is supportive. I know most of the school knows about you, but some people won't support us. They'll tear up the flyers or throw them in the trash."

"I'm sure it'll suck, but think about the kids who don't have the football team to back them. I think it's worth it."

She leaned her head on my shoulder as I walked her to class. "I love your attitude. It's going to get you far. Just not in high school." She veered off to the left for chem lab and I continued on to Pre-Calc.

## Chapter Eighteen—First Kiss

*Present*

"Grayson's on fire today." Bill pumped his fist and celebrated the fourth touchdown pass of the game.

The Bears were trailing by twenty-one points and no way would they catch us. Most of their players were moping on the other side of the field. Some had thrown their helmets under the benches in anger.

I sympathized with them. That was how I felt during the Bills game, but I could only stand on the sidelines and watch. I refused to show any emotion. If the cameras caught me having a temper tantrum, people would say "this is why women shouldn't coach" or "women are just too emotional for this game."

I high-fived Bill and the offense as they ran back to the bench. "He's doing amazing stuff out there, that's for sure," I said.

Grayson seemed more confident and focused. He played to the crowd, and the more they cheered, the better he played. This was not the same guy who wept in front of me and almost lost his job because he showed up to work drunk.

We pocketed another win, bringing our season to 6-2. We were tied for first place in our division and the press was anxious to chat. Grayson was charming as ever with them and Bill answered questions about the season.

I stuck around because the team was having trick-or-treat at the stadium for the team's families and I was passing out candy.

The Cheetahs went all out. The admin staff decorated the cafeteria so it looked scary, but not too much because most of the kids were young. I wanted to wear my Cheetahs sweater and khaki pants, but Hayley said I had to participate. She altered a dog costume to make it look like Crowbar, and we had a Cheetahs dog jersey made with my last name for Crowbar to wear. Totally over the top, but I knew the kids would love it. I checked my watch. The festivities would begin at six. I had time to eat my salad, watch part of the game, and get ready for the party.

"Great game, Coach," Marcus said.

"You all held them to only seven points. Great game, Coach," I echoed Marcus's congratulations. I liked Marcus because he was dedicated and wanted this team to succeed as much as I did. He was considered washed up by many analysts, so he wanted to prove everyone wrong. He was doing a hell of a job. "We'll talk about it tomorrow. Are you sticking around for the party?" I thought he had little kids, but maybe those were his grandkids. I told myself to pay closer attention to the personal lives of the people I worked with.

He rolled his eyes and pointed down at his frame. He played defensive tackle twenty years ago but slipped out of shape as the years rolled on. "I'm sticking around but I'm not putting on a costume so I'll be there as an NFL coach."

I put my hands on my hips and shook my head at him. "I'm disappointed."

"You sound like my wife," he said.

"I might be the only coach dressed up. You're all going to feel so left out." I was saying it to pump myself up the more I realized how few coaches were participating.

"I'm sure you're going to look great. I'll see you up there." He pointed up at the second floor with his clipboard.

"See you later," I said.

Crowbar and I grabbed dinner, then celebrated the win with a quick game of fetch. Crowbar loved children. Truthfully, I was doing this for him. He pranced around when I slipped on the Cheetahs jersey Hayley's mom made for him. His was easy. I was going to need help getting into my costume. I put on spandex shorts and a

T-shirt and looked at the furry full bodysuit I was going to have to wear for the next two hours.

I had the costume around my thighs when my phone chirped that I had a text. I overestimated how far I could step and fell, banging my thigh on the edge of my desk in the process. "Ow!" I turned over and rubbed my leg. My mood was instantly fouled by the impending bruise on my thigh. A rapid knock on my door startled me. "What?"

"Are you okay?"

I looked up to find Parker standing in my doorway. "I'm on the floor of my office tangled in this costume. I don't think I'm okay." I took a deep breath. It wasn't Parker's fault that I fell.

She came all the way into my office and let the door close behind her. Her body was covered in pale purple and bright pink body paint and silver glitter. Her costume left little to the imagination. It wasn't supposed to be sexy, but my mind and my body reacted as though she was wearing lingerie. The shimmering pearl-colored taffeta dress molded against her curves nicely. I couldn't stop staring at her.

"Here, let me help you up." She pushed back her wings and offered me both hands.

"Can I just stay here and die of embarrassment?" I asked. She looked amazing and I was on the floor with my black-and-brown fluffy costume twisted around my legs.

She knelt and looked over my body. "Where does it hurt?"

I pulled my hand back and showed her the red welt on the side of my thigh. "I hit the desk on my way down."

She hissed in a breath. "I'm starting to think that your bruises from high school were because you were klutzy, not because you played football."

I gasped at her teasing, then shrugged. "There might be some truth to that." I struggled into a sitting position. "Why am I wearing a full body dog costume? I'm going to die of heat exhaustion."

"Things could be worse." Parker stood and helped me off the floor. She was stronger than she looked.

"Worse? How?" I couldn't imagine anything worse. I put my arms in the sleeves and pulled the front up.

"You could smell like Brad."

"Oh. Good point." We both crinkled our noses recalling how bad Champ's costume smelled after Brad changed.

She smiled. "Do you need help?"

"Yes, please." I turned so she could zip me up. Her fingers on my back made me shiver. "How are you not cold? You're barely dressed."

"These boots are warm and a lot of people will be upstairs so I'm banking on body heat," she said.

"You always ran warmer than everyone else." That was a dumb thing to say.

She turned and found Crowbar stretched on the couch. "Hello, big boy." His long tail thumped against the couch cushion as Parker petted him. He rolled over and gave her his belly.

"Crowbar gets all the girls," I said. I pulled out the costume makeup Hayley packed for me. I prayed it washed off as easily as she promised it would. I started drawing lines to mimic Crowbar's spots.

"Do you need help with that, too?" Parker asked.

"Why? Am I doing a bad job?" I moved closer to the full-length mirror that hung on the back of the door. My lines looked like his brindle fur. She slipped into the small space between me and the mirror. She was too close, but I didn't move.

"No. I just figured it might be easier and faster if somebody does it for you." She took the makeup pencil from me. "Your face like his?"

I nodded, choosing not to speak while we were this close. Her blue eyes were still piercing and her lips full. Her face had slimmed down over the years but had gained a few laugh lines around her eyes and mouth. Her makeup was perfect. I should've insisted on doing it myself but I selfishly wanted to be near her.

"Black nose?"

I rolled my eyes and nodded. "The works. Make me look like him."

She laughed. "By the time I get done with you, nobody's going to recognize you."

"Most of the people here know Crowbar. I won't get away with much," I said. It dawned on me that her daughters weren't with her. "Where are Vee and Rose?"

"Grayson has them for a minute. Look up," she said.

I looked up so she could add eyeliner. I was only going to put face paint on, camouflage style like I was out hunting, but Parker was artistically painting my face. Having her this close to me was unnerving. I was already hot wearing the costume, but the nearness of her ignited my blood. "This fake fur prison is going to make the paint run."

She gave me a look. "Stop whining. You'll be fine. Unless you run five miles, you're not going to sweat this off. Trust me. I have children."

"That doesn't even make sense."

"If you had them, you would know that it does." She looked at the paint stick. "This is what we use. And it will wash off nicely with soap and water. I can't tell you how many times we've dressed up as pirates or jungle animals. Okay. We're almost done. Purse out your lips and don't talk," she said.

She didn't seem bothered by being in my space. I was glad I'd made myself clear at the dinner party because I wasn't sure I could behave. She leaned in until her lips were a breath away from mine. I froze out of desperation to feel her lips press against mine. She cupped my chin to keep me still. My body swayed slightly forward as though magnetically drawn to hers, as though the universe had plans for us, and for a moment we kissed. But it wasn't a kiss. It was a reminder of our youth. I pulled away before it became a part of our future. I was fully prepared to pretend it didn't even happen.

She pulled me back. "Sutton. I want this."

Even though my blood pounded and I wanted her to fully kiss me, I stopped her. "This can't happen. I can't do this again."

"But things are different now. Give me a chance to explain things, will you?"

God, those pleading blue eyes always made my knees weak. "Nothing good will come of this." I was hyper aware that I didn't say no.

A knock on the door separated us quickly. Emily, one of the trainers, poked her head in. "Oh, I thought maybe you needed some help."

Parker held up the makeup stick and calmly said, "We're doing a pretty good job over here." She stepped away and pointed to me. "What do you think?"

Emily smiled and nodded. "Nailed it. It looks like you got this, Coach."

I took the opportunity to step farther away from Parker. "I can put on my lip coloring but thank you."

She respectfully backed away, too, as though it finally sunk in that she had been in my space too long. "Of course." She gave me a quick up-and-down and smiled. "You look great. You'll be a big hit with the kids."

Parker left when Emily did. When she closed the door, I sprawled out in a chair to shake off the nervousness. Crowbar must've sensed my mood because he slid off the couch, stretched, and moseyed over to lick my hand. After thirty seconds of trying to understand what just happened, I gave up, knowing I had somewhere to be. I slipped the large dog head into position, careful not to ruin my awesome face paint job, and tapped my leg for Crowbar to follow. I attached a small saddle I made of two plastic pumpkins to Crowbar. He was going to be a hit. I'd been getting emails all week asking if Crowbar would attend the trick-or-treat event. According to Hayley, I was getting thousands of likes for every photo of him she posted. He had a bigger fan base than I did.

When I entered the cafeteria, Brandon saw me and immediately pulled his twins over to meet me. "You look amazing." Brandon laughed.

I wanted to bark but the kids looked nervous about getting close to either one of us.

"How am I the only one who dressed up?" I asked.

He looked down at his Cheetahs windbreaker and khakis. "What do you mean? I'm a winning coach from the Cheetahs. That's good enough."

Everyone else looked professional in their pressed pants and Cheetahs shirts and I couldn't have felt more awkward and out of place until Bill showed up. He was dressed as Aquaman and gave me a giant side-arm hug.

"At least I can count on Sutton." His gruff, now hoarse voice sounded hilarious. I couldn't stop laughing at his attempt to keep his long golden-brown wig from getting caught in his mouth or tripping over his oversized boots. It was the perfect icebreaker.

About half the players who stuck around were dressed up as well. Grayson was dressed in green tights, a green skirt, and a tight green T-shirt. I thought he was the Jolly Green Giant until I overheard him telling people he was Peter Pan. Parker's costume made more sense now. She was Tinkerbell. Their daughters were dressed completely differently from them. The oldest, Violet, was dressed like Katniss Everdeen and had a small bow and a quiver slung over her tiny shoulder. Rose was dressed like a witch. They ran over to me and asked if they could pet Crowbar. They barely waited for approval before hugging him tightly. Thankfully, he loved children and accepted their awkward hugs and slight fur pulling.

"Be careful. Don't hurt him," Parker said.

"You look incredible." Grayson laughed at us.

I playfully threw a piece of candy at him, ignoring the twist in my stomach at what just happened in my office with his wife. "Laugh all you want. Look at our line. Besides Bill, we're the next best thing here. Isn't that right, Crowbar?" He wagged his tail and gave a low woof.

"Good for you for dressing up," Grayson said. I felt guilty at the easy camaraderie we shared.

"Uncle Matt. You need to come over and meet Crowbar," Rose said. She adorably dropped the "r" off the end of his name. A nice-looking man kissed Parker on the cheek and knelt to talk to the girls. He had dark, wavy hair and twinkling eyes. I wondered if he was Grayson's brother because Parker was an only child.

"Are you Coach McCoy?" he asked Crowbar. The girls squealed and laughed.

"No, he's Crowbar and she's Coach McCoy." Violet pointed to me. "It's a joke."

He winked at me. I barked at him. He fist-bumped me and grabbed a piece of candy from the table. "Nice to meet you, Coach," he said.

He wasn't in costume. He was wearing a sweater, jeans, and chukka boots and had an air about him that screamed money. His hands were manicured and his watch was vintage. Expensive vintage. Maybe Uncle Matt was Grayson's agent. "Nice to meet you, Matt."

"Do you mind if I get a few photos with the four of you?" Parker asked. She pointed to her kids, me, and Crowbar. Nobody would recognize me anyway. "That's fine. Send me a photo. I need to show Hayley that I went through with the costume."

"I'll get a picture of just the two of you. Then she can post it."

I posed with Crowbar. "I'm sure she'll love that."

Parker nodded. "You both look incredible."

"So do you." I don't know why I blurted that out. I was trying to keep my cool about the kiss, but I felt even more guilty about it in front of her family. I cleared my throat and looked away. Grayson was deep in conversation with Uncle Matt so he missed our exchange. "Will you take them trick-or-treating in the neighborhood or is this it?" I asked Parker.

"It's already seven. It's probably time to get home, take baths, and hide the candy. I want them to get some sleep tonight," Parker said. She was holding Rose's hand who sleepily leaned against her. She loved motherhood. I could see it in her eyes and how her children clung to her for strength.

"You'd better go before that one falls asleep." I didn't know how to be relaxed around Parker with Grayson at her hip.

She pointed behind them. "Plus, you have quite the line behind us. Hopefully, you have enough candy."

I waved her off. "I'm sure there's tons here. What doesn't get passed out will be sitting in a glass jar in all the coaches' offices."

In a surprising move, she squeezed my hand. "Congratulations on your win, Coach."

"Thanks for your help today." I didn't watch them move to the next table. I didn't even remind her to send me the photo. I knew she wouldn't forget. I'd hear from her later tonight and the thought gave me a jolt that I couldn't ignore.

❖

I was on the phone with Hayley when Parker sent me the photos.

"Send them to me. I can't believe you didn't FaceTime me or at least send me a selfie," she said.

I told her how Parker helped me and it took a solid ten minutes to calm Hayley down and reiterate that we were only friends. I didn't mention the kiss we shared. I felt too conflicted about it. I knew Hayley would help me sort through my feelings, but I was too guilty to admit what happened.

"Any weirdness from Grayson?"

"Nothing. He barely looked at Parker."

"That's odd. He was so attentive the other night." She paused as she pulled up the photos. "Oh, my God. These pictures are incredible! I'm going to post the one of you and Crowbar, if that's okay."

"Parker said you would want to. Do you think people will call me a bitch or a dog or anything?"

"Why don't I just turn off comments?"

"Yeah, that's smart." I couldn't prevent people from copying and posting it, but they wouldn't be able to do it on my page.

"Listen, I'm glad you and Parker can share space again. I know it's hard for you, but I think seeing her again is making it easier to be around her. Plus, your date with the kindergarten teacher will help keep your past in the past."

I didn't know how I felt about my upcoming date. I was excited to see Ruby, but Parker kept popping up in my mind, a hundred times stronger after today. "It sucks that Ruby and Parker know each other. Hopefully, that doesn't complicate things."

"I stalked Ruby on social media and she is exactly the person you need in your life. She's cute, loves fun activities like skiing and snowboarding, and she likes beer. I mean, I couldn't have created a better person for you," Hayley said.

She stifled a yawn, so I kicked her off the phone. "Go to sleep. You had a long day. I'll call you after my date."

"I love you. Good job today."

We didn't even talk about my win, and honestly, I didn't even realize it until just then. "Thanks. I love you, too."

## Chapter Nineteen—The Gay Quarterback

*Past*

"We're doing this because the cheerleaders always cheer us on." I was annoyed because the entire football team was at the American Cheer Power to support our cheerleaders and I felt like I was the only one paying attention. Most of the guys were pumped not because of our squad, but because they thought they would get to talk to other schools' cheerleaders. Just like last year, they weren't allowed on the floor so their plan was shot and they were bored.

"It's their job to cheer us on. They signed up for it," Justin said. The guys high-fived him.

I rolled my eyes. "So did you, douchebag. When you sign up for the football team, you sign up to support girls' sports too. Try to be a team player, okay? Those girls do a lot for us."

"They're certainly doing a lot for me now." Wyatt pointed to a different squad on the mat forming a giant pyramid. "Maybe I should be a cheerleader."

I pushed him. "The football team wouldn't miss you if you did."

"Damn, Sutton. That's rough." Max covered his mouth with his fist to keep from laughing at Wyatt who looked embarrassed.

Wyatt knew he wasn't the best but he acted as though he was. The whole school knew him. His catches were phenomenal when he caught the ball, but his percentage was low. I'd rather have a solid receiver who caught the ball every time than someone who jumped high, did flips, and made showboating a part of football. He thought he was going places, but I knew college was his peak. He wasn't good enough for the NFL.

I looked at the schedule. The Oak Grove Puma Cheer Team was up next. When blue and silver burst out onto the mats, our entire section whistled and clapped for them. My anxiety was at an all-time high for Parker because I knew she was nervous. Even though the guys I sat with pretended they didn't care, they were up and yelling the cheers with them. Max was even doing the moves. I knew all the cheers, too, but I didn't want to embarrass myself. This was the only time I could look at Parker without anybody questioning where I was looking or why I was staring. Parker was at the top of the pyramid and when she flipped from the top and four cheerleaders caught her effortlessly, we all gasped. The routine looked super good.

"How come they don't do this during the games?" Max asked.

"Probably because all the attention would go to them and not us," I said.

"They're great. I thought Missy was kind of a badass bitch and now I know why. Look at her. She owns this!" Max said. He was right. We never saw these cheers at the games.

"Maybe we should ask them to do these routines before the games. They would really pump up the crowd," I said.

"I know I'm pumped," Wyatt said. His meaning was clear. I gave him another eye roll. He was being a tool and the cheerleaders' parents were right next to us. Wyatt was embarrassing me. "Their uniforms make my—" He paused and looked at me. "They make my heart pitter-patter. It's too bad we didn't plan better. We could've all dressed up as cheerleaders for them today to show our support."

"We don't have to dress up just to show our support. They appreciate us being here just like we are. Students from Oak Grove," I said.

Wyatt nudged me. "Says the quarterback who never wears costumes or uniforms other than football."

I pointed to my shirt. "I'm wearing a Pumas shirt. That's costume enough. Besides, costumes are for children," I said.

When the routine was done, we jumped and high-fived the parents around us. Most of them were dressed like us: Pumas shirts and jeans. There was one couple who wasn't and I would bet my life they were Parker's parents. Her mother was wearing a wool houndstooth pantsuit and designer heels that looked dangerous on these bleachers. She was accessorized with tons of flashy jewelry. It was borderline gaudy. Her dad wore slacks, a sweater, and loafers. They looked completely out of place with the rest of the families who were holding up large, obnoxious signs with glitter guaranteed to draw the team's attention.

"Way to go, Pumas!" Wyatt yelled in the quiet moment before the next cheer team began. The team looked up at us and waved. When my eyes found Parker's, I felt a jolt and gave her a little fist pump.

When the competition broke for lunch, we were allowed to go down to the main floor and chat with the cheerleaders. Max and I found our squad while the rest of the guys sought out new ones to talk to.

"That was great!" Max hugged the group. They all loved him. "Why don't you do these cheers at the games? They're amazing."

"We don't want to die on the track. At least here we have mats," Amberlynn said.

"You should take the field before we do. I can ask Coach to give you all a few minutes. It's impressive."

"That would be cool," Missy said.

"When are you up again?" I asked.

"They'll announce the second round in about half an hour." Missy turned back to the squad. "Go hang out with your families or wherever. Just make sure you're back in this spot in twenty-nine minutes for the results."

"Do you want to grab something from the vendor trucks out front? The lines here are too long and I could use some fresh air," Max said. We'd driven through McDonald's drive-thru for breakfast, but that was four hours ago. I wasn't hungry until he mentioned it. Parker was walking away with her parents. Talking to her any time soon was out of the question.

"How come Becca didn't join us?" Max's girlfriend loved cheerleading and said if she wasn't such a klutz, she would do it.

"Scholarship stuff."

"Sutton!"

I looked around when I heard somebody calling my name. My eyes landed on Missy. She waved me over to a group of cheerleaders I didn't recognize. Max and I walked over to them. "What's up?"

"I was just telling these lovely cheerleaders that we have a female quarterback, and they didn't believe me. Everyone, this is Sutton McCoy, our quarterback, and she's amazing," Missy said.

I looked at Max briefly. "Thanks. Hi, I'm Sutton."

"How good are you?" one of the cheerleaders asked.

I shrugged. "Good enough."

Missy grabbed my arm. "Oh, she's great. We've had two winning seasons with her as our quarterback."

There was nervous energy being in this mix and I felt my anxiety ramp up. "Hopefully, we can go to state next year." Max nudged me when the cheerleaders giggled. I didn't feel threatened by them. Their body language told me I was more than welcomed there, but they were too shy to speak.

"We need to get some food before they announce the second round results. We'll see you later. Good luck." He steered me away from the girls. "What the hell was going on there?" he asked.

"I don't know. Missy isn't usually so nice. Let's grab some burgers," I said. I found the cheeseburger truck and stood in line.

"Excuse me, Sutton?" A super cute cheerleader from the group we just talked to stood three feet from me.

"Hi."

"Hi, I'm Gemma. I'm with the Franklin Falcons from Dover County. Hi." She was nervous but determined.

I pointed to our line. "Are you going to eat lunch?"

She waved her hands at me and shook her head. "Oh, no. I'm too nervous. Especially now. Can I talk to you?" She looked at Max and then at me.

"I'll have a cheeseburger, fries, and a Coke." I handed Max a twenty and moved out of the line to see what Gemma had to say.

"I know you don't know me, but I wanted to know if you wanted to go out sometime," she said.

To say I was taken aback was putting it mildly. No girl had ever asked me out before. "Um, Dover County is across the state. That's pretty far." What a stupid thing to say. I tried again. "I mean, I'm flattered, but I'm interested in somebody else at the moment."

She looked crushed but recovered quickly. "Oh, okay. Missy said you weren't dating anyone."

"I'm not, but I'm working on someone."

"How about I give you my number anyway? I mean, if things don't work out with her?" Gemma asked.

It was at that moment that I realized life was going to work out for me. I might have been a baby dyke in a small world, but people were interested in me and that boosted my confidence. Even if Parker wasn't gay, there were plenty more lesbians out there for me. "Sure." I thought she was going to write her number on a napkin, but she wrote her name and number on my forearm and punctuated it with a tiny heart.

"I hope you call me," she said.

I sat on an empty bench and watched her walk away, stunned by what just happened.

"Here's your food. What was that all about?" Max slid a tray of food next to me on the bench.

"I just got asked out. By a hot cheerleader." I showed him my arm.

"Woohoo! That's my girl." He held up his hand and waited for me to slap it. I didn't hesitate.

"Hell, yeah." I was on cloud nine. I was about to shoot Max a devilish grin until I noticed that Parker O'Neal stood twenty feet behind Max. She had witnessed the whole thing. I gave her a nervous smile hoping I didn't come across as too much of an asshole. Her face showed no emotion. Not a smile or a frown. It was as if she didn't see me. She turned to her parents and pointed to a smoothie truck in the opposite direction of where Max and I stood.

## Chapter Twenty—The Marriage

*Present*

I froze with my phone in my hand. When Parker texted me and asked if we could talk, I didn't think she meant right now. It was eleven at night. I was curled up in bed with Crowbar. The phone rang four times before instinct took over and I swiped right. "Is everything okay?" I was afraid something was wrong. We weren't pick-up-the-phone-and-call-one-another friends yet.

"Everything's fine. I just have a lot on my mind."

"I'm surprised you're still awake." I was sure she had to get up early to get the kids up and ready for school. "There is school tomorrow, right?"

Her throaty laugh made every part of me tense up. "Yes, but once they are gone then I can get a quick nap in. It's hard to go to sleep on game days."

"Because you get so excited?" I was confused. I was surprised that I was still awake. Most Sundays after home games I dropped early.

"Because Grayson is gone all night."

I sat up. "What? Where does he go? Why is he not home?" I was shocked for her, but I was selfishly more concerned that he wouldn't make it to practice on time. At least players didn't have to report until ten.

"He hangs out with his friends. I don't care though. I like a nice, quiet evening. Going to the games is exhausting."

"Coaching it is pretty exhausting, too." I was teasing her a bit.

Her voice was low and her laugh quiet. "I bet. Fifty-three babies, not to mention the coaches and trainers you babysit, too."

"It's not that bad." But it really was. Football was very macho but also very emotional. A lot of guys played the game with their hearts on their sleeves and it showed. Most of the time I walked the sideline ensuring they were okay physically, mentally, and emotionally. "Grayson's pretty good at keeping the guys pumped up and focused."

"You've done a remarkable job. You were great with the Vikings, but having a say over everything is exactly what you do best."

Did she follow my career? "Why, Parker O'Neal, have you been stalking me?" I smacked my palm against my forehead because I used her maiden name. She didn't correct me.

"I always knew you were going to go far, so yes, I tracked your career. I was disappointed you chose the Vikings because come on, they haven't done anything magnificent since the seventies."

My laughter startled Crowbar awake. I put my hand on his back to calm him. He put his head back down on the pillow once he realized I wasn't getting murdered. "They took a chance on me, and for that, I'll be forever grateful. Plus, I got a chance to coach some good quarterbacks." I must have been exhausted because I asked her a question that I shouldn't have. "What else did you stalk me about?" Was I really flirting with my quarterback's wife? I panicked before she even answered. "No, never mind. Don't answer that. It's late and I'm tired."

"You never got married. I knew that before dinner the other night."

I was quiet. I could either be truthful or play it off. There was only one right answer, even if it was a half-truth. "I'm too busy to have a relationship."

"Come on, Sutton. You always wanted kids."

There was a pregnant pause. "That's true, but I didn't want to have failed relationship after failed relationship and not have anything to show for it. At least being a workaholic takes my mind off other things. Some people can have it all, and some people can't."

"I understand. Actually, I don't. I'm just saying that so you'll still talk to me."

I looked at the clock. It was almost midnight. What was I doing? "How are your parents? Grayson was kind enough to tell me that they talked about how much they hated me long after we were over."

"Our relationship is strained to put it mildly. They're good with the girls, but I'm careful not to let them control them like they did me."

"That's a good thing," I said.

"What's even better is that they are in Baltimore and don't have any plans to move to Connecticut anytime soon."

"Wait. Did they follow you around?"

She sighed heavily. "They did. First Miami, then Pittsburgh, then Baltimore. Thankfully, they really like it there and it's close enough, like a five-hour drive or one-hour plane ride, so they don't feel the need to move yet. And I emphasize yet."

"Your mother hated me. Hated me." I emphasized hated both times.

"My mother hated everybody I dated. Nobody was good enough."

"She was probably excited when you dated Grayson. I mean, college graduate, NFL quarterback. That's probably her dream come true."

I heard her rustling around and wondered if her voice was low because the girls had crawled into bed with her. I could picture them, tiny versions of herself and Grayson, all curled up with their arms draped across her body for warmth and comfort. I always wanted children, but the women I dated weren't exactly wife or mother material. Except one. "My mother has issues with everything I do. The girls want to play sports and she wants me to put them into pageants."

I gasped. "Like Little Miss Connecticut or Little Miss Bridgemont?"

"Yeah, but they aren't doing it. I'm not putting my children through the hell I went through."

I had forgotten that Parker participated in pageants from age five until fifteen. "But think of all the trophies they'd win. Cute little buttons like them." I laughed.

"Argh. That was horrible. I let the girls do what they want. Right now they are both in soccer, outdoor and indoor, but Vee wants to take dance and Rose wants to play football so this might be it for soccer. And both play the piano and go to French class."

"Your children are learning French? That's very cool."

"It's so easy for them to learn at this age. They are really like sponges."

"That's what Ruby said," I said.

"Ruby?"

"Yes, the kindergarten teacher at your school." It never occurred to me that Parker would be jealous, but I heard it in her voice.

"Oh, that Ruby." I could tell she was biting back a retort. "She's nice," she said.

"She says she's a Cheetahs fan. Her family has season tickets. It's nice to meet the super fans," I said.

"You probably have more super fans than you know. I'm sure you get a slew of women trying to hook up."

"That's what the spam folder is for." It bothered me that she thought I was interested in dating. She didn't know the relief I felt when Lexi moved out. I didn't care that Lexi cheated. I only cared that she took a lot of my things. I had nice things. I worked hard for my nice things. They made me happy. People didn't. "Look, I really need to go to sleep. Coaches get in a lot earlier than players. And I hope Grayson shows up on time because if he doesn't, I don't even want to know what Coach Tatum will do."

She blew out a heavy sigh. "I wish I could control him more, but his actions aren't up to me," she said.

It was weird and sad that she had no say in what her husband did. Why was Grayson out all night? I was hesitant, but I asked the obvious question. "Why isn't he home with you?"

"This is actually what I wanted to explain." She paused and the silence was killing me. "Grayson and I have an open marriage. Not a lot of people understand that, but it works the best for us right now."

I fumbled my phone and caught it before it landed on Crowbar's back. I was shocked. "Wow." Of all the things I was expecting her to say, open marriage wasn't on the list. "Wow." So much for me being cool about such a personal matter or showing support. "How long ago did you open your marriage?" I asked. That seemed like an okay question to ask.

"When Rose was still a baby. I've been too busy with the kids, so I haven't had the time to pursue anything recently, but this arrangement allows us to be our true selves."

It was totally vague and I wanted to know more. "Recently? But you have in the past?" I backpedaled immediately. "Wait. You don't have to answer that. It's not my business."

"A few times early on, but then I got busy with the girls. That and my situation and need for privacy is too much for some people to handle."

My heart felt like it was airborne. Of all the people in this world, I never would have thought Parker would be okay with an open relationship. "You've always been a private person. It makes sense that you would be private about this too."

"Neither of the women I dated agreed. They thought I was closeted, but I was protecting my family, not hiding."

"So Grayson knows you date women?"

"Of course."

I stood and paced. This was so much to process. I knew too much. My mind was telling me to hang up and run away, but my heart wanted more. "Sounds pretty lonely."

"It can be, but I stay busy and Grayson and I have a wonderful relationship. We both would do anything for the girls."

I heard the smile in her voice and knew she had made peace with their decision. It still blew me away. Sharing somebody I loved with another person would be hard for me to accept. Good for them. "As long as everyone is happy. That isn't what the problem has been with Grayson, right?"

"I didn't realize how late it is. You have to get up so early. We can talk another day." Discussing Grayson was clearly off-limits. "Thanks for listening, Sutton. I really appreciate it."

"You're right, it's late. And thank you for trusting me with your secret. Cone of silence, I promise. Sleep well, Parker."

"You, too."

I ended the call and sat there motionless even though my heart was racing. What was going on there? Not once had I ever heard a rumor about Grayson stepping out on Parker. Is that why she kissed me last week? Was she looking to start something with me?

I shook my head. I didn't know the rules of an open marriage. I just knew that I didn't think I could be with her because that probably meant the relationship would be behind closed doors again. I wasn't doing that again for anyone. I plugged my phone in and slipped back into bed. It wasn't my place to worry about them, but Parker still had a pull that was impossible to ignore.

Jamal had Grayson by the face mask. "Whatever's going on with you, you need to shake it off. Go take a walk." He pushed Grayson away and barked for Archie. "Get in there and show your starting quarterback how it's done."

Grayson ripped off his helmet and threw it across the field. He had shown up in a foul mood all week, but at least he was on time. Whatever was going on in the Moats' house wasn't going well and Grayson was terrible at hiding his feelings.

I walked over to Jamal and nodded in Grayson's direction. "What's going on with him?" I'd been studying films on the Jets, not watching practice.

"He's thrown every single pass either at the receiver's feet or too high. If he plays like this on Sunday, we'll lose for sure. I want Archie warmed up in case this sorry sack shows up to play instead of our star." Machismo was alive and well in football and it was hard to not roll my eyes at Jamal.

I jogged after Grayson because he didn't deserve being called out like that. "Hey, Grayson. Hold up." He turned but kept walking. I caught up to him and kept in stride. "Look, don't worry about Coach getting all up in your face. You know what this is like. You've been around the league long enough to know he's just blowing off steam." I abhorred making excuses for rude behavior, but I had to communicate with Grayson on a level he understood.

"I'm just tired of all the rules. All the time. Here, at home, in life."

I softened my voice. "Are you going to the team therapist? She's worked wonders with other players and coaches."

"I hate feeling like this," he said. His features were scrunched up into something that resembled physical pain.

I sent a text to Dr. Jennifer Gioia, one of the team therapists, to find out if she was available right now. She was. "Let's go see Jennifer. Maybe she can help you sort a few things out," I said. Grayson headed in the opposite direction. "I'm not asking." He turned back around and put his hands on his hips. The darkness in his stare was unsettling. "I want you to get help. I know something is eating you up and we have therapists to help. We all go to them. That's why we have two on staff. It's not a sign of weakness."

"Fine, but I need to get out of these pads," he said. He stomped off toward the locker room, removed his pads and cleats, and slipped on athletic slides. He grumbled under his breath the whole time. By the time we'd reached Jennifer's office, he'd relaxed somewhat.

I knocked on her door. "Hey, Doc. Do you have some time to talk to Grayson?"

"Of course. Come on in, Grayson."

She was the nicest person with a gentle disposition. During my sessions, I never felt like I was talking to a shrink. I felt like I was talking to a co-worker who had my back and supported my decisions. I was required to talk to her when the season started and it helped to get all my fears and doubts out and into the space between us. Three sessions later, I was good to go. I hoped she could do the same for Grayson. I squeezed his arm and closed the door, leaving them to fight his demons.

When I got back to the field, Jamal looked pissed. "Where's Moats?" His voice was getting hoarse from yelling at everyone.

"He's with the doc right now. Give him some space," I said. It was a demand. It was also the first time I flexed on any of the offensive coaches. He nodded and turned his attention back to the field. Archie was doing an okay job, but I was sure he was getting tired of hearing how much Grayson carried the team. I somehow had to get the coaches back to the basics. They needed a reminder that this wasn't the military. The men on the field had feelings and positive reinforcement was better than ass-kicking.

An hour later, Grayson trotted back onto the field with a better attitude. Whatever was eating him, Dr. Gioia helped fend it off. His throws were hitting their marks and he even joked with his teammates.

## Chapter Twenty-one—
## The Quarterback and the Cheerleader

*Past*

I jogged over to the cheerleaders who were stretching and getting ready for tonight's game. "I need a hair tie. Does anybody have a hair tie?"

"What?" Missy asked.

I was trying not to panic. "My elastic broke. I need a hair tie. Doesn't anybody have one? If I don't put my hair back, those assholes on the other team are going to rip it out."

"You can use mine. I have another one." Her voice was quiet, but her words spiked my pulse. It was the new girl, Parker something. She was shy, and pretty, and people flocked to her. She was the All-American girl with stunning blue eyes, long blond hair, and straight, white teeth.

When I saw her in my dad's office on the first day of school, I normally would've introduced myself, but there was something about her that made me want to both run away and be near her. It was perplexing. I watched as she slid the tie from her long ponytail. She didn't hand it to me but told me to get on my knees and turn around. "A ponytail is fine," I said.

"Nope. We're not going to give them any reason to get their hands on you."

I could tell she was French braiding my hair. Her fingers felt amazing and it was hard not to lean back or relax into her. All eyes were on us. I stayed on my knees and waited for her to finish. I wanted to say something clever and fun, but I was tongue-tied. The rest of the cheerleaders were walking through cheers, but Parker was focused on me. She quickly wrapped the end of my braid in the elastic and tucked the part that would've stuck out of the helmet up into the braid.

She patted my shoulder. "That should get you through the game."

I jumped up and took a step forward before turning to thank her. "You saved me tonight. I owe you big." I adjusted my helmet and ran over to the sidelines where my teammates stood.

"McCoy, you're out there with Max," Coach Larson barked. Max and I jogged to the Puma logo in the center of the field. We nodded at the right times and deferred the ball to the visiting team when we won the toss. It wasn't hard to miss Parker on the sidelines with her long blond hair. I almost wiped out on the run back to the sidelines because Max slowed down and I was looking elsewhere. My cleat scraped the back of his ankle.

"Ow. Sutton, pay attention," Max said.

"Fuck. Sorry!" I helped him with his shoe when we got over to the bench.

"Where's your head at?" He followed my glance. "Oh, I get it. The new girl." He shrugged. "I think there's a long list so you might want to get in line."

"McCoy! Johnson! Up for the kickoff," Larson yelled.

"Sutton's helping me with my shoe. Be right there."

Max made a big production of checking the laces and the fit before finding an opening for us on the sidelines. Special teams stopped them on the twenty-one-yard line. The Fort Range Pioneers were a tough team. We lost to them last year. I was ready for them this year though. They were heavy on offense, but light on defense. And they played dirty. They put late hits on players, especially quarterbacks.

We cheered when they missed the field goal. I grabbed my helmet and jogged out. I saw Parker and gave her a quick head nod. We got into position and I started the game by handing off the ball to our running back.

"Blue thirty-two, blue thirty-two." My offense set up. "Independence." Two seconds. "Independence," I yelled. The team pushed off the line and I stepped back in the pocket and delivered a beautiful spiral that Max caught twenty-eight yards down the field. We got another fifteen yards when their middle linebacker nailed me well after the pass was thrown. I was rattled but I bounced up and called the huddle like it didn't matter.

"Fuck, that looked rough. Are you okay?" Max asked.

"I need somebody to stay back in case that shit keeps happening." I was angry and slightly dizzy. I was probably concussed but didn't want to stop. By halftime, most of us were bloody. We were ahead because we kept our cool, whereas they kept getting penalties.

I wanted to collapse on the locker room floor but managed to stay upright by leaning against a locker while we listened to Coach Larson's changes. When he was done, I ran across the hall to the women's locker room to put on better pads that protected more of my body. I pushed open the door and startled Parker. "I'm so sorry. I didn't mean to scare you." Her eyes were wild and her chest heaved. "I'm not used to running into other girls down here."

She held up a broken hair tie and laughed. "I needed to redo my hair," she said. Looking into her blue eyes and at her perfect mouth, I suddenly felt no pain. "You're very tall," she said.

I took a step back because I didn't want to intimidate her. In full football gear, I was supposed to intimidate. I placed my helmet and the better pads on the counter. "I'm getting beat up out there. I've got to change my pads." I started to tug at the neck of my jersey.

She playfully rolled her eyes at me and rested her hands on her hips. "Can I help?" she asked.

"That would be amazing. Can you grab my jersey around the neck and pull it off? If you don't mind."

"Of course, bend over," she said.

I bent over so she could pull off my jersey. I quickly untied my pads and pulled them off. I was sweaty and still tasted blood in my mouth, but Parker didn't seem put off.

"Do you need help putting it back on?" she asked.

"Yes, but let me just rinse out my mouthguard real quick." It unnerved me that she was watching me and when I felt her hand on the back of my neck I almost crumpled. Her touch was amazing.

"Your hair is holding up nicely," she said.

I nodded and discreetly spit the water into the sink. It wasn't bloody so I didn't have to be embarrassed by that. "Thank you so much. You seem to be rescuing me a lot today." She helped me wrestle into my new pads and watched me intently as I laced up.

"Ready for the jersey?"

"Yeah. I'm sorry it's so dirty. Tough game."

"It's okay. This is what we do. We cheer, braid hair, and even help dress players." We both blushed at her words.

"Wow. I mean, I knew cheerleaders were helpful."

She giggled and pushed my shoulder playfully. "Not like that." She gathered up my jersey and held it in front of her.

It was a struggle, but we got it on just in time. The banging on the locker room door startled us both.

"Let's go, McCoy."

"Yes, Coach." I smiled at Parker and grabbed my helmet.

"Go get 'em, McCoy." She growled and made a little fist.

"I will." I opened the door and trailed my team back to the field. A few moments later I saw Parker slip into formation with the cheer team.

"What are you smiling about? This game is killing me." Max adjusted his helmet and stretched. He was getting pounded out there. He was used to it. I wasn't.

I nodded at Parker. "Her. She's so nice. She helped me in the locker room with my pads."

"She's hot, too." He smacked my knee and pointed at the field. "But let's get back to the game. We're up."

We won by three points. The crowd was wild, the coaches almost fought, and I was exhausted. We downed Gatorade and listened to Coach tell us all the good we did. I peeled off my uniform and sprawled out on one of the benches in the women's locker room wearing my compression shirt.

"We meet again."

I looked up and smiled when I saw Parker, but dropped it when two other cheerleaders, Missy and Amberlynn, walked up behind her.

"Good game, Sutton," Amberlynn said.

I waved thanks to her, too tired to speak.

"I don't know how you do it or why you do it. You probably have a million bruises." Missy always spoke her mind, and nine times out of ten, she was a bitch.

When it was apparent they were going to undress right in front of me, I sat up and grabbed my clothes to take a hot shower. I wanted to rest longer, but I didn't want them to feel uncomfortable. Sometimes I thought Missy did it on purpose just to see me squirm. When I came out to my dad, he told me to never be alone in a locker room with only one other person. At least there were three private showers. I grabbed one and hurried up. I could soak my sore muscles tonight when I got home.

"Hey, Sutton. Are you going to Tom's?" Amberlynn yelled.

"Yeah, I'll be there."

"Okay, you're here alone. We're leaving and we'll see you soon," she said.

The private stall had a lock, but I was still vulnerable, so I rinsed out my hair and quickly dried off. I wondered if Parker was going to Tom's. Just in case, I took extra time to style my hair and put on a tiny bit of makeup.

The parking lot at Tom's Pizza was full, but I found a spot on the side of the road. It was the place to be because not only did it serve cheap, mediocre pizza, it also had a bowling alley, an arcade with games from the nineties, and dance-off machines. I high-fived several people on my way inside. "Great game, McCoy!" and "Awesome win!" followed me until I found a spot in my booth.

"I called you," Hayley said. She scooted over closer to Harrison to make room for me.

"I haven't even looked at my phone," I said. I grabbed a slice of pizza and ate it in four bites. That game took all my energy and I needed to replenish ASAP.

"Max has been asking a lot of questions," Harrison said.

I looked at him. "What kind of questions?" He looked innocent, but I knew what he meant.

"You know, about a certain cheerleader," Hayley said.

I shrugged like it wasn't a big deal and grabbed another slice. "Yeah, so?" I gave her the now is not the time look.

She caught on and changed the subject. "Your lip is a little swollen," she said.

"My whole body is banged up so I'm not worried about a little cut." Honestly, I was more worried about my ankle that I rolled at the end of the game. I needed to ice it.

Over Harrison's shoulder, I saw Parker walk in. She looked amazing. Her blond hair was down and flowed around her shoulders. She was wearing jeans and a thin blue sweater. A jacket hung over her forearm, and she clutched her purse to her side to prevent it from hitting people. The place was packed and loud. When our eyes met across the restaurant, I felt something stir inside me. We didn't know each other, but we weren't strangers. We were friends waiting to happen. Maybe it was because she was the first girl who had literally made me forget about everything, or maybe it was because I wanted us to be something. Either way, I knew it wasn't just me, because she gave me a small wave and kept eye contact before getting pulled in a different direction.

## Chapter Twenty-two—
## The Troubled Quarterback

*Present*

"Can you come over?" Parker's voice sounded shaky.

"Are you okay?" I stood out of panic and excused myself from the meeting. Maybe Grayson got hurt or maybe he hurt her.

She took a deep breath. "We're fine, but we need your help." It was almost eight at night. We were flying to San Francisco in two days.

"Sure, give me half an hour and I'll be there." I walked back into the team room. "Listen, I have an emergency and I have to leave. Are we good on everything?" Everyone nodded.

"Are you okay? Do you need any help?" Brandon's face was etched in concern.

"I'm fine. I just need to…" I paused not really knowing what I needed to do. "I need to leave. I'll see you all in the morning." I tapped my leg and Crowbar jumped up. It was the fastest he'd moved all day. He probably felt my anxiety. I grabbed my bag and locked my office.

I was at their house in twenty-five minutes. I cracked the windows for Crowbar and told him to be a good boy and to wait in the car for me.

Parker opened the door. She'd been crying and I had to ignore the need to pull her into my arms. I was going to kill Grayson if he was responsible for it.

"Come on in. We're in the living room." Her voice lowered. "The girls are upstairs in bed."

Grayson was sitting with his head in his hands. When he looked at me, I knew he had been crying, too. Ah, fuck. It would be a matter of time before I started. Crying was my weakness. I sat on the couch and watched as he rubbed his hands over his face several times. I was legit worried.

"What's going on?" I asked Grayson. I was on my last nerve. I looked at Parker. "Seriously, somebody needs to start talking and fast because I'm about to freak out." She sat next to me and took my hand. I didn't pull away because she obviously needed me, but I also didn't want to get my ass kicked. I looked at Parker in alarm.

"It's okay," she said.

Grayson stood and leaned against the fireplace. His crossed arms told me it would be a while before he broke down. I was trying to ignore the feel of Parker's warm hand in mine.

"Is everyone okay?" I asked.

"Physically fine," Parker said. She slowly let go of my hand and stood next to Grayson. "We need your help and we don't know what to do without catastrophic fallout."

Well, that scared the living shit out of me. "Okay. Talk to me." I leaned back on the couch as though I was a friend who casually stopped by even though I was sweating and my stomach kept contracting out of sheer nervousness.

"We've been living a lie," Grayson said.

"Okay." I nodded as though I understood completely but still had no idea what was happening. Parker must not have told him that she told me about their open marriage.

"I don't even know where to begin," he said.

I shrugged as though it wasn't a big deal. "Start at the beginning. That's always the easiest."

He made a noise that was a combination of a laugh and a sob. "First of all, I love Parker and Violet and Rose. I don't want anyone to doubt that."

"Okay."

"But I can't go on like this," he said.

"Like what?"

"The pressure is too much. I just can't do it."

"Do what? Be a husband? A father? A football player? Please narrow it down a bit." I tried hard to keep the panic from bubbling up again. All those options were different kinds of catastrophes. Parker was calmly rubbing his back.

"We've decided to get a divorce," Parker said.

I was floored. "Okay. What happened? Why now?"

"Back in college, I met someone," Grayson said. "But I was with Parker and we had a dream of making it to the NFL and having the perfect family. I was on a path that was decided for me years ago." He started pacing. "Now I don't know what to do."

"Do you want to get back with that person? Is that what this is about?" Who was this person? He nodded. I leaned back in relief before what he said really sunk in. "Wait. You want to divorce your wife to be with someone else?" I blew out a deep breath. So many feelings were swirling inside me. I looked at Parker. "How are you doing?"

She gave me a weak smile. "I'm okay. This was a choice we both made. It's a long time coming. But we need your help because this is killing him and I don't want him to lose everything over this."

I was shocked that she was so supportive of him. Again, I didn't know the rules of an open relationship, but I was pretty sure successful ones didn't end with divorce. Parker stood there, cool and calm with her tears in check.

"Does the divorce have to happen now? I know that sounds insensitive, but you're at the tail end of the season. A divorce now will affect everything in your life from the game to how people treat you socially. Remember when Jakob Phillips had an affair and left his wife? It came out in the middle of the season. The Packers never won a game with him as starting quarterback. They benched him and eventually released him." I realized it sounded like I was more worried about our careers than the personal lives of the people in this house. "I'm not trying to be dismissive of everything you're going through. But you do have responsibilities outside of this house."

Grayson groaned and rubbed his hands over his face. "I know. And I'm going to retire to minimize the damage. I just need to get to the end of the season."

"That's why we called you. We need help navigating the fallout," Parker said.

I looked at them. They both were anguished. I had to be honest. "A divorce at this point in the season will hurt your credibility as a player. One of the reasons you came back to the NFL was because of the money, right?" Grayson nodded "You want to set your family up for the future. This will hurt your endorsements and it will hurt the team. Honestly, I think the best thing to do is wait until the season is over and make this happen as quietly as possible."

Grayson nodded even though he looked devastated. "I thought you might say that. This is killing me. I wouldn't be here if it wasn't."

"Is this why you're having a rough time at work?" I asked.

"Yeah. I know I sound like a complete idiot right now," he said.

I stood. "You don't, Grayson. Love is hard and sometimes we make choices when we're young that we regret. I would really like for you to think about flying under the radar until after the season. Don't go out. Don't get caught with her in public. Everybody has cell phones and they take photos and videos and sell them to the highest bidder. It would destroy your family if word of this got out." I could feel myself getting angry, so I slowed down. "Do the right and respectful thing. Don't cave to a moment of weakness that could affect everything you've built up to this point." I felt for Parker and the girls, but I also couldn't be mad at Grayson for finding love. I was here to offer advice as a coach about what would cause minimum damage. "After the season, there will be less blowback and trust me, it'll come."

"Do you get harassed a lot for being your true self in the NFL? Have people been cruel about you and your relationships? It has to be hard for you."

His question didn't faze me in the least. I'd been asked it a hundred times since I joined the league. "I think people are upset that a woman is in charge more so than a lesbian. I get plenty of crap for being gay, but honestly, if I were straight, they would probably give me more shit. I guess most people think that being a lesbian means you know a lot about sports." I shrugged.

There was a look of pity on Parker's face, but it was directed at Grayson, not me. "Living authentically is hard." She turned to me. "You're so brave."

I walked over to Parker. "Are you really okay with all of this?"

"Like I said, this wasn't only Grayson's decision." She truly seemed to be at peace. I was missing something here. The whole situation gave me a weird vibe. "I want us both to be happy. Right now, we aren't. Grayson is a good man, and a great dad. None of that will change. And I deserve happiness, too."

Her words made my heart clench. According to her confession on the phone, she hadn't had sex in a long time. She must have resented him because she stayed home with the kids, while he was off screwing somebody he was in love with.

"Why didn't you do this sooner?" I lowered my voice to let them know I wasn't judging them.

"My parents wouldn't allow it. They were very judgmental when I first brought up that we were going through some things," Parker said.

"Your parents are assholes," Grayson said.

It wasn't my place to say anything, but I was so with Grayson on that one.

"They aren't perfect, but they have tried to give me the best life possible." Parker shot back. It was a weak retort, but we didn't comment.

"Let's get back on track. What do you need me to do? I'll do whatever I can to keep this between us. The team doesn't have to know. The fewer people who know, the better."

Grayson stood in front of me and put his hands on my shoulders. The weight of his hands was uncomfortable. "Sutton, I don't think you're getting it. I'm gay."

I stood in front of him and gaped for a solid ten seconds. "What?"

"You met my boyfriend on Halloween."

"Uncle Matt?" I barely got those words out. My teenage years came rushing back and flooded my mind with horrible memories. Grayson stealing my girlfriend only to end up leaving her years later. "Who knows? Do the girls know?"

"No, but they are starting to figure out that something is going on. Nobody knows for sure but us and Matt's parents. My parents don't know."

"Where is Uncle Matt now?"

For the first time all night, Grayson smiled. "It's just Matt. The girls call him Uncle Matt because they've known him since they were little, but you can call him Matt."

"What does he think about all this?"

"It was too hard to be apart, so Matt moved up here and we decided it was time to move forward with our relationship."

I wanted to explode. Grayson and Matt had made a decision for Parker and they hadn't even consulted her. She sacrificed everything for their relationship. No wonder she was heavily involved in her daughters' lives. While he gambled with their privacy, Parker had to play the docile wife who followed him wherever the NFL sent him.

"What do you think about what I've said? Do you think you can keep your relationship with Matt quiet for two more months?"

"It'll be hard but if you think that's for the best, then I will. I know he'd like to know what's going on. Do you mind if I invite him over?" Grayson asked Parker.

"Of course not. Sutton's car is already in the driveway. The neighbors will just think we have company over."

Grayson texted Matt while Parker excused herself to check on the girls. I sat on the couch. I was stunned. It had only been a week since Parker told me about their open marriage. I was still processing that. I realized then that their marriage wasn't really open. From what I understood, an open marriage meant the marriage was still alive. Parker was just Grayson's beard.

When Matt showed up, he and Grayson retreated to his office. Parker came downstairs. She saw the closed office door and walked directly into my arms with quiet tears streaming down her face. I managed to get her over to the couch where I held her and let her cry. I didn't know when I started crying but I didn't even care. We needed this cleansing. When her sobs subsided and she sat upright, she gave me a sad smile.

"I'm so sorry. For everything." She touched my face and wiped my tears away. Parker was a pretty crier. I ended up with splotches on my skin. The only visible sign that she had been crying was red-rimmed eyes.

"So open marriage really meant he got to keep his relationship with Matt, more or less?" I asked. She nodded. "How long has this been going on?"

"On and off since college. Matt is a great guy. He's wonderful with the girls. I think that's made it so much harder on Grayson because he can see what his life could look like."

"And that's why he pushed for divorce?" I asked.

"That's why he agreed to one," she said.

"It was your idea?"

"Yes." She put her hand on my thigh. "The last few months have been really confusing for me. Reconnecting with you, seeing Grayson so happy. I've felt trapped for so long. I don't want to feel that way anymore."

I put my hand over hers. "Don't take this wrong, but why on earth did you marry him knowing he cared so much for somebody else?" I left myself out of the equation. Now wasn't the time.

She looked defeated. "I can't tell you the last good decision I made on my own."

I wanted more of an explanation, so I waited.

"I was young, and my parents had raised me to be a certain way. My whole life I'd been told homosexuality was a sin. And when I met you, I knew there was no way the feelings I had for you were wrong. When my parents split us up, I was too young and naive to realize I could've done things on my own. By the time I realized that, I'd lost you and Grayson. The only thing I had left to keep me going was my children."

"Why didn't you divorce sooner?" Why was I doling out relationship advice when I had failed so hard at every one I ever had?

"I didn't want to risk Grayson's reputation. He worked hard and he always gave me everything I wanted. Don't get me wrong. Grayson and I have been best friends for years. This hasn't been a loveless marriage. It's just been a sexless one. For me at least," she quickly added.

"Some people have sacrificed more for so much less. Marriage isn't only about sex. I get where you're coming from." I needed to leave this house. I was sliding down the slippery slope of my past and I needed to regroup.

"Sutton, I know I hurt you and I know things are really strange right now, but I never stopped thinking about you." Parker carefully placed her hand on my knee. The look she gave me was raw and intense. Everything was happening too quickly. I leaned back. My body tingled from her nearness. She was entirely too close and on purpose.

"What are you doing, Parker?" My voice was low. I cleared my throat.

"Do you ever think about us?"

I folded my arms in front of me to add a barrier. "I do. I did. You really broke my heart, but we both have moved on." Truth would be a splash of cold water and maybe she would take a step back. I wanted her, but I didn't want the scandal that came with the indiscretion. "I know you are vulnerable right now, but this isn't real." I pointed at her and then me several times back and forth to emphasize what wasn't real. Us. There wasn't an us. I didn't want to be an old pattern she fell back into.

She put her hands on my forearm. "I know I hurt you, but I can't stop thinking about you. I never did. It was like that before we even moved here. When Grayson said the Cheetahs reached out, I panicked. He didn't know you were coaching here, but I did."

I stepped away from her. "This can't happen, Parker. You're still married and I'm coaching your husband. I honored the secret when we were kids, but I'm an adult now and I'm not going back into the closet for anyone. Not even you." But fuck, it was hard not to fall for her all over again. But life was scary and hers was quicksand. One bad decision and I would be neck deep.

She took a step back. "So, what happens when I'm divorced?"

I threw my hands up. "Then you're free to date whomever you want."

"Anybody?"

"Anybody available. Look, we can't have this conversation. It doesn't make sense. We've grown so much and we're probably not even compatible anymore."

She smirked and I realized I gave away too much. "I doubt that." She walked over to me and put her fingers on the soft spot above my breast where my heart fluttered like hummingbird wings. "We've always had chemistry, even now, but it's more than that. A part of me is still in here."

I swallowed hard. It was a big part, but something I wasn't going to tell her anytime soon. She might've realized her marriage was over years ago, but it was still fresh to me. "I'm not entertaining anything until the season is over and the ink on your divorce papers is dry." She was still smirking at me and I panicked. "Even then, who knows, maybe Ruby and I will give it a shot."

Her blue eyes narrowed angrily. "You've been hot and cold with me. Sometimes you flirt with me, and other times you act as though I don't matter anymore. Which one is it?"

I felt powerless and weak-kneed this close to her, but I needed to be the responsible one. "We're different people now. I'm not the same lovestruck teenager that I was fifteen years ago. You made sure of that. You have children, a mortgage, a whole different life."

"Some things never change, Sutton. I know you're still attracted to me. Maybe we are very different now, but don't you think it's worth pursuing?" she asked.

I wanted to succumb to her logic, but I knew if I did, my whole life would unravel and I wasn't ready to let go. "It's not fair. You don't get to live out this avenue of your life and then when it's dead, jump into my lane. That's selfish and cruel."

"I promise that's not what I'm doing. My marriage has been dead a long time. Seeing you again was no small part of me realizing that."

She touched my face. I automatically leaned into her hand and closed my eyes for half a second. I wanted this so much. My past and present were colliding and for half a moment, I felt euphoric. Nothing else mattered but right now. I should've pushed away when I felt the soft whisper of her lips against mine. It was an invitation. I let my heart have this moment. The image of Grayson and Matt in the other room flashed in my mind and I pulled away.

"I'm not ready to do anything right now. You have to respect that."

She gave me a soft smile. "I understand, but I hope you're open to something in the future."

I didn't know how I didn't crumble. Years of hardening my heart and throwing myself into my job came through in the moment I needed it most. "I don't know what to say. You have to give me time. And you need to get this settled before anything can happen here." I motioned my finger between us even though I knew the moment she beckoned, I would call. "I need to go. Crowbar's in the car and I still have films to study. Are you good? Are you okay with Matt here?"

"He'll leave soon, but yes, I'm good."

I paused when I got to the front door. "Whatever you do, don't tell your parents anything. Even when it's time for the divorce." I knew in my heart that they would destroy Grayson at the expense of their daughter and granddaughters. "I'm sure they will find out in time, but let's hope it's after he's professionally retired at the end of the season."

She grabbed my hands. "Thank you. I knew you would know what to do. I'm sorry it had to come out like this, but he was starting to unravel and needed help."

"I never—" I stopped. We were both extremely vulnerable and emotional right now. Words were only going to get us into trouble. "I'll talk to you soon." She hugged me. It felt wonderful to have a selfish moment even under these circumstances. She always felt right in my arms. "Let me know if you need anything."

She looked tired but also relieved. I was sure she thought the burden was gone, but really, it was just beginning.

## Chapter Twenty-three—Scrambling

*Past*

"You need to get laid," Hayley said. I elbowed her ribs. She oofed and rubbed her side. "No, I'm serious. Then we can talk about sex and stuff."

"You're still a virgin so I don't know why we need to discuss anything." I was seventeen and perfectly happy playing football, going to school, hanging out with my friends. I didn't need any complications. Plus, I wasn't sure what getting laid really meant for me. Was it penetration? Was it oral? And regardless of what Hayley thought, she wasn't an expert. She just broke up with her boyfriend because he was fooling around. She got on the pill for him, ready to sleep with him and found out he was hooking up with some sophomore. "You probably need to take all your straight talk to another straight person because I'm not going to be able to help you at all."

"But you could give my future boyfriends some advice." She winked slowly at me.

Hayley and I talked about everything. We had for years. We talked about masturbating, how often we did it, what we thought about during it, but when it came to sex, I didn't share the same enthusiasm she did. She wanted to talk about boys, but I didn't. "Somehow, I have a feeling you will work it out just fine with your boyfriends."

She flopped down on my bed. "Isn't this supposed to be the best time of our lives?"

"Junior year? No. It's only supposed to be okay. It's senior year that's going to blow us away," I said. I moved my books off the bed and lay beside her. "I have a good feeling about this year."

She rolled over to face me. "I do, too. I feel this energy around us. Like big things are happening. That's why you need a girlfriend. A serious one. And I need a boyfriend."

I held her hand. She was so broken up about Jamie cheating on her that I thought for sure she would take a break to regroup and mend her heart. I was wrong. "Why do you need a boyfriend?"

"To fuck with Jamie. To show him I'm okay."

I laced my fingers with hers. "Listen, it's okay that you're not okay. He did a shitty thing and everyone knows." Hayley had a great heart, but she hated to show weakness. "Maybe now we can hang out at the mall more or get back to our weekend routine of watching every single sports-themed movie ever made." I missed her.

"But if you find somebody to date, then we could double date," she said.

"With whom? You're not dating anyone." I sat up. "Or wait. Are you?"

She blushed and looked away. I squeezed her fingers. "What's happening and why am I the last to know?"

"I like two guys."

The hetero world was a giant mall with so many options for Hayley. The kiosk of lesbians in my world wasn't always open and hardly had any options. A cute, perky girl like Hayley wasn't going to stay single for long. I was probably going to be single until college. "Tell me which ones and I'll tell you if I approve."

"Okay, so I like Drew in my Careers class. You know who I'm talking about, right? I think you had a class with him last year."

The summer had been good to Drew. He grew six inches and filled out. He went from just average Joe to hottie, and he was making his way through the cheerleading squad. I knew he was only in it for sex.

"Next! Drew's too much of a player."

"Yeah, but he's hot. Like superhot and all muscly."

"There are plenty of hot guys who aren't players. Who else? You said there were two guys."

She sat up. "You have to work with me here. He's completely different from anyone else I've ever been interested in."

Hayley didn't have a type. She liked them all. As long as they paid her attention, she was interested. It made me nervous. "Tell me. I won't get mad."

"Why would you say that?"

"I don't know," I said defensively. "I just wanted you to know that I won't judge you or think any less of you. As long as it's nobody on the football team."

"I kind of like Zay."

"The tall, lanky, emo dude? With black hair and piercings and eyeliner that's better than mine?"

She huffed. "See? Judgy much?"

"I'm sorry. You're right. I'm an ass. Tell me why Fall Out Boy is so dreamy." I deserved the smack on my arm and giggled.

"He's just nice. And he's hot in a rock star sort of way."

"Good. You deserve someone who is nice and hot."

She waved me off. "Enough about me, let's talk about you and the girls. I know you like Parker, but she seems to be wavering back and forth between Harrison and Nick."

Hearing that made my stomach drop. Parker was so pretty and sweet and those guys were just dudes looking to score. Sometimes it sucked being the team captain. You knew everything about everyone on the team. "Yeah, I know. I can still dream though, right?"

"No. We need to find someone you're into who will like you back, not date your teammates and tease you. Oh, I know! Let's look through the yearbook. You can point out all the girls you like."

"I feel like that's offensive," I said.

Hayley grabbed my yearbook and opened it between us. "Calm down. It's just us. We do this all the time."

"Okay. Are we starting with the clubs?" Parker wasn't in last year's yearbook, but I knew I was going to compare every girl to her.

"Let's start with the freshmen," Hayley said.

They were this year's sophomores so they were only a year behind us. I couldn't imagine dating a freshman now. I thumbed through the pages and found two ninth graders who I thought were pretty. I was starting to get discouraged even though we just started. We moved on to sophomores. It was easier because I knew most of the people in our class so I wasn't judging based on a tiny photo. At the same time, it was harder because I already knew who in our class was gay.

"Oh, she's cute. Ashlee Markle. She's in theater. A thespian lesbian." Hayley pointed to a cute brunette with short hair and a brilliant smile.

I groaned at her bad joke. "Wasn't she Frenchie in *Grease*?" I vaguely remember seeing the play and the hype about it. "She's cute but she's dating Dusty." Too bad.

"Moving right along." Hayley flipped the page and dropped her finger on a volleyball player. "Ooh. Tay Minton. She's definitely gay, but maybe doesn't know it yet."

I leaned closer for a better look. She didn't give me the warm feelings that Parker did, but something stirred low in my belly. Maybe it was the permission that Hayley gave me to look at the girls in our school. "She's cute and seems pretty confident." I filed her away in my mind and made it a point to talk to her the next time we ran into each other at school. She was the only sophomore.

The juniors, this year's seniors, got my blood pumping. Hayley and I found six possible candidates. I knew most, but I never thought about being attracted to them until Hayley gave me permission. I didn't know if any of them were actually gay, but Hayley was convinced most were.

"Shut the fuck up! Sienna is totally wearing rainbow dog tags!" Hayley held the book close to my face as though I hadn't already zoned in on it the second she pointed it out.

"It's a black-and-white photo. We don't know if they're actually rainbow," I said.

"Of course they are. This is so exciting. Maybe she's the one. You should ask her out. Then maybe we can double date. You should be dating and kissing and doing all the things that lesbians do." She wiggled her fingers in front of me.

I laughed. "That's probably not how it's done, but it would be nice to have a girlfriend." Sienna was quiet, nice, cute, but she wasn't my dream girl. For years I had a description, but never a face. Not until Parker O'Neal showed up with her long blond hair, bold blue eyes, and quiet disposition. I turned to Hayley. "This feels weird. I've always wanted an organic meeting. Like I see this girl across the football field and she's stunning. And she's impressed that I'm a football player. She doesn't care that I get banged up and bruised because she knows it's my passion."

Hayley looked crushed. She leaned her head against my shoulder. "I can't wait until we're older. We're going to be so fucking happy and married and our kids will play together and be as close as we are."

"It sounds so far away." I wasn't desperate for a girlfriend, but I was ready for one. I knew Hayley meant well, but it was different for me. Since we were thirteen, Hayley had dated at least a dozen guys. Not only was she an incredible person, but she was straight. I was just going to have to wait until a girl walked into my life who was ready to start something with me.

## Chapter Twenty-four—First Touch

*Present*

"Hey, how are you?" I couldn't tell Hayley anything about what was happening, and I hated it. I knew she would be hurt, but she would understand. It had been ten days since the Moatses dropped their bomb on me, and honestly, Grayson was doing better. An obvious weight had been lifted and he had done a one-eighty on the field. I texted Parker regularly to see how she was doing. I kept my texts short, but with feeling.

"I haven't heard from you in forever. Are you okay?" Hayley asked.

"I'm good."

"You're great! I swear you're going to the playoffs." Hayley was always my biggest cheerleader.

I wanted to believe her, but I also didn't want to jinx us by thinking that far ahead. "I hope so. We still have a lot of work to do. We have five more games until the playoffs and we have to win four out of five."

Hayley sighed. "Three and two will give you a wildcard. Listen, I called because I wanted to find out what you're doing for Thanksgiving. Are you able to get away?"

I inwardly groaned. How could I forget about one of the biggest holidays? "Honestly, I don't know what I'm doing."

"Well, we would love to have you and your dad and Judy. Or just you, or just them. Somebody to watch the kids, really." Hayley laughed. "Also, I miss you. I know football season is busy, but I need you."

I missed her, too, and my mental health needed rejuvenating. "I'll be there. I'll call Dad later and invite him as well. I can't promise I'll stay all day, but I need to wrestle with some kids."

"They would love that. And so would I. Are you driving home?"

I clenched the steering wheel tighter. I was on my way to see Parker, but I couldn't tell Hayley that. "Yeah. Me and Crowbar are going to watch games and fall asleep on the couch."

"Sounds perfect. Trust me. The boys are driving me bonkers. I'm living vicariously through you for the next ten years," she said.

"I'll send you a text when I talk to Dad. Thanks for inviting me."

"Thanksgiving is for family and friends. You're always invited. You know that."

"I love you." I did and it broke my heart that I couldn't share a massive part of my life with my best friend right now.

"I love you, too, and I'll see you soon," she said.

I hit the end button and a wave of guilt washed over me. I cracked the window for fresh air. What was I doing? Who did I think I was? I wasn't a professional who should've been doling out advice in a very sensitive situation. I was inserting myself because I still cared for Parker. I didn't want to admit that maybe there was still something between us, but here I was, making a beeline for Parker's since Grayson sneaked over to his apartment with Matt. It was 9:04 p.m. and like I told Hayley, I should've been home watching films, but instead I was in fresh clothes, my hair down, and pulling into Parker's driveway.

"Hi, come on in." Parker's eyes lit up when she saw me.

"How are you doing?"

"You know what? I feel good. I'm at peace."

She looked incredible. Worn, comfortable jeans hugged her hips and tapered down to black booties. The black V-neck sweater showed a hint of cleavage. I kept my eyes on her face, but my peripheral vision picked up the smooth, creamy skin of her neck and bit of her collarbone. She was sexy without even trying. "That's good to hear."

"Come on in."

I knew they had met with a lawyer, and I was dying to find out how it went, but I didn't want to ask.

"Can I get you a drink?" she asked. She plucked a wineglass off the table with her slender fingertips and motioned for me to follow her into the kitchen. "This is a merlot."

I needed a clear head. "No, thanks. I need to be sharp for tomorrow." I knew that if I started drinking now, I would continue until my excitement of being close to Parker dulled and that would take at least a bottle. I couldn't afford to drink that much tonight. She handed me a glass of ice water.

"Let's have a seat in the living room. Are you ready for the game?"

I gave her a look. "Let's not talk about football. Tell me about your day. You sometimes volunteer at the school. What do you do when you aren't being a mom or a wife?"

"As much as I love my children, it's nice to have adult time. I have Pilates on Mondays and Fridays. I have book club on Wednesday nights. The rest of the time I'm either fielding calls for Grayson's charity or volunteering in the classroom. My life is very simple," she said.

It was far from that. I had a simple life. "I definitely don't think it's that."

"You're right. It's not simple, but it's going to be soon. We met with the lawyer today."

"Oh?" I told myself to act only mildly surprised. I knew Grayson left after films today for personal reasons. "How'd that go?"

"It went well. The girls and I will stay here at the house. We're figuring out custody because we want equal time. I'm sure the sooner we get it done, the happier we'll all be."

I wanted to know more, but I had to be delicate about it. "I have so many questions, but I know it's not my place."

She finished her glass and kicked off her boots before folding her legs underneath her. "There's not much to tell. You know everything really."

"What about you? Why didn't you put yourself first? I know you said it was because your parents were jerks about it, but that's a huge sacrifice."

She ran her fingertips delicately over the cashmere throw she pulled from the back of the sofa to cover her lap. "I felt it was punishment." That didn't sound like the Parker I knew.

"For what?"

"For going against my parents, for hurting you, for making bad decisions one after another."

Her mouth tilted down at the corners. I reached out and touched her hand. "Hey, high school was a long time ago. We were kids on different paths. You're doing what's best for yourself and your family. Do you think what happened between us was wrong or that what's going on with Grayson is wrong?"

She covered my hand with her own and squeezed. "No, of course not. I'm proud of him. I'm even proud of myself for finally seeing what we were doing. I hate that the girls will be affected by this, but it's the best for our relationship as their parents."

"What about you? What happens to you?" I didn't move my hand.

"I'll still run Grayson's charities. I'm not worried about me. I want to make sure the girls are good. The lawyer recommended some therapy for all of us to get used to the idea of being a split family."

"They know and love Uncle Matt, right?"

"They do. So much. And he adores them. Plus his parents love the girls so I know they are going to be loved and well cared for. I'm worried about my parents' reaction to all of this."

I clenched my jaw to keep from spouting horrible things about her parents. That was her battle. "What do you think's going to happen?" I was fearful of the O'Neals. They had money and the power of the church behind them. If nothing else, they could destroy Grayson in the press, which would affect Parker and the girls. "I mean, do you think they would disown you? You're their only child."

"I really don't know. They've gotten even more 'churchy' over the last few years. Maybe they suspect about Grayson, but they definitely know about me."

What did that mean? "Know about you how? What do you mean?"

She pulled her hand back and linked her fingers together and rested them gently on her lap. She was always so graceful, even as a teenager. "My sexual identity. I'm tired of trying to fit in a mold that the whole world wants me to fit in. I understand Grayson's frustration. Only he has it ten times worse because he's in a sport that doesn't accept gays."

"Hopefully, that's changing. I think if Grayson comes out to the world on his terms and not in a way that has him scrambling around, it will help other players. Homophobia exists everywhere, but the younger generation is more tolerant."

She leaned her head back on the couch and sighed. "You've always been so strong and proud. I always envied your life. Your dad was so supportive. And your friends. You're even still friends with guys you played football with."

"I can't believe that some of your cheer friends haven't reached out on social media to use you." I smiled at her to let her know I was joking.

She laughed. It made my stomach quiver again. "I finally had to block Missy because she was incessant. I guess she's still in Oak Grove. She's been married twice and has at least one child. She wanted more of my time than I could give her. And all the perks that football wives got."

I crinkled my nose. "What kind of perks do you get?"

Another laugh. Another quiver. "I'm sure you get a lot of products that companies want you to endorse."

"I never responded to any of my emails. I know we have a whole public relations team that fields stuff like that to our agents, but I always delete them." It never dawned on me that my voice would be heard. Now that I was the first at something, the world would be listening. "Think of all the macaroni and cheese commercials I could be doing."

"That's your social responsibility? Mac and cheese commercials?"

I pretended to be shocked. "We all eat it. Why wouldn't I promote something so All-American?" This entire exchange was cheesy, pun intended, but I could see her shoulders relax and the worry lines around her mouth and forehead soften.

"My girls love it. And there are healthy options."

"Or maybe I should work with a publishing company so I get free books donated to my charity."

She sat up straight so fast that I leaned back. "You should ask your agent to look into that."

"I should answer my agent's calls more. I'm sure he fields a lot of requests. I've been spread so thin this year that it's impossible to pick and choose. I need sleep, you know." I finished my water. "It's getting late. I should go." I didn't know if Grayson was coming home tonight and I felt guilty for being here. I darted to the kitchen and put my glass in the sink. I felt Parker's body heat before I even turned around.

"Sutton."

The way she said it made my weakened resolve fall apart. I pressed my palms against the counter for a moment to gather any strength I could before I turned to face her. Her eyes always told the truth when her guard was down. The last sixteen years weren't easy on her. I hated that there was a part of me that hoped she was suffering. The woman in front of me was in agony.

I pulled her close and ran my fingertip along her jaw. She was still my first love. Still the woman I wanted most in this world. I could tell she was holding her breath, waiting for me to decide. The universe brought us together once and fate stepped in the second time.

"Parker."

A slight whimper escaped her parted lips as she cupped my face in her hands and brought my mouth down to hers. The first kiss was tender and soft as we adjusted to one another. She was more assertive now. It was a massive turn-on.

"I want you. It's always been you," she whispered when we broke apart for air.

Our kiss went from gentle to explosive in the span of fifteen seconds. I couldn't get close enough. Not only did I knock my walls down, but I kicked them out of the way to get to her. She felt so familiar in my arms, but I noticed subtle differences as well. Her breasts were fuller, her hips had widened, but her waist was still small and her skin so smooth. I kissed her neck and reached down to unlatch the button of her jeans. I was moving too fast after practically giving her a PowerPoint presentation of the reasons why we had to wait.

Instead, I slid my hand under her sweater and smiled at her body heat. I had touched dozens of women in my life, but I had Parker's body memorized. The small mole on her ribcage, the way chill bumps followed my touch like it was a race to get to the sensitive spots first, and the way she bit her bottom lip when my hand got closer to her breast. She smelled like sweet orange blossom and a hint of vanilla. I slid both hands down the curve of her lower back, into the band of her jeans, and squeezed her ass. I pulled her flush against me, wishing our clothes were off and we were somewhere private. I wasn't the shy teenager who worried if I was doing something wrong anymore. Parker's body squirmed against me for friction and her small, breathless moans made every part of my body hum with desire and need. I was two seconds from pulling her into the study when a rapid, but low, insistent knock on the front door interrupted us.

"Why aren't they answering the door?" a man's voice asked.

Parker put her hand on her chest and stared at me in alarm. My imagination exploded. Grayson was in a wreck, or he got pulled over. Or it was Bill who had found out about Grayson and my involvement in his marriage. To be fair, other coaches had hidden worse behavior in the past. I followed Parker to the door. She opened it.

"You never answered your phone. We've been calling all night," a woman said.

Fuck my life. The O'Neals stood in the doorway with suitcases in hand. I had no choice but to stand there and wait until the recognition hit them. Ginger O'Neal did not disappoint. Her lips curled back in a sneer. If I didn't have the upper hand of having recognized her first, I would have cowered.

"Hello, Ginger. Hello, Samuel." I grinned like the cat who ate the canary and leaned my shoulder against the wall as though I belonged there.

"What is she doing here? I thought she was out of your life, Parker," Ginger said.

How did they not know I was the offensive coordinator for the team their son-in-law played for? The announcers said my name all the time during games. "I coach her husband now." I returned her sneer with a smirk. She scoffed, huffed, and smacked her husband in the chest.

"Do something, Samuel."

"Nobody's doing anything, Mother. Sutton is a part of our lives now. She's our friend, Grayson's coach, and belongs here just as much as you do," Parker said.

"It's so good to see you both again after all these years. You look well." I wanted to bolt, but I didn't want them to control my actions anymore. I was an adult and everything Parker said was true. Maybe we were more than friends after what just happened a minute ago, but they didn't need to know that.

Parker gently pushed me out of their way. "Mom. Dad. Come in. What are you doing here? We weren't expecting you until the weekend."

"Obviously." Ginger scoffed.

I pulled myself up to my full height and looked down at them. Funny how they used to scare the shit out of me. "I was just on my way out. Good night, Parker. I'll see you later."

"Bye, Sutton. I'll see you soon." Parker's voice was a full octave higher.

I could feel their stare boring into my back as I walked to my car. "We tried calling but apparently you were busy. Why is she here? Where's Grayson?" Ginger asked.

I didn't hear Parker's answer as I shut the car door. I got out of the driveway as fast as I could without burning rubber. I called Grayson. "Sorry to interrupt, but your in-laws just showed up, presumably unannounced."

"Shit. They're early. They offered to come up for Thanksgiving. I didn't know Parker changed the date."

"She didn't. She was very surprised they were there. You might want to head home."

He sighed. "Thanks for the heads up."

"Only a little bit longer." I disconnected the call and wondered if I was going to be in trouble from the league or the team for orchestrating this arrangement. My contract was for two years so even if they fired me, they had to pay me. But if they fired me, no other team would touch me.

Ten minutes later, I pulled into my driveway. The weariness of the day finally hit. Crowbar slid off the couch to greet me. I let him out one last time and crawled into bed. My limbs felt heavy. I crawled into bed with Parker on my mind, but sleep overtook me before I could play out any scenario that could have happened before her parents showed up.

## Chapter Twenty-five—First Meeting

*Past*

"Do you get a cheerleader assigned to you or was that a lie from the movie?"

I laughed at Hayley's reference to the movie we'd watched last week. I was torturing her with every sports-themed film in existence. "Maybe that happens in Texas, but not here. We're not that important. Football isn't life in Oak Grove." It was my life, but not the blood of a town like so many movies portrayed. Hayley and I were hanging out in the bleachers watching the new squad figure out basic cheers. Varsity and junior varsity cheer teams were on the field. There were ten cheerleaders on varsity and about fifteen on JV. "They look so young," I said.

Hayley grabbed my cheeks. "You look younger than they do."

I pulled away. She loved doing that to me. "I look like I'm supposed to. They look twelve. Look at the JV team."

"Some of them are freshmen. That makes them about fourteen. Maybe they're like the Olympic gymnasts and never hit puberty," Hayley said.

"That's rude." I scowled at her. I hit puberty at ten. It was a nightmare. Hayley didn't start her period until she was fourteen. Also, a nightmare. She was the last of her friends to start. The stress of worrying there was something wrong didn't help.

"You know what I mean."

"How come you never tried out for cheerleading? You've got the energy for it."

She snarled at me. "That's offensive. I'm not going to be any football player's doormat except for yours."

"Damn straight." I loved her. I would always love her. Even if time made us drift apart later in life, I knew we would always be able to pick up where we left off. True friends and siblings could do that. Hayley was the closest thing to a sister I had. I couldn't imagine my life without her in it. "Promise me we'll always be friends. Even if you run off and get married. Promise me we'll always be close." She linked her arm around mine.

"I will love you more than my husband and six kids."

"Six? Wow. That's a lot."

"I'll have my own basketball team and one substitution." She nodded and I believed her.

"Except you're really short and unless you date the Incredible Hulk or Thor, your children will be genetically disposed to be soccer players or horse jockeys."

"Maybe they'll be famous actors. They obviously don't need to be tall," Hayley said.

"Good point." We watched the cheer team divide into groups.

"I love that Missy's about to lose her shit with them." Hayley pointed to the head cheerleader who stood with her hands on her hips barking at the scared squad in front of her. "How important are cheerleaders? Do you even hear them out on the field?"

"Their job is to get the crowd into the game, not us. We're already there. You know how rude teenagers can be. Also, no, I can't hear them. I have Coach yelling at me and the opposing team yelling at me. I hope to God when I'm older, people stop yelling at me."

Hayley patted my leg. "You'll be yelling at them. I promise you that." She wiped off the dirt on my knee. "You probably should've changed. And let your hair down. Some of the cheerleaders don't know who you are." She turned to me and squeezed my arm. Her body language screamed excitement and I groaned before she even said anything. "You should go down there like 'Oh, hey, I'm the quarterback. Anyone interested in dating the quarterback?"

"Yeah, that sounds like it'll work." I rolled my eyes and was rewarded with a gentle shove.

"Would you date any of them? I know you like sporty girls, but some of the cheerleaders are super cute," Hayley said.

"Excuse me. Are you watching them? They are sporty, too. They tumble, do backflips, forward rolls, get tossed in the air, and land on their feet like cats," I said.

"We should go down there and parade you in front of them."

I looked at her in disbelief. "Why? Why are you pushing this?"

She shrugged. "Because I love you and the quarterback should get to date a cheerleader. I think it's a rule."

I laughed. "It's not a rule. And don't worry. I'll find somebody."

She took my hand. "But it's high school and I want you to be happy and have fun with all of us. Going out in groups is fun, but alone time is funner."

"More fun. Alone time is more fun."

Rolling her eyes, she huffed. "Whatever. You know what I mean. Surely, one of those cheerleaders is gay."

I ignored the JV team because they were too young for me. "We know Missy and Amberlynn aren't. I'm clueless about the rest." I didn't have gaydar yet. Maybe it was something I would gain once I spent more time with lesbians and gays, but for now, everyone was straight. I sat up when Missy waved me over. "Does she mean me?" I pointed to myself. She nodded. I stood and marched down the bleachers and out onto the field.

"We're all getting together to make posters for the football team's first game. Do you want to join us? It's before school in the art room. Ms. Elling said we can use all the posterboard and glitter and paint we want," Missy said.

What a weird request. Why would she assume I'd want to hang out with them? She must've noticed my confused look because she elaborated.

"And by you, I mean the whole football team. It would be good for the new cheerleaders to meet the entire team. I'll bring doughnuts and I'm sure we can have the cafeteria brew coffee for us. The lunchroom ladies get in so early."

"A meet-and-greet? That's a good idea. I'll bring it up to the guys tomorrow. When do you want to do it?"

She bounced on the balls of her feet as though for two minutes she couldn't abandon cheering just to have a conversation. "The first game is Friday so why don't we try on Wednesday morning? It's not like they need to do anything other than show up."

"Okay, sounds good. I'll talk to them."

"Thanks, Sutton."

Missy bounced away and pulled the team into a huddle. Hayley mouthed something to me but I ignored her and motioned for us to leave. She met me on the side of the bleachers.

"What did she want?"

"She wants the football team to meet the cheerleaders for breakfast one morning."

"Is that weird? I mean, don't you all know one another already?"

"Not everyone. And she's bringing doughnuts. I mean, she could've started with that and I would have committed right then."

"Are the guys really going to help?" Hayley said.

I snorted. "I can barely get them to do drills. What do you think?"

"It's nice that she's trying, right?"

"Thanks for coming. I have name tags for everyone to wear," Missy said. She waved a stack of white labels with a red border that read *HELLO, my name is*.

I passed them out to the team. Last night I reminded them to behave and be nice. Coach Larson told them he was showing up, too. I knew that he wasn't. Just the threat that he would be there was enough to keep the guys in line. I wrote my name in big block letters. Wyatt used five stickers, one for each letter in his name. I was positive everyone knew his name already because Coach was forever yelling at him to pay attention to the field, not the cheerleaders.

I managed to grab two doughnuts before they disappeared. Missy must've spent a fortune. I excused myself from the table where Max and I were trying hard to draw two junior varsity cheerleaders into conversation. I grabbed another cup of coffee from the cafeteria's urn. A slightly burnt but comforting smell wafted around me when I hit the spout. It looked like jet fuel and I was sure it tasted as bad. Two sugars and two creamers couldn't kill the bitterness, but I needed the caffeine to get me through Algebra in thirty minutes.

"It's horrible coffee and yet here we are, lining up for more."

I turned to find the new girl standing in line. "Anything to keep me awake. Are you on the squad?" We both knew I knew she was, but she played along.

"Yes. I'm new to Oak Grove. I'm Parker O'Neal. And you're Sutton." I smiled at her smugly. She took the time to find out my name. That was promising. But then she pointed to my name tag. "It's hard to miss."

"Right." I blushed and took a sip of coffee that was unbearably hot. I turned my head and coughed as it scalded my throat. Fuck, that hurt.

"Are you okay?" Parker asked.

I waved her off as though this happened a lot. "I'm fine. Still not awake and still making bad choices." The smile she gave me took my breath away. I was already nervous to talk to her, but now that we were in each other's personal space, I felt skittish and wanted to bolt back to the table. "How's cheerleading?" Hayley would kill me if she knew that was my opening question.

"It's good. How's football?"

"Painful, but I'm excited about the new season." I took another sip of coffee and tried to mask the burn but failed.

"You should probably wait to drink that," Parker said.

"I keep telling myself the caffeine will wake me up, then I forget it's hot as fu—" I stopped myself. I wasn't around the guys. I was standing in front of a new cheerleader and I was trying to make an impression. "It's just too hot."

She smiled. Her smile was beautiful and made my stomach do backflips. She wasn't like the other girls at Oak Grove. She seemed more refined and delicate. Even her clothes weren't casual for school. I was wearing jeans and a T-shirt and she was wearing pants and a sleeveless top. Her arms were toned and tanned. She looked amazing. Her flats screamed money whereas my Converse should've been tossed over the summer. I looked worn and I had never been so self-conscious in my life.

"Have fun making posters. I'll see you on the field, quarterback," she said.

What she said wasn't even flirty, but I felt a bounce in my step like I was Missy getting ready to direct a cheer. I sat next to Max again.

"Who were you talking to?" Max asked.

"New girl."

Max gave me a look. "I know it's the new girl. What's her name? Where's she from?"

"Her name is Parker and I think she's from heaven."

He bumped my shoulder and laughed. "Maybe she's the one."

I couldn't stop staring at her. She sat down with the defensive tackles and made small talk with them as they painted their signs. They laughed with her, but every few seconds, her eyes drifted my way. "Yeah, maybe she is."

## Chapter Twenty-six—Touchdown

*Present*

In my adult life, only two people have ever lifted me off my feet. A linebacker from Texas A&M scooped me up and out of the way when students rushed the field after we won a college bowl, and head coach Bill Tatum swung me when we made the playoffs. Both were painful, but exhilarating moments in my life.

I felt the tears on my cheeks before I realized I was crying. My career was riding on this season. We made it. I sat on the players' bench, found a towel, and cried. No, I sobbed. I knew cameras were on me, and I didn't care.

Massive palms slid into my view. "Let's go, Coach. We aren't done yet." I looked up into Grayson's smiling face and put my hands in his. He pulled me to my feet and hugged me. He was sweaty, dirty, and happy. I assumed that he would want the season to end, but he played like a wild animal out there fighting for yardage. Reporters were clamoring for an interview from him, but he checked on my well-being before talking to anyone.

"I'm good, Grayson, thank you. Go do some interviews."

He shook his head. "Not without you." He pointed to the towel. "Dry your tears. We're going to be interviewed. Together." He waited until I was presentable and pulled me over to an NBC reporter who was waiting for the exclusive.

"Grayson, how does it feel to take an expansion team to the playoffs?" Nikki James had been with NBC for over ten years. She was one of the first women on the field reporting from the sidelines.

"It's the best feeling. Who knew I could do this?" He pointed at me. "She knew. Coach McCoy never let me give up. She was there at my lowest point and helped me see how important leading this team was. I did a complete one-eighty about two months ago thanks to her."

"Coach McCoy, big praise coming from your biggest player. What do you say to that?"

"Grayson is a natural leader. Without him, we wouldn't be here right now headed for the playoffs."

"It looks like you'll be playing the Rams. How do you feel about it?" she asked.

"I've had my eye on them since the beginning of the season." It was before then, but I didn't want to come across as a football geek even though I was.

"What's next for you, Coach?"

"More late nights, a fast new year, and hopefully, another win."

"Do you think you can beat the Rams? They're in the number one spot in your division."

I shrugged and nodded. "They're tough and have a great offense. We're hoping to give them a run for their money."

Nikki picked up the cue that we were done. "Good luck, Coach, and congratulations."

I shook her hand and followed Grayson to the middle of the field where I shook hands with the losing team's coaches. I understood their crestfallen looks and the numbness that came from losing a game you had to win. We ended the season with 11 wins and 6 losses and still had to fight for a wildcard spot in the playoffs.

Bill and I walked down the hallway to the locker room. "I'm so proud of this team," Bill said.

We walked into the locker room and everyone was waiting to spray us with champagne. I was drenched by the time I got out of there. Bill, Marcus, and I had a press conference in twenty minutes. It was enough time to take a quick shower and get the alcohol off me. I grabbed a change of clothes and raced to the women's locker room. Two trainers were there changing into their street clothes.

"Congratulations, Coach!" they both said.

"Thanks!" I grabbed a fresh towel and got cleaned up in record time. I almost slipped and fell when I jumped out and saw Parker leaning against the counter. I clutched the towel closer. "What are you doing here?" I forgot to lock the door in my haste, but noticed it was locked now. "There are people down here."

"You mean Emily and Tess?" Parker thumbed behind her. "They were leaving when I walked in. You should be more careful about locking the door down here. Anybody could wander in. You're not being very safe."

Parker and I had agreed to cool it until the season was over. It was hard, but fair since I advised Grayson and Matt to do the same. I kept telling myself that I'd waited over fifteen years for her. I could wait another few more weeks. We talked on the phone daily, FaceTimed late at night, and texted every chance we got.

"Is everything okay? Where are the kids?"

"With my parents." She walked slowly toward me and stopped when I took a step back. "I came here to congratulate you and to let you know we filed the paperwork this morning."

I groaned. "Why didn't you wait until we were done with the season?"

She looked me up and down appreciatively and did nothing to hide it. Her eyes lingered along the hem of the towel. She took a step closer. This time I stood where I was. I was seconds from pulling her into my arms and skipping the press conference altogether, but I still had to do my job. She looked amazing, though, in a tight black sweater, gray slacks, and black boots. Her hair was pulled up in a bun with sexy tendrils framing her face. She was so sexy.

"We both agreed it was time. The kids are adjusting to the news that we won't be in the same house, but they understand that Grayson will be around all the time and available whenever they need him."

I was surprised they didn't wait. Somebody at the courthouse would see the paperwork and talk to the press. It was inevitable. As much as I wanted to be in this moment, I had to get upstairs. "Listen, I have about ten minutes to get ready. I can't talk to you right now."

"I've learned the best way to get your attention is to be in your space. I'd say I'm sorry, but I'm not," she said.

I blew out a deep breath. "I'm going to change now. This towel is dropping to the floor in three, two..."

She held up her hand. "I'm only leaving because the next time I see you naked will be because you want me to."

It was unnerving how quickly she got to me. I flipped the lock and dropped the towel. I got ready as quickly as possible. I sneaked in right as Bill was introducing us and sat as if I timed it perfectly.

"I have to give a lot of the credit to both coordinators, Coach Marcus Atkins and Coach Sutton McCoy," Bill said.

It took everything I had to stay in the moment. Bill teased me at my lack of focus and we all laughed. Nobody cared. We were going to the playoffs, and everyone wanted to celebrate. The reporters were happy for us, and after twenty minutes of never-ending questions, Bill called it. We had a busy day tomorrow. Film was at ten and Bill told us he didn't want to see anybody there earlier than that.

I whistled for Crowbar and zipped home. My energy level was high. I changed into sweats and a T-shirt, heated spaghetti, poured a glass of wine, and curled up on the couch with Crowbar. My phone dinged and I ignored it. I finished my glass of wine and moved to water. When my doorbell rang, I thought for sure my neighbors Tom and Lottie Griffith with their deep tans were there to let me know they were back from Florida.

Parker stood in my doorway. "I tried calling, but you didn't answer your phone. Oh, my God. I sound just like my parents."

I didn't know what to do. I clutched the doorknob and looked down at the welcome mat. I was tired of fighting. Her, myself, the past, the future. I knew exactly what I wanted. "Come in."

"I parked around back and nobody followed me," she said.

I nodded and walked to the kitchen, switched back to wine, and held up the bottle. She smiled. I grabbed another glass and poured a healthy amount into both glasses. "It's fine. The news is out or will be tomorrow."

"Sutton, it's going to be okay. It's very amicable. We know we need to be there for our children. He's happy. I'm happy. And the weight of all of this has been lifted. From his shoulders, from mine. It's time for me."

Her fingers were devoid of any jewelry and that scared me. I walked to the other side of the counter to put three feet between us. Even though the papers had been filed, was I okay being the rebound girl? Is that what I was?

"Can I get you some spaghetti?" I asked.

She waved me off and put one of her hands on her stomach. She was nervous. "Let's go into the living room." I made Crowbar leave the couch and pulled off his blanket so Parker didn't get any hair on her clothes. She patted his head before sitting on the spot he just vacated. "So, what's going on?" Was my voice normal? My chest felt like it was vibrating.

"This is a nice place." Her tongue touched the side of the glass before she took a sip.

"It's just to get me through the season. Honestly, I wasn't sure how the season was going to turn out. I'll look for something more permanent this spring."

"It's very minimalistic. I appreciate that so much. My kids have their toys, games, clothes, and shoes everywhere. This is immaculate."

"One of the benefits about not having kids. My place is always ready for company," I said. We sat quietly drinking our wine. She had something to say and I was going to wait it out.

She drained her glass and looked at me. "I think you know why I'm here, Sutton." The rawness in her voice made my insides turn to mush.

I wanted to fight and tell her no and that I wasn't ready, but it would be a lie. I'd been ready since the day she left me. "How do you know you're making the right choice?" The last thing I wanted was to move too fast and lose her all over again.

She stood right in front of me. "I've always known. We both have."

I felt her hand on my knee. She wanted me and I wanted her. We had waited half our lives to be together again. I opened my eyes and tried to blink back the tears that had gathered.

She touched my cheek. "I'm so sorry, Sutton. I know I screwed up. I never meant to hurt you and I know I did." I grabbed her hand

and pulled her toward me. She straddled my lap and cradled my face in her hands. "I'm sorry," she whispered before kissing my cheek. "I'm sorry." She kissed the corner of my mouth. "I'm sorry." She claimed my lips.

I grabbed her hips and pulled her to me. I couldn't get close enough to her. She was so familiar but so exciting. This wasn't the shy teenager who was nervous to touch. This was a woman who knew exactly what she wanted.

"I'm sorry," she whispered before pressing her hips down and kissing my lips hard.

I tasted merlot and warmth. My hips rolled into hers and my hands slipped under her sweater. Still so warm and inviting.

Her hands left my shoulders to pull the sweater over her head. She dropped it behind her. "I'm sorry."

I cupped her face and brought it closer to mine. "You don't need to apologize. The past is forgotten." I kissed her, sucking in her bottom lip and scraping it between my teeth. She made a slight gasping sound and plunged her tongue into my mouth. She gave me everything she could in that kiss. I ran my hands up her neck and wrapped them in her hair. I was overwhelmed and I needed for us to be naked and in my bed, not on the couch. I stood with her in my arms. She automatically wrapped her legs around my waist. I told Crowbar to stay and carried her to my bedroom, kicking the door shut in my wake. "Are you sure about this?"

She touched my swollen lips. "I've never wanted anything more than this moment."

I lowered her onto the mattress and ripped off my T-shirt and kicked off my sweats.

She held her hands up. "Wait."

I froze not knowing what to do. Did I push too far too fast? "What?"

"I want to look at you. You're even more beautiful than you were when we were younger."

I melted but stood still. I wasn't as lean as I was in high school, but I was stronger. I slid out of my boxers and took off my bra. I watched Parker unbutton her pants and I helped slide them off. Her blue lace bra and panty set made my mouth water. Seeing her like this confirmed what I'd assumed: she was still petite, but her curves were more pronounced and her breasts fuller. She took my breath away.

"You're still so beautiful, too."

She bit her bottom lip and looked at me. It was hard to talk since this was such an emotionally charged moment, so I lowered myself between her legs and kissed her. I pulled her knees up and over my shoulders and pressed my pussy against hers. The thin strip of lace between us barely registered. We moaned at the same time. I wasn't sure if my heart could take tonight, but I wasn't going to give up now. I'd wanted this for too long. Her moans grew louder, stronger with every roll of my hips. I watched as her blue eyes darkened and her mouth parted slightly. I pulled one side of her bra down to capture a rock-hard nipple in my mouth. I sucked hard and soothed it with my tongue. Parker writhed beneath me. Her nails raked my back.

"Let me take it off," she said.

I leaned up to help unlatch the hook and within seconds, the bra was on the floor. I stood and ripped her panties off. I grabbed the remote to the fireplace in my room and turned it on. It gave the room the perfect amount of light and romance and gave Parker's naked body an ethereal glow. As frenzied as I was thirty seconds ago, a calm hit when I realized she wasn't a dream and was here with me.

"Are you cold?" I asked.

"Do I feel cold? I'm burning up, Sutton," she said.

I traced my fingertips over the chill bumps on her stomach until she shivered. I kissed her again and moved so that I rested between her legs. I forced myself to go slow and treasure each touch, but the more I caressed, the hungrier I became. "You've always been so warm." I started a trail of kisses from her neck, down to her collarbone, and across her breasts. I sucked her nipple into my mouth.

"More," she whispered.

I alternated between the two, sucking and squeezing. Parker's moans became louder, and she grabbed my shoulders. I felt her slight push and moved down her body until my head was between her thighs. Her body quivered as I ran my hand up and down her thigh.

"Sutton, please." Her look was unguarded and full of love. My heart swelled and I vowed to do everything to please her.

I kissed her thigh and ran my tongue over to her mound. I spread her apart and licked soft skin. I held down her legs and continued licking and sucking until I knew she was ready to come. I slowed and slipped two fingers inside. She arched her back and I moaned. Her hips greeted my thrusts, but I knew it wasn't enough. I moved up her body so I could look her in the eye as I entered her again. She touched my face. I moved faster and faster until she had no choice but to hold my shoulders and crash into her orgasm with a shout. Her whole body shook. I wasn't done. I flipped us so I was underneath. I slipped my hand between our bodies and massaged her pussy while my tongue delved inside her wet, welcoming mouth. She moved so that she was on her knees and her palms were on either side of my head.

"I love you," she said, staring into my eyes.

A giant rush of feelings exploded inside me and the only thing I could do was kiss her so that she couldn't see the emotion on my face. I was afraid of those words. Instead, I put all my energy into pleasing her. I slipped inside her first with two fingers, then three.

"Oh, my God." Parker breathed against my cheek.

She took several deep breaths and I waited until I felt her walls relax before I moved my hand. I didn't want to hurt her. When I started thrusting, she threw her head back and rocked against me. Nothing mattered except this moment. I felt my past and my present colliding.

I touched her face with my free hand so she would look at me. "Is this okay?" I asked.

She turned her head to kiss my palm. "Don't stop. Don't ever stop." Her voice was hoarse and her eyes hooded. She was in the hazy space between orgasms. It was beautiful to watch her find and embrace pleasure.

I plunged into her fast and hard. She slid her hands forward until her head rested on my shoulder. I wrapped one arm around her waist and held her against me until she came again. My muscles were strained and I was sweating, but I wasn't done yet. I needed to taste her again. I wanted to feel her lose control again. The more I touched her, the more I needed her. I rolled her over and kissed my way to the sweet spot between her legs. Tiny beads of perspiration covered her body. Her legs fell open and her hips lifted to greet my mouth. Her hand was on the back of my head pressing me into her. I couldn't remember the last lover who openly took everything I gave. I ran my tongue up and down her drenched, swollen slit. Her appreciative moans encouraged me. I gently pulled on her clit with my mouth and when her thighs tightened around my head, I sucked harder until the third orgasm ripped through her body. I placed tiny kisses on her legs until she released my hair. I crawled up and pulled her into my arms. I had no words.

She clutched me, held me close to her as if she let up just a little, I would disappear. "I'm not letting you go this time," she said.

"I know you don't want to." I trusted her feelings. I just didn't trust her actions.

"I know I'm going to have to do a lot to convince you that I want you in my life, and I know I have a lot to do to make up for the way I hurt you before. I'm just looking for a chance at us again." Her voice was low and throaty.

I shivered at her words. Was I ready to confess? Was it safe for my heart? I'd built a wall around it for so long that I didn't know if what I was feeling was real or a fantasy. Would tomorrow be different? Just because she was here tonight, didn't mean we had a tomorrow. Parker had a long road ahead fielding questions about her personal life from every avenue. And once the world found out the reason, they would be relentless. I didn't answer her but ran my fingertips up and down her arm.

"What time do you have to be at work tomorrow?" she asked.

"Bill said he didn't want to see anybody until ten. What time do you have to be home? And how were you able to get away?"

"I told my parents I was going out with my friends since Grayson was celebrating with the guys."

Her words were a pit in my stomach. I hated lying. "How long did the lawyer say it would take for the divorce to finalize?"

"We waived the mandatory waiting period so the lawyer thinks about a month," she said.

"That's not long," I said. We were both quiet. "As incredible as tonight is, we can't do this again until after the divorce is finalized."

"I understand." She put her hand on my chest. "But I want you to know that our divorce has been in the works for a long time, and I've been thinking about you for so many years." Her voice wavered at the end of her sentence.

I wanted to trust her, but I'd been guarded for so long. "We can wait a month. We've waited this long." I looked at the time. It was nine o'clock. "What time do you have to go?"

She looked at the clock. "I still have another hour." She kissed me softly and sucked my bottom lip into her mouth. There was something so perfect about kissing the person who taught you how to kiss in the first place. It was familiar, and incredibly exciting.

Her hands fluttered down my body, and I braced myself, knowing that I wasn't going to last. Her mouth was hot against my cooling skin and when she ran her tongue over my clit, I bit back a loud moan. She wasn't gentle and I didn't want her to be. I grabbed the sheets and held on as she reminded me what I'd missed for so many years. I came twice before I had to stop her. My body was out of practice, and I knew time was our enemy. When we couldn't delay her leaving any longer, I held her by the front door and wondered if this was real or a dream. I allowed a sliver of happiness to weave inside my heart when she said this was a new beginning and we were just getting started. Again.

## Chapter Twenty-seven—The New Girl

*Past*

My dad left as Hayley was arriving. She high-fived him on her way in. "Kill it, Mr. McCoy." She grabbed a Pop-Tart from the cabinet and threw it in the toaster oven. "Nothing beats the high of the first day of school. I've been up since four. How do I look?" She twirled in her black combat boots, ripped jeans, and a cute band shirt we'd gotten at Hot Topic last weekend.

I put my forefinger up to my lip as though studying her intently. "The perfect embodiment of an angsty teenager who hates authority. I love it." I looked down at my athletic shorts and T-shirt and sneakers. "What do you think about mine?"

She threw the hot Pop-Tart on a plate and pointed upstairs. "Totally unacceptable. I mean, you're the school quarterback. It's junior year. You need to try harder." I followed her up the stairs. She pulled out nice jeans and a popover sleeveless shirt. "This is adorable and will make you look less like the quarterback and more like a kickass junior. Also, lose the ponytail. You won't take the field until after school," she said.

I bought the shirt at the start of summer because it was on sale, but forgot it was in my closet. "Okay. You're right. It's the first day. I should try harder." Everyone knew I was the assistant principal's daughter and the quarterback. It was time to live up to my reputation.

"And even though you're tan and shit, put on some makeup. Let's show the world your baby blues." She pinched my cheek and motioned for me to follow her into the bathroom. "And don't wear a sports bra."

"Do you know how much crap the guys will give me when they see me like this?"

Hayley jerked my chin to keep me looking at her instead of my reflection. She waved a mascara wand in front of me. "Hold still. Just a bit will make the biggest difference."

I huffed as though it was an inconvenience, but secretly I loved it. I missed things like this with my mom. Mom wanted to show me how to apply makeup so it looked natural before she passed away, but I was too stubborn and didn't want to think about my mom not being around so I ignored her attempts. I thought she would survive and that we had time. I was wrong. "Thanks for doing this."

"That's what family does and you're basically my sister." She hugged me.

I ended the hug early because I didn't want to start crying. The first day of school was always emotional. My dad was clueless, but I struggled not having my mom here for support. The first day was a day of new beginnings. My mom used to leave notes in my lunch like "Be strong, be fierce, be you." Then she would drive me to school playing loud eighties hairband music. I pretended to hate it, but I knew all the words and sang along under my breath.

"We'd better get going if we want to get a good parking spot," Hayley said.

"How do I look?"

Hayley fluffed my hair. "You'll do." She ate the rest of the Pop-Tart and checked her teeth for food. "I hope Mr. Cork lets us get away with murder." Our AP English teacher made learning fun. And it helped that it was the last class of the day. We also had French together right before lunch. Our lockers were in different hallways, but I was sure she would move her things into mine by the end of the week.

"I love him. It's too bad Madame Bleek is such a bitch though," Hayley said. She and Madame Bleek butted heads daily. Ms. Bleek wanted us to learn how to conjugate verbs and learn all the parts of a sentence in French, and Hayley wanted to curse and have conversations about food. It was funny to watch, but also stressful.

"Maybe if you let her teach instead of always trying to mess with her, we both could enjoy the class more," I said.

She nodded, then shook her head. "I know I'm an ass, but so is she. Come on. Let's go."

❖

"Where are you going, QB? Whoa. Look at you." Max looked me up and down and gave me a low whistle.

Heat spiked my cheeks. I bumped his shoulder. "Hayley wouldn't let me wear workout shorts and a T-shirt on day one."

"Good call. You clean up well."

"Go to class. I'll see you later." I had first period with Max, but I needed to drop off my dad's phone. He left it on the kitchen island in his haste to leave.

I turned the corner and walked into a very busy front office. A thin veil of panic covered the room. I scanned the place, hoping to see my dad so I could get in and out quickly. Ms. Clarissa was busy with two students, the office aide was trying to make copies of something but the copier wasn't cooperating. One of the admin assistants was on the phone making very big hand gestures while the other one was rapidly flipping through folders in a filing cabinet. I smiled at the familiarity of it all. First day was a rush even in the front office.

What I wasn't expecting was a very cute blonde sitting on a chair outside my dad's office. I was awestruck. I knew everybody and didn't have a problem talking to people. But there was something about her that made me want to simultaneously run away and also get to know her. I was confused. I smiled at her and walked into my dad's office.

"Looking for this?" I held up his phone.

"Thanks, honey." Even though I was holding it in my hand, he patted down his jacket pockets as though he would never do something as irresponsible as leave his phone behind.

"Are you even ready for today?" I thumbed behind me. "It's chaos out there. You should probably hide in here."

He raised his thin eyebrows at me. "It's already been a day and school starts in five minutes." He pointed at me. "Don't be late."

"I won't." I paused and turned back toward him. "Who's that girl sitting out front? I don't think I've seen her before." I tried to be as nonchalant as possible.

"She's a new student from Buffalo, New York. Just got into town last week." He didn't elaborate, but I wanted to know more about her.

"Oh. What grade is she in?" She looked to be around my age. When I smiled at her, she gave me a soft smile back. She had long blond hair and the prettiest eyes. She screamed money but didn't seem to be snotty like the other kids whose parents were wealthy at our school.

My dad pointed at me as an idea struck. His eyes widened. "Hey, why don't you take her around for a quick tour and then sneak her into assembly? I called for Gabby to come down and show her around since they are in homeroom together, but she's taking forever."

All my senses jumped to attention. "Okay. She can show me her schedule. No problem." For the second time today, my dad asked me how he looked. "You look great, Dad. Now go encourage those young, impressionable minds and make a difference." I followed him out, completely freaked about meeting the new girl, but also extremely excited about it.

"Well, it looks like Gabby came through after all." He pointed to Gabby and the new girl walking out of the office together. The excitement quickly vanished and was immediately replaced by regret. Had I just stopped and introduced myself, I could be getting to know her, one-on-one. "Maybe she'll be in one of your classes. She's a junior, too. Get to homeroom. I'll see you in a few minutes." The first bell rang which told us we had two minutes to get to homeroom. I made my way to class and said hi to several people along the way. I still didn't know the new girl's name. I only knew she had homeroom with Gabby. Would she be in any of my classes?

Where did she live? Oak Grove had two high schools and if she was going to Oak Grove, then she had to live within five miles of me. I walked into homeroom to applause and stopped at the front of the room.

"Oh, yeah. Looking good, boss," Wyatt yelled.

When I realized they were clapping for me, I flipped them off. Mr. Sanders couldn't see my hands, but my team could. I was embarrassed, but I loved the respect they gave me. Being a part of the team was more than just having a group to hang out with. I had brothers and dudes who looked out for me.

I slipped into a seat and said hi to Trish Calloway, who helped do morning announcements on days we didn't start with an assembly.

"How was your summer, Sutton?" she asked.

"It was good. Lots of running and working out. How was yours?"

"Worked. Saving money for college, you know," she said. She worked at Dairy Queen, but I had seen her at a few parties.

I nodded. "Are you working after school, too?" I felt bad because most people I knew had to get a job when they turned sixteen. My dad wanted me to do things that would look better on my résumé so I volunteered with Coach Larson during the summers at peewee football games.

"A few days and on weekends. Hey, when can we get together to talk about the upcoming season?"

The bell rang and I turned to face front. "Hit me up after class."

"Welcome back, students." Mr. Sanders slipped his glasses over his nose and started roll. The energy of the first day of school was only rivaled by the last day. "The sooner everyone settles down, the sooner we can head to the auditorium." That got us to quiet down. We filed out of the classroom and made our way to the first day assembly.

I found Hayley in the crowd and sat with her. "New student alert," I said.

"Boy or girl?" Hayley asked.

"Girl and she's gorgeous." I scanned the crowd for the new girl. We had three new transfers and lost four students. I saw her sitting next to Gabby in the bleachers to my left and discreetly pointed her out. "There. Blond. Second row."

"She's really cute, but she looks bitchy or bored. I can't tell," Hayley said.

I smacked Hayley's knee. "She's new and doesn't know anyone. Give her a break." It was hard to look away. There was something about her that made me pause. Sitting there with her messenger bag on her lap, she was the most beautiful girl I'd ever seen.

"Hello. Earth to Sutton." Hayley leaned into my direct view of the new girl.

"What?"

"Stop staring. You're starting to drool."

I frowned at Hayley's interruption. When the juniors jumped up to shout, I lost her in the crowd.

"Come on. Yell! We need to show the seniors we mean business!" Hayley jerked me to my feet and screamed at the seniors across the gym. I wanted to yell with the team and my classmates, but my heart was with the new girl who took my attention and my breath away.

## Chapter Twenty-eight—Fair Catch

*Present*

Monica Meadows pulled me aside after the Cheetahs lost the division championship game. "Coach, what a tough loss, but an amazing journey. Do you have any regrets?"

It was hard to hear in the stadium since they were celebrating and we were trying to have a conversation through a veil of silver and blue confetti.

"Absolutely no regrets. This team surpassed the expectations I had for them. I'm so proud of everything we've accomplished. How many teams can say they went from ground zero to the division championship game their first year ever? It takes years for a team to gel, but somehow, we not only had a winning season but did amazingly well in post-season." I was sad we were so close but couldn't get there, but also happy that we made it this far.

"Congratulations on your success with the team. You brought in Grayson Moats and proved to the NFL that not only could a woman take a team this far but could motivate a once retired quarterback to return to the game. Is he really retiring?" she asked.

When she put the microphone back in my face, I stuttered. I didn't want to say anything until it was official. Maybe in the last three minutes his agent released a statement, but I didn't know. "I'm afraid you're going to have to talk to him about that."

"Great job, Coach McCoy. Good luck next season."

"Thanks for all your work down here on the field, Monica." She hugged me on national television, and I didn't care. More reporters were flagging me over, but I really wanted to talk to the team. They needed me more than any network.

"Coach, come on in." Bill waved me into the locker room.

My heart went out to the players who were crying or upset about our loss. The emotional side of football was harder to break down. As somebody who had put their heart and soul into this game, I knew it was a tough loss to swallow.

"I'm proud of each and every one of you," Bill said. "You gave the team everything and it showed. This season was a victory in our hearts. I want you to know that what you did here was remarkable and you are all winners. Keep your heads held high." We applauded the players, the coaches, and the trainers who were with us. We didn't make it to the Super Bowl, but I couldn't imagine things could be better than this. "Let's go home."

I left before the guys started undressing. The season was over. That meant everything.

Parker and I had one incredible night last month, but we had kept to our agreement. Even once news of the divorce was leaked, we waited. It was hard but I knew it would be worth it to fully give ourselves to each other.

"McCoy, Pierson, and Trust. We're meeting with the media in ten. Pierson, remind Moats he's expected in twenty," Bill said.

We all knew he was retiring. Now that we were a proven winning team, players were going to line up to play for us. I fixed my makeup and brushed my hair. I was hyped up. I waited with Marcus outside the press room. We both knew our résumés just got way more attractive. I wasn't going anywhere, but I wasn't so sure about him.

"I can't believe it's over," he said.

"What an incredible season." I gave him a hug. When Bill and Jamal showed up, we walked in together. It was a quick question-and-answer session. I stayed when Grayson took the podium.

"Yes, the rumors are true. I'm retiring. It's been a hell of a ride but it's the best move for me and my family." Grayson answered each question with poise and positivity. I was weirdly proud of him. After twenty minutes, he stepped away from the podium and away from football.

The team threw him a retirement party the Friday before the Super Bowl. News of his divorce was quickly swallowed up by the hype of the big game. Now that Grayson was retired, his personal life wasn't in the limelight. It was the best result the Moats could have hoped for.

Every single teammate and coach showed up for Grayson's party. The girls stuck by his side. For the first time in Grayson's career, Parker hung back. She stayed close because of the girls, but she was distancing herself from him. Change was happening. I kept my distance and spent the evening hanging out with Matt. I got to hear his side of the story and the hardships he muddled through while waiting for Grayson. He had tried other relationships but failed. Grayson was his true love and he said he was worth the wait. I wondered if he knew about me and Parker until he caught me watching her across the room.

He nodded at her. "She's happier than I've ever seen her."

"What?" I smiled and bumped my shoulder against his. "I mean, we're not together. Yet. Officially."

"You might be keeping a respectful distance, but love looks good on her." Matt glanced my way. "And on you."

For the first time, I let myself feel happiness about me and Parker around another person. It blossomed inside me and burst into a kaleidoscope. I blushed at how liberating it felt. "Thank you."

Archie approached us and Matt gave him a bland smile. "Coach McCoy, do you want to come to my Super Bowl party? Lots of people, huge screen, great food," Archie said.

"I'm hanging out with my dad, but thanks for the offer." I felt bad for Archie. I was sure he thought he was going to take Grayson's place, but that wasn't going to happen. Our scouts had found a few quarterbacks coming up in the draft, but we had our eye on a benchwarmer from Jacksonville who had massive potential and wasn't being utilized. If we bought out his contract, we could use the draft for defensive backs. "Speaking of which, I should get going. I need to pack so I can get out of here first thing in the morning." We were off for a few days and I planned on spending the weekend with my dad and Judy. Dad and I had always watched the Super Bowl together and I had no interest in messing with tradition.

When I was driving a text from Parker popped up. *You looked beautiful tonight.*

I purposely wore three-inch heels and a dress for Parker's enjoyment. I was still shorter than most of the players even though I towered over the coaches and wives. I drove home smiling. It was a good night. I had the weekend off and I was driving to my dad's in Rhode Island in the morning. I called Hayley as I drove because she deserved to know the whole story.

"You've been holding out on me. I get that you couldn't tell me about the divorce, but you still suck."

I sighed. "There's more."

"Oh, God. This sounds bad. It's bad, isn't it?"

"It's not really my story to tell, but part of it is mine so I think I can tell you. This can't get out though." I could practically hear her roll her eyes at me.

"Okay, I pinky swear or whatever the kids say now."

"Well, they don't say that. Okay." I squeezed the steering wheel and braced myself for the barrage of questions that she for sure would pelt me with. "Grayson's gay." I winced waiting for the explosion.

"What?" Her volume level didn't disappoint.

"He's gay. So is Parker. Or at least she's bi. I never asked her how she identifies."

"Well, I figured that about Parker, but wow. Grayson?" I heard rustling around and knew she was pacing. "Are you kidding me? What the fuck? How long has he known?"

"I don't know, but he and Matt have been dating since college."

"Uncle Matt?" Her volume was back. "What about Parker? How is she doing? Wait. Did she know?"

"She's known since the beginning," I said.

"Oh, Sutton. This is a lot to take in. I feel so bad for them. What about the kids? How are they doing?"

"According to Grayson and Parker, they are adjusting well. They've known Matt their entire lives. Grayson and Matt have an apartment near the house. They'll have fifty-fifty custody."

Her voice got low. "What does that mean for you?"

I blew out a breath but stayed silent.

"You're going to jump on that, aren't you?"

I needed to be honest. Tears welled up. I couldn't lie to Hayley. "I already did."

"You did what?" she yelled. She was going to wake the boys.

"I'm sorry I couldn't tell you." My voice hitched and I stopped the sob that bubbled up in my throat. I swallowed hard and took a deep breath, but I couldn't stop the tears. I was crying for my past, my present, and my future. "It wasn't my story to tell and I couldn't tell you that without telling you the rest." I was babbling, but I hated lying to Hayley.

"Sis, you need to pull over. It's okay, but you can't drive when you're crying like this." Hayley was right. I pulled into an empty parking lot with bright lights.

"Okay. I'm stopped now."

"Good. Tell me the whole story now."

I spilled the entire thing. I started with the kiss on Halloween and ended with tonight and Matt telling me how happy Parker and I looked. Hayley knew my confession was hard but instead of berating me, she stepped up like she always did.

"It's okay, Sutton. You've waited a long time. Have you talked at all?" Hayley asked.

"I told her we could talk when the divorce was final."

"This is a lot to think about. I'm still trying to wrap my head around the fact that Grayson is gay. What a mess."

"I know, but they are working on a solution on what's best for the family."

"Wow, just wow," she said.

"That's exactly what I said when they told me. It's a lot to think about." I started my car back up and got back on the road. "I'm headed home now. Get some sleep. We'll text during the game. It's been such a long week."

"It's been a long season," she said.

"A long life."

Minutes later, I slid into the garage and parked. I scrolled through the other messages on my phone. I had several text messages but scrolled until I saw Parker's name. I opened the text thread and dropped my phone when I read her message.

*The divorce is final. When can we talk?*

It was after midnight, but I was too excited and texted her back. *I'll be home Monday by noon.*

The bubbles made me smile. She was still awake. *I'll bring lunch. See you then.*

Judy made a ton of appetizers for the game even though it was just the three of us watching it. Dad and I cheered the great plays and booed the bad calls. Watching the game was bittersweet. It should've been us, could've been us, but the better team won.

"Should've been you out there, kiddo," Dad said.

"Amen. But we certainly gave them a run for their money."

"How do you feel about the Cheetahs? Are you going to stick with them?"

"Starting at the beginning makes all the difference. I feel like being part of this greatness only happens once in a lifetime," I said.

"You've done an amazing job."

"He brags about you to anyone who will listen," Judy said. She handed him a beer and kissed him on the lips. She gave me a beer and squeezed my shoulder. Our relationship was new, but I liked her. She gave my dad a peace that I hadn't seen in forever. When the Titans won the Super Bowl, I was happy for them, but couldn't shake my jealousy.

"Welp. There's always next year."

I rolled my eyes. "Dad, that's the most overused phrase in the NFL."

"I think in any sport." He turned off the television. "So I heard that Grayson and Parker are getting a divorce."

"Yep. It was just finalized."

He turned so he could see me better. "How do you feel about that?"

I knew what he was really asking. "I feel like it's the best thing for their relationship. It's an amicable split, Dad."

"Is she back in your life?"

"Yes, and no, the divorce isn't because of me."

"I like Parker, but she broke your heart and I don't want the same thing to happen again. I know you're an adult now, but you'll always be my little girl and I don't want you to get hurt."

I shrugged like the fate of my future and my heart wasn't a big deal. "If it doesn't work out, then I'll move on." I could tell he wanted to say something, but he pursed his lips instead. I was thankful that he was respectful of my decisions no matter what he thought of them.

"I want you to find love. Once you do, it'll change your life forever. Hopefully, you'll have it with Parker, but if not, just know there are so many women out there who would love the opportunity to spend time with you. You're such an amazing person, Sutton. Never forget that."

He squeezed my hand and excused himself to help Judy with cleaning up. We'd spend the rest of the night getting caught up before I left early in the morning. I wanted to drive home tonight, but I also knew it was important to spend time with them. They'd been together for six months and from the looks of it, bits and pieces of Judy were sprinkled in his house. The throw pillows were frilly and something my dad wouldn't have picked out himself. The clock in the kitchen had apples instead of numbers and the knitted throw on the back of the couch looked like it was homemade and crafted with love.

After tossing and turning in the guest bed for an appropriate amount of time, I ate a quick breakfast, grabbed Crowbar, and rushed back to Bridgemont. I told my dad I needed to get back to wrap up some loose ends. When we pulled up in the driveway, my heart stopped before the car did. Parker was here. I looked at the time. It was ten thirty. I wasn't expecting her until noon. I checked my reflection in the visor, let my hair down, and got out of the car. She wasn't in her car and she wasn't waiting at the front door.

I opened the door and found her waiting inside like she belonged there and it was just an ordinary day in my life. Only it wasn't. Crowbar wagged his tail and headed straight for her. I needed to catch my breath first. I was weak-kneed again.

"Hi," I said.

"I hope you don't mind that I let myself in through the garage with the code." She winced as if it was a bad decision when it was the best possible surprise.

"That's totally fine. I'm glad you did."

"I'm early, but I couldn't wait." She walked toward me, shyly, gracefully, completely vulnerable.

I hadn't seen her look at me like that in fifteen years. The tears fell. I couldn't stop them. The space between us, once full of history, bad decisions, and regrets, was clear. Nothing was stopping us. I pulled her in my arms and held her. She felt right.

"Let's sit. We have a lot to talk about," I said. We sat on the couch and I positioned myself so we were facing one another. "So, you're single again."

She smiled and my pulse jumped. "I've been single for three days," she said. She held my hand. "But I don't want to be. I want to try again with you." She held up her hand when I tried to interrupt. "No, you're not the rebound person. You're the one. You've always been the one." She brought my hand up to her chest and placed it over her heart. "You've always been right here. Even when I was too scared to admit it to the world." She brushed her lips across mine. "I'm not scared anymore."

"This is going to get messy. I want what's best for you and the girls."

"They want us both to be happy. Right now they are with Grayson and Matt until Wednesday."

"How are they going to feel about you? Specifically dating me?"

"At least a third of the students at Wellington have same-sex parents. It's something they've grown up with. I can't tell you how many books are available to help parents with this very thing," she said. She straddled me and locked her fingers behind my neck. "I need you to trust me again. I know it won't be easy and I don't blame you at all. But I'm here, and unless you kick me out right now, I'm staying until Wednesday."

I wasn't going to play coy during such a heartfelt moment. Everything I wanted was right in front of me. We both went about it the long way, but just like my dad and Hayley told me, if Parker and I were meant to be, then it would happen. Who knew it would be fifteen years later? I wanted to take the plunge. I deserved it.

I kissed her hard. She gasped but matched my energy within a second. Her tongue parted my lips and plunged into my mouth. I moaned at the intimacy of it. I pulled at the hem of her sweater and she immediately removed it. She was wearing a pink tank with no bra. Her nipples strained against the fabric. I ran my fingers over her breasts gently at first until she pressed herself into my hands. Her hips rocked into mine and I knew she wasn't looking for a soft touch. I took off her tank, then tossed my sweater on top of it. I flipped so her back was on the couch. I didn't even think to take her back to my bedroom. There was no time. I needed her naked body against mine as quickly as possible. I needed that connection now. I pulled off her leggings and panties. I sank into her warmth, her desperation, her love. This was real. She pushed and pulled against my body, bringing me closer, directing me where to touch her. I pushed her thighs up and licked her pussy hard and fast. She grabbed the couch cushion and moaned. Her other hand wound in my hair and held me against her. She was wild and uninhibited, beautiful, and finally mine. I'd waited a lifetime for her.

"I love you, Sutton," she cried out. She bucked hard against me and I held her hips down and sucked her clit into my mouth. "I need you inside me." I slipped two fingers inside as far as I could go. She tilted her head back and the sexiest moan poured from her lips. "Oh, God, yes." She braced herself by grabbing the back of the couch. A powerful orgasm shook her body. Her body quivered and she gasped to catch her breath.

"You're amazing," I said right before I kissed her. She threw her arms around me and held me close. Her body was slick with perspiration, and I knew once she came down from the high of orgasming, she was going to be cold. "Let's go to the bedroom so we can get warm and talk." I gently pulled her up and wrapped her in the blanket draped across the back of the couch.

"Talk?" she asked and kissed me softly.

"I'm sure there will be words."

She winked and opened the blanket that was wrapped around her.

I playfully gasped. "Did you just flash me?" I grabbed the ends of the blanket to pull her close as I walked backward. I unfolded a corner and peeked. "Oh, I like."

She kissed me softly. "You like a little or a lot?"

I picked her up and carried her to the bed. "I love a lot."

"Love?" She touched my face.

My breath hitched. "Definitely love." I turned on the fireplace for heat and followed her to the bed. "I love you, Parker. You've always had my heart, even when we were on different paths."

"I promise I'm never letting go. I belong with you." She straddled my waist.

I ran my hands up and down her thighs. "I've missed you so much. I never wanted anyone else."

She kissed me tenderly and moved down my neck to my collarbone, then ran her tongue over my breasts. She scraped her teeth over my hard nipples and ran her fingers down to the junction of my thighs. I parted my legs, anxious to feel her inside me. She was already deep in my heart. The physical connection was magnified because we were finally free to be in love. I rocked my hips against her hand, trying not to come immediately, but I gave in. We had every single day for the rest of our lives to go slow. I shouted and shook, and when I was done, I pulled her into my arms and held her tight.

"I've missed you so much," I said.

"I'm never leaving you," she said. Her words were said with such conviction.

I pulled the covers over us and even though it was barely afternoon, we fell asleep in each other's arms.

Hours later, I felt her warmth leave me. "Where are you going?"

"I'm going to order food so we can sustain this for the next forty-eight hours."

I watched her slip on one of my sweatshirts and walk out of the bedroom, her tiny ass cheeks peeking out from below the hemline. She returned with her phone and two water glasses and crawled under the covers.

"What sounds good to eat?" she asked as she pulled up an app on her phone.

I nibbled on her neck. "You."

She turned her head. "Besides me."

"Me."

She laughed. "Besides us."

This was my perfect moment. We were in bed talking about the simplest thing, and I wouldn't trade it for anything. Our journey was anything but easy and the road ahead was sure to have pitfalls, but nothing mattered except this moment.

"I'd cook, but you don't have any food in the house. How is that possible?"

I shrugged. "I'm never home."

"Hopefully, that changes because after fifteen years apart, I'm going to need to see you more than a few times a week," she said.

I knew two things that would happen in this relationship. I wouldn't be at the office until eleven every night because I knew she would be waiting for me, and even if I had to be there, she would support me. "I promise to put you first. Always." I loved my job, but I could coach football anywhere.

She cupped my face in her hands. "I know you will. We've been through too much. I trust you, Sutton. With my heart, with my life, and with my family." The determined look on her face made my stomach flip flop. I put her phone on the nightstand.

"But I was going to order food." She laughed when I nuzzled her neck. "We're going to wither away before this relationship takes off. What are you doing?"

I nestled my body between her legs, eliciting a soft moan from her slightly swollen lips. "I'm making up for lost time, remember? We have a lot of catching up to do."

## Epilogue—Lose the Game, Win the Girl

"I'm throwing the ball to you so I need you to catch it and lateral pass it to our amazing running back, Vee," I said to Hayley who nodded solemnly at the players in our huddle.

"I've got this. You can count on me. Vee's going to run it in for a touchdown and we're going to win this game. You ready, honey?" Hayley asked.

Vee growled like a cat, fittingly so. The Pumas were me, Parker, Hayley, Matt, Mason, and Vee. We were up against the self-proclaimed undefeated Cheetahs. Grayson was the quarterback with Max, Dad, Rose, and Kaleb rounding out the rest of the roster. Cameron was cheering on both teams and digging in the sand, or maybe he was eating it, I couldn't tell. The game was tied and this was the last play before Mike and Judy called us up for dinner.

"Don't run until I get the ball in my hands." Mason was my center. I looked at him. "Hand me the ball when I yell Independence." We lined up against the Cheetahs. I stood behind Mason. "Red fourteen. Red fourteen. Independence!" Mason turned and handed me the ball. I scrambled out of the way of my dad who quickly broke through the line and was hot on my trail. I tossed the ball to Hayley who caught it and gently flicked it to Vee.

"Run, baby, run!" Hayley yelled.

She almost made it. Grayson picked her up right before she crossed the end zone and ran her back the other way over his shoulder for a touchdown in their favor.

"If only she'd dropped the ball," Parker said. She stood between me and Hayley with her hands on her hips shaking her head. "Daddy's little girl right there."

"Cheaters! Not the Cheetahs!" Hayley yelled.

We watched as they celebrated twenty feet away. "Boo! Hiss! Boo!" I grabbed Cameron and put him on my shoulders. I high-fived Mason on a job well done.

"Dinner's ready. Come on up!" Judy waved us over before we had a chance at redemption.

"At least we'll get to the table first," I said.

"Let's drop their food in the sand," Hayley said.

"Harsh, my friend. Harsh."

"Hot dog, hot dog. And chips." Cameron clapped his tiny hands together sending sand down my hair and shirt.

"You're getting Auntie Sutton dirty."

I grabbed his tiny hands and extended his arms as far as they could go and jogged up to the table. He giggled the whole way. "Okay, big boy, go see your daddy. He'll fix you a plate."

"Nope. Let's go wash up first," Hayley directed him into the house.

Parker and I washed our hands in the kitchen sink. "I feel bad that we're dragging sand all over this house," I said. I had one more week of vacation left before my second season with the Cheetahs so Parker and I decided to take the kids to visit my dad and Judy. Hayley and Mike decided it sounded like fun. When all was said and done, we rented an Airbnb with five bedrooms for the week that was about a half a mile down the beach from my dad's house. We'd begged Max to stay with us, but he had business in Boston and could only give us an afternoon.

"It's a beach house and probably ten percent sand. And look at how happy your dad is. I don't think they care."

I put my arm around her shoulder. "He loves having the kids around."

Since the divorce, Parker's parents stopped talking to her. I only cared because I knew she was hurt. Not-so-secretly, I was glad they weren't in the picture. Maybe if they got comfortable with our relationship, they'd be welcomed back, but right now, they were poisonous.

"He's so good with them. Rose called him Papa after Cameron did and I swear he teared up," she said.

The kids called Judy Gigi and she adored it. Before Dad, she was married for twenty years, but she never had children.

Parker squeezed my waist. "We'd better get out there. I don't think those heathens are going to wash up. I don't want to get the burger that fell on the ground."

"You saw that, too?"

She put her fingers to my lips to shush me. "Don't say anything. The poor guy wants to be good at something other than work."

Parker thought I was lying about Mike's inability to play sports until she met him. She was always kind but didn't hesitate to take his place in any game if it involved something athletic like hand-eye coordination or simply running.

"Winners get to eat first," Grayson yelled and beat on his chest.

"Stop being a guy." Matt playfully pushed him out of the line.

"Women and children first. Excuse us. I've got a hungry little man who's been yelling for hot dogs the last three minutes." Hayley cut in front and grabbed the plate Mike handed her with a hot dog for Cameron and a cheeseburger for her. It wasn't the one that fell. "Thanks, hon." She kissed Mike's cheek and sat at the picnic table with Cameron beside her. When Mike served Grayson the one that fell, Parker and I busted out laughing.

"What's so funny?" he asked. He covered the patty with a tomato slice and a ton of ketchup. "I mean, you lost. I'm surprised you can see through your tears of defeat and blinding rage at losing to me. Again." He took a giant bite and all I saw was a guy eating sand.

I kissed Parker. "We let you win."

He pointed at us. "And you're great losers."

"Would you be nice?" Matt said. He sat next to Grayson and stole a chip from his plate.

"I'm calling it a tie. There were several fouls that last play. We'll have to play the tie-breaking game another time. I need to leave in about thirty minutes," Max said.

"Aw, do you have to go?" I pouted.

"I go where the money is." He held out his palms and shrugged.

"You're amazing. You're the only person I know who's going to retire by forty," I said. I loaded my plate with potato salad and watermelon and sat next to him.

"No, I'll be filthy rich by then and I won't want to retire," he said.

"Come sit down, babe. You grilled enough food to feed us the entire week." Hayley patted the other side of her.

"And you did a great job." I held up my cheeseburger as though toasting him. We all did. I had a wonderful family, a career I busted my ass for, and the love of my life. I was the luckiest person here. I smiled when Parker put her head on my shoulder.

"What are you thinking about?" she asked.

I looked at her. "You." I loved that I still made her blush.

"You look so happy." She touched my arm softly.

"I really am. Like I legit think I'm the happiest person in the world," I said.

"I believe you."

"It's about damn time," Hayley said. She squeezed our hands. "I love you both and I better be staring at forever." She gave us the mean mommy look. Parker and I laughed.

"She's my forever," I said. I was never going to hide or be embarrassed by my love for Parker. We'd gone through too much. Parker sighed. It was a good kind of sigh. One that made my heart quicken and fill with love just when I thought I was already full.

"Always and forever," Parker said.

"We're all pretty lucky," Matt said.

Grayson puffed out his chest. "But only some of us are winners."

I put my arm around Parker's shoulders and kissed her. "You might have won the game, but I finally won the girl."

# About the Author

Multi-award-winning author Kris Bryant was born in Tacoma, WA, but has lived all over the world and now considers Kansas City her home. She received her BA in English from the University of Missouri and spends a lot of her time buried in books. She enjoys hiking, photography, and spending time with her family and friends.

Her first novel, *Jolt*, was a Lambda Literary Award Finalist. *Forget-Me-Not* was selected by the American Library Association's 2018 Over the Rainbow book list and was a Golden Crown Finalist for Contemporary Romance. *Breakthrough* won a 2019 Goldie for Contemporary Romance, *Listen* won a 2020 Goldie for Contemporary Romance, and *Temptation* won a 2021 Goldie for Contemporary Romance. Kris can be reached at krisbryantbooks@gmail.com or at krisbryant.net.

# Books Available from Bold Strokes Books

**Catch** by Kris Bryant. Convincing the wife of the star quarterback to walk away from her family was never in offensive coordinator Sutton McCoy's game plan. But standing on the sidelines when a second chance at true love comes her way proves all but impossible. (978-1-63679-276-7)

**Hearts in the Wind** by MJ Williamz. Beth and Evelyn seem destined to remain mortal enemies but are about to discover that in matters of the heart, sometimes you must cast your fortunes to the wind. (978-1-63679-288-0)

**Hero Complex** by Jesse J. Thoma. Bronte, Athena, and their unlikely friends, must work together to defeat Bronte's arch nemesis. The fate of love, humanity, and the world might depend on it. No pressure. (978-1-63679-280-4)

**Hotel Fantasy** by Piper Jordan. Molly Taylor has a fantasy in mind that only Lexi can fulfill. However, convincing her to participate could prove challenging. (978-1-63679-207-1)

**Last New Beginning** by Krystina Rivers. Can commercial broker Skye Kohl and contractor Bailey Kaczmarek overcome their pride and work together while the tension between them boils over into a love that could soothe both of their hearts? (978-1-63679-261-3)

**Love and Lattes** by Karis Walsh. Cat café owner Bonnie and wedding planner Taryn join forces to get rescue cats into forever homes—discovering their own forever along the way. (978-1-63679-290-3)

**Repatriate** by Jaime Maddox. Ally Hamilton's new job as a home health aide takes an unexpected twist when she discovers a fortune in stolen artwork and must repatriate the masterpieces and avoid the wrath of the violent man who stole them. (978-1-63679-303-0)

**The Hues of Me and You** by Morgan Lee Miller. Arlette Adair and Brooke Dawson almost fell in love in college. Years later, they unexpectedly run into each other and come face-to-face with their unresolved past. (978-1-63679-229-3)

**A Haven for the Wanderer** by Jenny Frame. When Griffin Harris comes to Rosebrook village, the love she finds with Bronte de Lacey creates safe haven and she finally finds her place in the world. But will she run again when their love is tested? (978-1-63679-291-0)

**A Spark in the Air** by Dena Blake. Internet executive Crystal Tucker is sure Wi-Fi could really help small-town residents, even if it means putting an internet café out of business, but her instant attraction to the owner's daughter, Janie Elliott, makes moving ahead with her plans complicated. (978-1-63679-293-4)

**Between Takes** by CJ Birch. Simone Lavoie is convinced her new job as an intimacy coordinator will give her a fresh perspective. Instead, problems on set and her growing attraction to actress Evelyn Harper only add to her worries. (978-1-63679-309-2)

**Camp Lost and Found** by Georgia Beers. Nobody knows better than Cassidy and Frankie that life doesn't always give you what you want. But sometimes, if you're lucky, life gives you exactly what you need. (978-1-63679-263-7)

**Felix Navidad** by 'Nathan Burgoine. After the wedding of a good friend, instead of Felix's Hawaii Christmas treat to himself, ice rain strands him in Ontario with fellow wedding-guest—and handsome ex of said friend—Kevin in a small cabin for the holiday Felix definitely didn't plan on. (978-1-63679-411-2)

**Fire, Water, and Rock** by Alaina Erdell. As Jess and Clare reveal more about themselves, and their hot summer fling tips over into true love, they must confront their pasts before they can contemplate a future together. (978-1-63679-274-3)

**Lines of Love** by Brey Willows. When even the Muse of Love doesn't believe in forever, we're all in trouble. (978-1-63555-458-8)

**Manny Porter and The Yuletide Murder** by D.C. Robeline. Manny only has the holiday season to discover who killed prominent research scientist Phillip Nikolaidis before the judicial system condemns an innocent man to lethal injection. (978-1-63679-313-9)

**Only This Summer** by Radclyffe. A fling with Lily promises to be exactly what Chase is looking for—short-term, hot as a forest fire, and one Chase can extinguish whenever she wants. After all, it's only one summer. (978-1-63679-390-0)

**Picture-Perfect Christmas** by Charlotte Greene. Two former rivals compete to capture the essence of their small mountain town at Christmas, all the while fighting old and new feelings. (978-1-63679-311-5)

**Playing Love's Refrain** by Lesley Davis. Drew Dawes had shied away from the world of music until Wren Banderas gave her a reason to play their love's refrain. (978-1-63679-286-6)

**Profile** by Jackie D. The scales of justice are weighted against FBI agents Cassidy Wolf and Alex Derby. Loyalty and love may be the only advantage they have. (978-1-63679-282-8)

**Almost Perfect** by Tagan Shepard. A shared love of queer TV brings Olivia and Riley together, but can they keep their real-life love as picture perfect as their on-screen counterparts? (978-1-63679-322-1)

**Corpus Calvin** by David Swatling. Cloverkist Inn may be haunted, but a ghost materializes from Jason Dekker's past and Calvin's canine instinct kicks in to protect a young boy from mortal danger. (978-1-62639-428-5)

**Craving Cassie** by Skye Rowan. Siobhan Carney and Cassie Townsend share an instant attraction, but are they brave enough to give up everything they have ever known to be together? (978-1-63679-062-6)

**Drifting** by Lyn Hemphill. When Tess jumps into the ocean after Jet, she thinks she's saving her life. Of course, she can't possibly know Jet is actually a mermaid desperate to fix her mistake before she causes her clan's demise. (978-1-63679-242-2)

**Enigma** by Suzie Clarke. Polly has taken an oath to protect and serve her country, but when the spy she's tasked with hunting becomes the love of her life, will she be the one to betray her country? (978-1-63555-999-6)

**Finding Fault** by Annie McDonald. Can environmental activist Dr. Evie O'Halloran and government investigator Merritt Shepherd set aside their conflicting ideas about saving the planet and risk their hearts enough to save their love? (978-1-63679-257-6)

**Hot Keys** by R.E. Ward. In 1920s New York City, Betty May Dewitt and her best friend, Jack Norval, are determined to make their Tin Pan Alley dreams come true and discover they will have to fight—not only for their hearts and dreams, but for their lives. (978-1-63679-259-0)

**Securing Ava** by Anne Shade. Private investigator Paige Richards takes a case to locate and bring back runaway heiress Ava Prescott. But ignoring her attraction may prove impossible when their hearts and lives are at stake. (978-1-63679-297-2)

**The Amaranthine Law** by Gun Brooke. Tristan Kelly is being hunted for who she is and her incomprehensible past, and despite her overwhelming feelings for Olivia Bryce, she has to reject her to keep her safe. (978-1-63679-235-4)

**The Forever Factor** by Melissa Brayden. When Bethany and Reid confront their past, they give new meaning to letting go, forgiveness, and a future worth fighting for. (978-1-63679-357-3)

**The Frenemy Zone** by Yolanda Wallace. Ollie Smith-Nakamura thinks relocating from San Francisco to her dad's rural hometown is the worst idea in the world, but after she meets her new classmate Ariel Hall, she might have a change of heart. (978-1-63679-249-1)

**A Cutting Deceit** by Cathy Dunnell. Undercover cop Athena takes a job at Valeria's hair salon to gather evidence to prove her husband's connections to organized crime. What starts as a tentative friendship quickly turns into a dangerous affair. (978-1-63679-208-8)

**As Seen on TV!** by CF Frizzell. Despite their objections, TV hosts Ronnie Sharp, a laid-back chef; and paranormal investigator Peyton Stanford, have to work together. The public is watching. But joining forces is risky, contemptuous, unnerving, provocative—and ridiculously perfect. (978-1-63679-272-9)

**Blood Memory** by Sandra Barret. Can vampire Jade Murphy protect her friend from a human stalker and keep her dates with the gorgeous Beth Jenssen without revealing her secrets? (978-1-63679-307-8)

**Foolproof** by Leigh Hays. For Martine Roberts and Elliot Tillman, friends with benefits isn't a foolproof way to hide from the truth at the heart of an affair. (978-1-63679-184-5)

**Glass and Stone** by Renee Roman. Jordan must accept that she can't control everything that happens in life, and that includes her wayward heart. (978-1-63679-162-3)

**Hard Pressed** by Aurora Rey. When rivals Mira Lavigne and Dylan Miller are tapped to co-chair Finger Lakes Cider Week, competition gives way to compromise. But will their sexual chemistry lead to love? (978-1-63679-210-1)

**The Laws of Magic** by M. Ullrich. Nothing is ever what it seems, especially not in the small town of Bender, Massachusetts, where a witch lives to save lives and avoid love. (978-1-63679-222-4)

**The Lonely Hearts Rescue** by Morgan Lee Miller, Nell Stark, Missouri Vaun. In this novella collection, a hurricane hits the Gulf Coast, and the animals at the Lonely Hearts Rescue Shelter need love, and so do the humans who adopt them. (978-1-63679-231-6)

**The Mage and the Monster** by Barbara Ann Wright. Two powerful mages, one committed to magic and one controlled by it, strive to free each other and be together while the countries they serve descend into war. (978-1-63679-190-6)

**Truly Wanted** by J.J. Hale. Sam must decide if she's willing to risk losing her found family to find her happily ever after. (978-1-63679-333-7)

**A Good Chance** by Ali Vali. Harry, Desi, and Desi's sister Rachel are so close to getting everything they've ever wanted, but Desi's ex-husband is coming back to get his revenge and rip apart their chance at happiness. (978-1-63679-023-7)

**A Perfect Fifth** by Jaycie Morrison. Streetwise pianist Zara Keller and Lady Jillian Stansfield couldn't be more different; yet their connection brings a new awareness of who they are and what they truly want in their lives—including each other. (978-1-63679-132-6)

**Catching Feelings** by Ana Hartnett Reichardt. Andrea Foster expected to catch a lot of pitches from the Alder Lion's star pitcher, Maya, but she didn't expect to catch feelings. (978-1-63679-227-9)

**Defiant Hearts** by Lee Lynch. In these stories, you'll find your lovers, friends, and lesbians you wish you knew—maybe even yourself. (978-1-63679-237-8)

**Love and Duty** by Catherine Young. All Princess Roseli wants is to marry her three lovers, but with war looming, she must instead marry Princess Lucia to establish a military alliance between their planets. (978-1-63679-256-9)

**Murder at Union Station** by David S. Pederson. Private Detective Mason Adler struggles to determine who killed a woman found in a trunk without getting himself killed in the process. (978-1-63679-269-9)

**Serendipity** by Kris Bryant. Serendipity brings jingle writer Annie Foster and celebrity pop star Bristol Baines together, and their undeniable attraction keeps them close, but will their different paths drive them apart? (978-1-63679-224-8)

**The Haunted Heart** by Jane Kolven. A ghost, a ring, and a quest to find a missing psychic—it's a spell for love. (978-1-63679-245-3)

**The Rules of Forever** by Nan Campbell. After reconnecting at their high school reunion, Cara and Lauren agree to embark on a textbook definition friends-with-benefits relationship, but trying to keep it uncomplicated is harder than it seems. (978-1-63679-248-4)

**Vision of Virtue** by Brey Willows. When virtue and desire come together, be prepared for sparks in this next installment of the Memory's Muses series. (978-1-63679-118-0)

**BOLDSTROKESBOOKS.COM**

Looking for your next great read?

Visit BOLDSTROKESBOOKS.COM
to browse our entire catalog of paperbacks, ebooks,
and audiobooks.

Want the first word on what's new?
Visit our website for event info,
author interviews, and blogs.

Subscribe to our free newsletter for sneak peeks,
new releases, plus first notice of promos
and daily bargains.

**SIGN UP AT**
BOLDSTROKESBOOKS.COM/signup

Quality and Diversity in LGBTQ Literature

*Bold Strokes Books is an award-winning publisher
committed to quality and diversity in LGBTQ fiction.*

www.ingramcontent.com/pod-product-compliance
Ingram Content Group UK Ltd.
Pitfield, Milton Keynes, MK11 3LW, UK
UKHW041416180426
11947UKWH00007B/166